T

THE MADMAN OF
PINEY WOODS

CHRISTOPHER PAUL CURTIS

THE MADMAN OF PINEY WOODS

SCHOLASTIC PRESS / NEW YORK

Library of Congress Cataloging-in-Publication Data

Curtis, Christopher Paul, author.
The madman of Piney Woods / Christopher Paul Curtis. — First edition.
pages cm
Companion book to: Elijah of Buxton.
Summary: Even though it is now 1901, the people of Buxton, Canada (originally a settlement
of runaway slaves), and Chatham, Canada, are still haunted by two events of half a century
before — the American Civil War and the Irish potato famine, and the lasting damage
those events caused to the survivors.
ISBN 978-0-545-15664-6
1. Blacks — Canada — Juvenile fiction. 2. Irish — Canada — Juvenile fiction.
3. Post-traumatic stress disorder — Juvenile fiction. 4. Freedmen — Juvenile fiction.
5. Veterans — Juvenile fiction. 6. Immigrants — Canada — Juvenile fiction. 7. North
Buxton (Ont.) — Juvenile fiction. 8. Chatham (Ont.) — Juvenile fiction. 9. Canada —
Juvenile fiction. [1. Blacks — Canada — Fiction. 2. Irish — Canada — Fiction.
3. Post-traumatic stress disorder — Fiction. 4. Freedmen — Fiction. 5. Veterans —
Fiction. 6. Immigrants — Fiction. 7. North Buxton (Ont.) — History — 20th
century — Fiction. 8. Chatham (Ont.) — History — 20th century — Fiction.
9. Canada — History — 1867-1914 — Fiction.] I. Title.
PZ7.C94137Mad 2015
813.54 — dc23
2014003493

10 9 8 7 6 5 4 3 2 1   14 15 16 17 18

Printed in the U.S.A.   23
First edition, October 2014

The author has used certain Canadian spellings to establish the setting of this novel.
Map art copyright © 2014 by Mike Schley
The text was set in Historical, Felltype Roman.
Book design by Kristina Iulo

To my beloved wife, Habon, thank you, thank you, thank you.

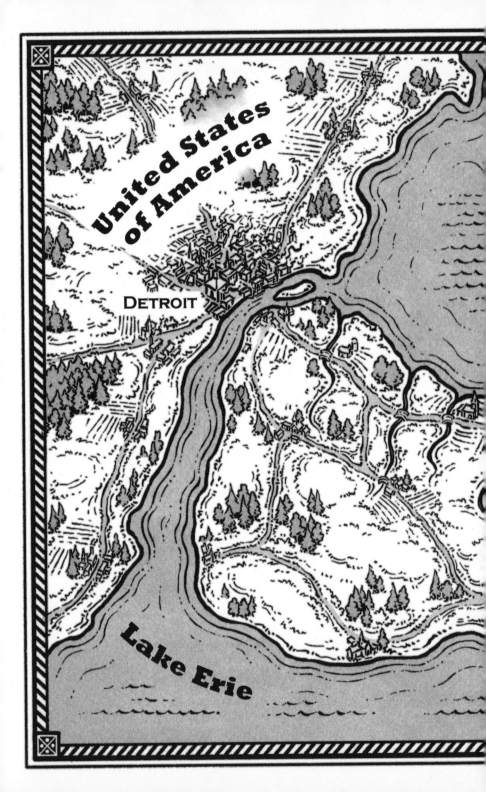

PART ONE

BUXTON
» AND «
CHATHAM

→ CHAPTER I ←

The American Civil War, 1901

BENJAMIN "BENJI" ALSTON OF
BUXTON, ONTARIO, CANADA

The old soldiers say you never hear the bullet that kills you. They say that as if there's some sort of comfort in those words.

The Johnny Reb who'd been hunting me down for nearly an hour was going to shoot me from behind and I wouldn't hear it, but that wasn't very comforting. I was as flat on my belly as I could be, but kept pressing my body down, trying to melt myself right into the ground.

He'd slowed down; he knew I'd stopped and he was doing what any good hunter would: being careful. But he didn't have to be. I'd lost my weapon right after he shot me in my side, and at the same time lost my urge to fight.

More than anything, I wanted to go home. I wanted to see my mother and father and yes, even my brother and sister again. If only one more time.

There was so much I needed to set straight with them, so many words I'd meant to say but hadn't.

I'd tell my father one of the reasons I'd left Canada

and sneaked south to fight for the Union Army of the United States of America was because of how his father had been beaten to death by a slave owner. I hoped he'd be proud that his first son had died so that others would live free.

I'd tell Mother how much she meant to me.

I'd tell her how the main reason I'd come south to fight was that after I helped win the war for the Union I'd work on solving the mystery of *her* mother and father. Even though she hadn't seen or heard anything of them since she'd escaped slavery a million years ago, my dream has always been to find them for her.

It would cause me a real gut-ache, but I'd even apologize to my brother and sister, Stubby and Patience. It's probably not their fault, but I find it irksome when Mother and Father and so many other people in Buxton get this surprised look of amazement whenever Pay and Stubby show off something they've made. Who cares that everyone says they're geniuses when it comes to working with wood?

I know Mother and Father go out of their way to praise anything I do, but I've never seen that genuine look of amazement directed at me. I've never heard anyone take a sharp gasp of surprise about anything I've done. I've never seen people exchange quick glances of disbelief over anything I've written or said.

Mother told me with time I'd find my calling, that my siblings were unusual because they'd discovered theirs so early. But now, it was too late for me.

The Johnny Reb let out a long, low whistle, probably calling more of the Confederate murderers to come help him find me.

I knew what a horrible choice I'd made just six weeks ago. If only I could go back.

Oh, why? Why hadn't I listened when the boss of the *Toronto Globe* offered me the job of being the paper's number one reporter and headline writer even though I'm only thirteen years old?

If only I could take back my foolish hasty words when I told him, "Thank you very kindly, sir, but there's a battle being fought in the United States of America to free the slaves, and there are recruiters in Michigan who need all the help they can get. This time next week, I will be a drummer boy in Mr. Lincoln's army!"

Now, I wished more than anything that I'd never heard about being a drummer boy, even if it was what all the bravest boys in Buxton dreamed about doing.

But this Southern traitor who was hunting me down was going to spill into the soil, along with my blood, all the dreams I'd worked so hard on. It would all end here in the dirt outside of Macon, Georgia. My plans of becoming the best newspaperman in North America were over.

All the headlines and leads I'd practiced writing in my head every day were for nothing.

A waste of time.

From the corner of my eye, I could see the rebel standing on the trail, not twenty feet from me. Neither one of us moved. Then he started moving away, looking for broken twigs or footprints, something, anything that would lead him to me.

It wouldn't be easy for him; the forest has always helped me. I lay as still as death, my nose pressed so tightly to the earth that little pieces of dirt and rotting leaves rolled up my nostrils when I breathed in and rolled back when I breathed out. They tickled me, but laughing was the farthest thing from my mind.

I waited forever.

And ever.

Then I let myself believe the impossible: He was gone! He'd missed me! All the life that had been draining out of me started flowing back! I trembled from the soles of my feet to the crown of my head. To be safe, I slowly counted to one hundred.

Just to be sure, I did it a second time.

Then a third.

I raised my head.

He'd missed me! I was still alive! This seemed too good to be true!

It *was* too good to be true.

His voice came from behind me, so close that he could have whispered, but no, he gave that cursed rebel yell, and it felt as if a lightning bolt chucked from the heavens cut me clean in two. My head jerked up; I couldn't help myself.

"Yee-haw!" the Confederate murderer hollered. "I sho 'nuff knowed that you all was gonna move, little black boy! Now you all's gonna find out what we'uns do to y'all Yankees what wants to come down he-uh to steal our grandpappy's land and take away them slaves what loves us so-o-o-o much! Yee-haw! You all needs to get ready to meet yer maker! Y'all got any last words, huh, Yankee? Yee-haw! Yee-haaaaw!"

I kept my eyes closed. My head dropped back to the ground like it weighed a ton.

I was ready.

He pressed something smooth and cool to the back of my neck, right at my hairline.

The old soldiers say you never hear the one that kills you. And I suppose maybe there is some comfort in knowing that.

But I heard everything. So there was no comfort to be found.

He pulled back a bit, then fired. It hit with a loud thump right in the area between my neck and skull. A flood of light exploded from the back of my head and ran throughout my body.

This was so unfair.

And I was surely going to let him know.

"Oww! Are you crazy? That hurt!"

I jumped up and rubbed the spot where he'd shot me. A lump on the back of my neck had already begun swelling.

"You cheated!"

He was laughing.

I snatched the bow away from him. "Where's the arrow?"

The way he was laughing got me madder and madder. "It ricocheted off your head and flew all the way into the woods!"

One thing was settled. Spencer Alexander was about two seconds away from being seriously whipped by his own bow. The only question was how bad the beating would be. If he'd taken the plum off the end of the arrow, I'd really pummel him. If the plum was still on, I'd show a little mercy, something he hadn't shown me.

I spotted the arrow, the tip still covered by the plum. At least he hadn't cheated that way.

"Spencer?"

"Huh?"

I swung. The bow whistled, then made a sharp crack when it caught his leg.

He didn't waste any time; he ran down the trail and I was right behind him.

I was able to hit him twice before he saw that if he got off the path and ran through the woods, I'd have a tougher time hitting him.

"Benji! Wait! I'm sorry!"

I missed again.

"It's too late for sorry, and what kind of accent was that? You think all white southern American people say 'yee-haw' and 'you all' every other word? And have such bad grammar?"

He yelled over his shoulder, "I was just trying to be authentic."

"Well, then, Spencer Alexander, I hope you're ready to take this authentic Buxton butt whipping!"

I swung two more times, but he was dodging so closely between trees that I slapped more oaks and maples than my cheating friend.

The spot where he'd shot the back of my neck throbbed as we ran through the woods.

I swung again, but instead of hitting Spencer, the bow wrapped around a sapling and snapped back, giving me a stinging blow to my upper lip.

I stopped and covered my mouth with my hand. I tasted blood.

Spence turned around and leaned on his knees, trying to catch his breath. "Serves you right, Benji; you know I was just —"

Two plum-tipped arrows wobbled from the woods right toward Spence. One caught him in the chest, and the other went square into his ear.

Pilot and Randall drew back two more arrows.

Pilot said, "The choice is yours, Johnny Reb: a slow, long starving death in prison, or a quick shot to the heart here."

Spence rubbed his ear and yelled, "You cheated, Pilot! You know we said nothing above the shoulders!"

I said, "Pilot cheated? Who shot me in the back of my head . . . point-blank?"

"That was different. You flinched, and I accidentally shot."

"I flinched? I didn't even move."

"Besides," Spencer said, "we're all square; you whacked me three times with my own bow!"

I snapped his bow over my knee. "Well, now you don't have to worry about that."

"I'll never play American Civil War with you again, Benji Alston. You take things too serious. If you *were* with the North, they never would've won the war."

Pilot said, "This is getting boring. I feel like a swim."

Spencer can always be counted on to do what's right. He stuck his hand out. "Sorry, Benji, I just got caught up in the chase. It was like you were a rabbit and I was a fox — as soon as you put your head down, something inside quieted my good sense and the next thing I knew, the arrow was flying."

I shook his hand. "Sorry I whipped you with your own bow. I'll get Pay and Stubby to make you a new one."

"Yee-haw! Reach for the skies, you all Yankee dogs!"

Big Twin and Little Twin peeked out from behind two trees, their arrows aimed at me and Randall.

Pilot said, "That's it, I quit. Let's go for a swim."

That was the end of the American Civil War as it was fought in the woods of Canada in 1901.

The whole thing was a waste of time, but I *was* able to get a good headline out of it:

JOHNNY REBS LOST THE WAR THIRTY-SIX YEARS
AGO AND LOSE IT AGAIN TODAY. SOME FOLKS
NEVER LEARN!!!

→ CHAPTER 2 ←

Little Better Than a Workhorse

ALVIN "RED" STOCKARD OF
CHATHAM, ONTARIO, CANADA

Grandmother O'Toole says structure and consistency are the backbones of a righteous life, so at the exact same day and time of each week, she and I walk to purchase the week's groceries.

These excursions are a good and true measure of how much I have matured over the years. To the best of my recollection, they began around the time I was seven years old, well before I'd trained myself to think using the scientific method. If they had started after my education, it wouldn't have taken me so long to wonder why, instead of walking straight down Main Street to buy the groceries, we took a detour that kept us off Main for one block before we returned to it.

Without fail, every Saturday morning at seven thirty-five, we would leave home and walk four blocks directly east on Main Street. When we got to Second Avenue, we'd turn left and go north for a block, passing Harrison's Furniture Shoppe. We'd turn right on Holmes Street, heading east again for a block, and once we reached Third Avenue, we would turn back right, head south for a block, and back to Main. Then we would turn left and continue east for another eight blocks to reach Shanahan's Groceries.

We had been doing it for so many years that the whole exercise seemed completely normal to me, never mind that we were walking three blocks out of our way and passing Langston's Groceries, said to be a perfectly fine grocery store, only to walk another eight blocks down to Shanahan's.

Our behaviour was much like Mr. Younger's old workhorse: The poor beast had walked a certain way home from the fields for years and couldn't change its route even though the Youngers' barn had burned down and they had long ago moved. The horse was walking a way that didn't make any sense, but he was comfortable doing it. With the help of a fireman, I finally reasoned that Grandmother O'Toole and I were doing the same thing.

But even as young as seven, I had an inkling that something wasn't right with our walks. It was at that tender age that we'd made our usual Saturday morning turn north on Second and were in front of the furniture store when, as we passed, I looked into the window of Harrison's.

What I saw made me stop dead in my tracks. I called, "Grandmother O'Toole! Wait! Come back!"

She said, "What nonsense is this? Ye've no money for buying overpriced furniture. Keep walking."

But my surprise had been real and deep enough that I ignored her. I pointed at the window and said, "There! Look!"

She came back, looked into the window, and said, "Well?"

I pointed, and even though she told Father otherwise, I truly wasn't trying to be disrespectful or impudent; what I saw in that window caused heartfelt surprise.

I'd always pictured Grandmother O'Toole as a towering silo of a person. I thought if she was standing in the east at six in the morning, the sun's rays would have difficulty reaching earth until she decided to move. But as my eyes beheld the two people reflected in the shop window, my head spun.

There was no doubt who the boy with the dazed expression and the bright red hair was. It was obviously I. Who, then, was the tiny, sad, tired old woman standing next to the boy? The woman who was peering so intently into the window with her right hand shading her eyes? The woman in rather shabby clothes who was only a wee bit taller than the redheaded lad; the woman who couldn't have weighed more than ninety-five pounds?

I said, "Grandmother O'Toole, that's you! *And we're the same size!*"

14

She swung her cane at me, but if I see it coming, I'm usually able to dodge it.

Soon after that, on another Saturday morning, the smell of smoke was heavy in the air as we left home. The ruckus we'd heard earlier in the morning had been Harrison's furniture store burning to the ground. When we made our turn onto Second Avenue, the street was completely impassable. Firemen were still pumping water on the smoking remains of Mr. Harrison's store.

One of the firemen said, "Hello, Mrs. O'Toole, Alvin. Afraid you're a bit late. If you'd've come earlier, you'd really have seen quite a blaze."

I said, "Hello, Mr. Thompson. We didn't come to look at the fire, sir; we're on our way for groceries."

"Groceries?" Mr. Thompson gave me a peculiar look.

He said, "Why didn't you just keep heading down Main? Langston's is right there, you know; why come this way?"

Those words were as revelatory to me as the sight that led the little boy in the fable to say, "But the emperor has no clothes!" As soon as Mr. Thompson asked that question, our route to groceries became obviously strange to me as well. Why *had* we made this detour for all these years?

I looked at Grandmother O'Toole, but she was glaring at the fireman. My skin flushed. About the only people she hates more than black Canadians are Canadians in uniform; this could turn into a terrible fight.

She seemed to grow right before my eyes, becoming silo-sized again. "Why's the way I walk to the grocery store any matter to ye? Perhaps if ye were as concerned about what goes on in yer house with yer wife and daughters when yer gone, ye'd not be so keen to be prying into other people's business."

She grabbed my hand, and relief washed over me that she said no more. We went back to Main and walked the block we'd never walked before.

When we passed Langston's grocery store, Mr. Langston's son, Huey, was standing in front, sweeping the sidewalk.

He called, "Good morning, Mrs. O'Toole; good morning, Alvin. Terrible about the fire, isn't it?"

She pulled me along by my collar and hissed at me, "If ye say one word to him, ye little magpie, I'll strap ye within an inch of yer blessed life, then tie ye to a tree in the South Woods so's that black savage Lion Man can come and eat all the meat off yer very bones. "

Most times she ended that story by saying that all Father would find was my skeleton at the base of a tree. Today she was too angry to give the usual ending.

We walked right by Huey Langston and I kept my eyes

down, saying a prayer of gratitude that an ugly confrontation had been avoided.

I could have saved my gratitude.

Huey Langston called after us, "Would either of you like to sample these grapes that just came in?"

Grandmother O'Toole stopped as if she'd been slapped. She released the collar of my shirt and walked back to Huey Langston. She hadn't shrunk from her talk with Mr. Thompson.

She snapped, "So tell me, you think we need yer charity, do ye?"

He seemed surprised. "Dear me, no, Mrs. O'Toole; it's just that the grapes are exceptionally sweet, and I thought . . ."

Grandmother O'Toole said, "Pardon me if ye would, before ye foul the air with any of the balderdash tha' 'tis rattling about in your head, and tell me, is yer father still among the living?"

"Well, yes, Mrs. O'Toole; he's not doing well, you know. Poor man will be ninety-five years old in September."

Grandmother O'Toole said, "Would ye be so kind to deliver a word or two to him for me?"

Poor, innocent Huey Langston said, "Why, of course! Hearing from old friends and customers is one of the few things that brings a smile to Dad's face."

A knot began tightening in my stomach.

"Wonderful!" she said. "But I was neither a friend nor a customer of the rotten old bugger. I know it's convenient for ye to forget, but yer lovely, ailing father wouldn't serve us, wouldn't even let us in the door. So would ye kindly tell him that Sinead O'Toole says that tonight she'll pray hard that the lamb of God stirs his hoof through the roof of heaven and kicks yer father square in his arse straight down to hell? Could ye pass that along to the fine old gentleman for me? Perhaps 'twill help speed the old rotter on his way."

Grandmother O'Toole's lungs must be similar in size to those of an elephant, for as Mr. Huey Langston stood there sputtering, she dredged up a huge wad of saliva from her chest and splashed it on the window of Langston's Groceries.

She dragged me toward Shanahan's Groceries. I don't know who was more appalled, me or Huey Langston.

A few blocks down Main Street, I found my voice. "Grandmother O'Toole! How could you say those horrible things, and why did you do that to the Langstons' store? Father will die of embarrassment. He is the judge after all!"

She stopped and grabbed my shoulders.

She said, "Listen, ye little redheaded monster. Ask yer father about those people. Those good, God-fearing Canadian Langstons. Ask him if he remembers what they were like not so many years passed. Ask him about the sign the upright Mr. Langston had in that very window of his shop."

I knew I was stepping over my bounds, but I had to say, "Sign? What kind of sign could make you treat someone so rudely?"

"Ask yer father why we used to have to go all the way to London or even down into that cursed Buxton to shop. Have him tell ye why we had to pay some other Canadian person to shop for us in Langston's before Shanahan's opened up."

"What?"

"Oh, so ye don't know everything, do ye?"

"Grandmother O'Toole, what are you talking about?"

"'Tisn't my job to explain these things to ye. Ask your da. Let him tell you about the sign that hung in that window not twenty years past, big as anything, that said, WE SERVE NEITHER BLACKS — NOR DOGS — NOR IRISH."

"What? *Really?*"

"I swore those many years ago that my shadow would never darken the doorstep of that store. Now that carbuncle of a son wants to act as though all's forgiven and forgotten. Well, 'tis not. It will burn within me till the day I die."

"I didn't know they did that. How could they not let people in because of where they're from?"

Grandmother O'Toole was hopeless. Any sort of sympathy or understanding I might have felt toward her flew away when she said, "They did it because they're fools. That's why I hate these Canadians even more than I hate the English."

Then she brought up one of her favourite subjects to moan about — the Saint Lawrence River and Grosse Ile, where she and her family first landed in Canada.

"'Tis beyond the personal, laddie. Yes, the Canadians murdered many of us on those ships in the river, but if you're approaching things with the mind of a divil, which is all they're capable of, that can be understood. They didn't want the jail fever to spread and they didn't care who they hurt to stop it.

"But that filthy sign in that window is what opened my eyes to show these Canadians are lower than even the scabbiest Englishman."

She banged her cane on the sidewalk. "How dare they? How dare they put a good white Irish soul in the same light and breath that they put one of those black heathens from Buxton? 'Tis the grandest of insults; for that they'll never be forgiven."

Even though I was only seven years old when it happened, I still remember how clearly I wished I could spend my Saturday mornings somewhere else.

→ CHAPTER 3 ←

The Tree House

BENJI

"Can you believe this, Benji?"

What a silly question. No one would believe this.

The second I saw it, two feelings started tussling inside me: pride and envy. And those are two feelings that never sit comfortably in the same spot at the same time.

Spencer said, "From down here it looks better put together than my own home. Look at the way those joints are perfectly tight, and how those windows fit. And the shingles! They're so spot-on, it looks as though they were painted on instead of being real pieces of cedar. This is amazing!"

Me and Spencer were standing at the base of a sixty-five-foot tall maple, our heads thrown back and our mouths open, showing that same stupid look of amazement everyone gets when they see something Stubby and Patience have made from wood.

"Boy!" Spence said. "Let's go up."

Spencer couldn't stop pointing out how perfect everything had been put together.

"Even the boards for the ladder have been shellacked and routed! Why would they go through all of that trouble?"

"They're showing off," I said. "They don't have a bit of humbleness between them; they're grandstanding."

Spencer said, "I don't think so. If they were trying to show off, seems to me like they would've built this right on the road so folks could easily see it, not hidden so deep in the woods."

"Are we going to talk about this or go up?"

We climbed the ten boards to the tree house. When we got to the trapdoor at the top and climbed through, instead of leading into the house, it opened onto a porch with a railing and two rocking chairs!

"A porch?" Spencer said. "They put a porch on a tree house? And look how solid it is."

He jumped hard and nothing moved, nothing. The tree house was braced so strong that it might as well have been sitting right on Buxton's soil instead of being put in the boughs of a maple, twenty-five feet off the ground.

Spence laughed and said, "A screen door too? Did you have any idea your brother and sister were this skilled?"

Who didn't know? Mr. Craig, the master carpenter, had told Mother and Father they felt and understood wood like no one he'd ever known.

I said, "I get the point; they're very good."

I hoped that didn't sound like a compliment. It wasn't meant to.

"I can't wait to see what's inside."

Spence opened the screen door. I followed him in.

It was dark and cool inside. The only light that found its way into the tree house sneaked in through the four windows, one on each wall. It took a while for our eyes to get used to the dark.

The giant maple went right down the middle of the house, coming out of the floor and leaving through the ceiling. In one corner sat their wooden toolboxes, Patience's with two horses carved on the top, and Stubby's with a train.

"Those two have got a lot of nerve coming into our woods and building this without asking," I told Spence. "A lot of nerve."

"I can't believe how beautiful this is; they must have started during the first thaw. They've been working really hard on this for a very long time."

"Doesn't matter," I snapped. "If we let them get away with this, who knows what's next? Why, they might even try to put a . . . a . . . sawmill in, and then what happens? There'd be people from all over Elgin County invading our woods to get lumber cut."

Spencer didn't understand how serious this was. He laughed and said, "Maybe they'll let us use it some of the time."

"Let us *use* it? Let *us* use something in *my* own woods? No, Spencer Alexander! This thing has got to go."

"Benji, haven't you noticed? This tree house isn't going anywhere for a good long time. It's built like a brick crap house; I think it could last for a hundred years."

He still didn't understand. And I didn't have a hundred years to wait.

"Then *we'll* tear it down."

"*What?*"

"You heard me. We'll tear it down."

He saw I was serious and said, "Aww, Benji, let's just —"

I said, "We're friends for life. You *have* to help me."

"I don't know, Benji. If we tore the tree house down, it would be like we stole it from them."

I hate moments like this! Times when you're arguing with a forensics champion who lives and breathes public speaking, and all of the good points seem to be on his side. It's like every argument you come up with gets sunk as soon as you launch it.

"Wait!" I said. "Instead of getting axes and tearing the tree house down, we could bring it down in sections very gently, then we could put it right back up!"

Spencer looked at me for a very long time, then shook his head.

"Benji Alston, that is the worst idea I've ever heard in my life. I've got a better idea. Instead of tearing it down and putting it back up, why don't we pretend we took it down, go swimming, then come back and pretend we put it up again? You're sounding very addled, you know."

"You didn't give me a chance to finish," I told Spencer. "We'll take it down, then put it back up, but . . ."

I paused, a trick I'd learned from Mr. Swan, who's the best storyteller in Buxton. You find yourself paying even more attention and getting even more excited when he pauses in unexpected places in his stories. I was giving Spencer the same chance.

He looked at me and if there was *one* trace of excitement anywhere inside him, he was really good at hiding it.

I finished, "But! When we put the tree house back up, *we'll put it back upside down*! Can't you see what a hoot that would be? They'd cry like babies! We could hide in the woods and watch; it would be great fun!"

"Benji, can't you see how long that would take? This is a fortress."

"We'll have four days. Patience and Stubby are supposed to go to Toronto to visit Uncle June with Father. We'll have plenty of time."

"Four days?"

"Four."

Spence scratched his chin and smiled. "I'm only doing this because we're best friends. But you'll be greatly in my debt, Benji Alston, greatly."

Spence laughed and offered his hand.

As soon as we shook hands, I was a bit disappointed that since Spencer is supposed to be so good with words, he hadn't done a better job of talking me out of this. It did seem like a lot of work for nothing.

If I wrote this as an article for my paper, I'm afraid the headline would have to read:

PAIR OF IDIOTS SPOTTED SHAKING HANDS
UNDER TREE HOUSE.

Oh well, in for a penny, in for a pound.

We took the shingles off first and then, using the mule and a block and tackle, brought each half of the roof down separately.

Taking the tree house down was a cinch; we had it resting on the ground with less than a day's work. Putting the whole thing back upside down was a house of a different colour.

→ Chapter 4 ←

The True Story behind Curly Bennett Losing His Mind

RED

I couldn't believe what I'd done. For one who tries to live by the scientific method, I had fallen horribly short. The beauty of scientific thinking is that it can be applied to events not related to science. Therefore, if I would have simply and impartially observed all of the data, I would not have been so startled when the truth became clear.

This much was obvious: Curly Bennett's father was back to drinking and, judging from my observations, he was drinking hard.

He was neither raging in town nor urinating in or otherwise fouling the wells of those with whom he had some type of disagreement, but the signs were there just the same: Curly's mother's seamstress shop had been closed since Wednesday, Curly had missed nearly a week of school, and when I went to their cabin, he answered my knock but wouldn't open the screen door. In addition to this, he was wearing his hat inside the house.

"Hey, Red."

"Hey, Curly."

Most times, Curly would step out on the porch and exchange a few words with me, but he kept himself in shadows behind the closed screen door.

We looked at each other before I finally said, "So how are you doing?"

"I'm fair to middling."

"Are you coming to school at all this week?"

"I ain't sure."

"A few of the lads and I are going fishing later this evening and were wondering if you wanted to join us?"

"Naw, I'm just . . . Who's going?"

"Hickman, the Baylis boys, and me."

"What 'bout Petey?"

"I'm not sure; no one has asked him."

"Why not?"

"There's no reason. I suppose I could."

"Well, if all the people you said *and* Petey Demers are going fishing, walk by here and whistle and I'll go too."

Curly was known for peculiar behaviour, so this didn't strike me as strange.

"All right, if Petey comes, I shall whistle from the woods behind your house. Make sure you dig up some night crawlers."

"You make sure Petey's there." He closed the screen

door, then pushed it back open a crack. "Don't let Pa see none of you."

Everybody knew the fewer dealings one had with Curly's pa, the better.

"I'm not stupid."

I could make out a smile on Curly's face through the screen.

"I know, you just look that way."

I shook my head and walked toward the road.

That evening, Bucky and Buster Baylis, Hickman Holmely, and Petey Demers waited on the road while I walked the path to Curly's shack. They refused to come with me; they took the sign that read ALL TREZPASERS WILL GET SHOT very seriously.

There were no lamps lit at the Bennett cabin. No one was sitting in the chairs out front, so I stayed in the woods and sneaked around to the back. I brought my fingers to my lips.

Before I could whistle one note, a thick arm wrapped around my neck from behind, blocking any attempt to breathe and causing my feet to dangle off the ground.

My heart stopped!

A voice growled, "What you doing sneaking 'round my house, boy?"

Curly set me back on my feet and laughed softly.

"What is wrong with you? I nearly died of fright! I thought your father had captured me!"

When he set me down, the hat he was wearing was knocked askew, and I could see that his right eye was swollen shut and his lip was puffy and appeared overly ripe.

Curly quickly pulled the hat over his face again.

He said, "Did Petey come?"

"Yes; why are you showing all of this interest in Petey so suddenly?"

"Who said I was interested in Petey?"

"Well, you never . . ."

He punched my arm. "So, we going fishing or we gonna sit and chat like this is afternoon tea, Your Honour?"

Curly called me that whenever he wanted to put me in my place. Since Father is a judge, he probably thinks it's an insult.

He picked up a tin can that I assumed held night crawlers and headed toward the road.

There were so many questions that needed asking, but my breathing had not yet returned to normal from the scare I'd taken. I rubbed my throat and quietly followed.

The lads were still at the side of the road. As soon as they saw us, they stood and started pelting Curly with the same questions I wanted to ask.

"Hey, Curly, we ain't seen you at school; what's the matter?"

"Why you got that hat pulled so low?"

"How come your ma's got her shop shut up?"

"Sharon said you're about to move; is that true?"

"Why haven't you been hunting with your brother?"

Curly brushed their questions aside and said, "By the time I answer all your prattles and nonsense, the fish will quit biting."

He looked directly at Petey. "Ain't you got no questions to ask, Petey?"

Petey shrugged. "I figure if you got something to say, you'll say it."

Curly edged up to Petey.

"Matter of fact, I do got something to say. I got a couple questions for you."

Petey just looked at him, wondering like the rest of us what this was all about.

Curly said, "You're pretty tall, ain't you?"

Petey looked down into Curly's eyes in such a way that any answer would be redundant.

Curly said, "Just how tall are you?"

Petey said, "Six feet, three inches. Why?"

Curly said, "I was just wondering how high they could pile crap before it would tip over."

Those intemperate words made every one of us on the road that night freeze. Petey could be played with, but only up to a point. I was sure Curly had reached that point and gone far beyond.

I tried changing the subject. "You get many night crawlers, Curly?"

An object in motion tends to stay in motion, and the same can be said of many an argument. Curly was determined to start something and wasn't waylaid by any of my distractions. He swung and hit Petey in the chest. It wasn't a light punch like he'd given me; he put all of his weight behind it.

Petey staggered a little, then looked hard at Curly.

Hickman said, "Ha-ha, what are you doing, Curly? That's Petey."

It wasn't clear if Hickman intended that to mean this was Petey our friend or this was Petey who, at only sixteen years old, was the second-most brutal brawler in all of Chatham, but either way, the meaning was obvious: Curly was treading a dangerous path.

Petey and Curly were the only two of us who'd ever spent any time inside of the jail. Father told me he'd put Curly behind bars to put the fear of God in him and try to stop what seemed inevitable, and all of Chatham knew Petey had been jailed for beating two grown men near to death. At the same time!

I didn't know which was more shocking, when Petey began walking back toward Chatham without doing anything or when Curly started after him.

To stop this before it became tragic, Hickman and the Baylis boys grabbed Curly.

Hickman said, "Curly, what is wrong with you? Go apologize."

Curly breathed heavily from his mouth and slapped their hands away.

I said, "Curly . . ."

He ran toward Petey and swung as hard as he could at the back of Petey's head.

I immediately wished I'd warned Petey.

What followed was the sickening sound of bone crashing into bone.

Petey stumbled forward and fell.

Buster Baylis said, "Oh, dear! That proves it; Curly Bennett has lost his mind!"

The time it took Petey to sit up and wipe the dirt from his face was when I finally put it all together and reached the only sensible conclusion: Curly had not lost his mind at all; this made perfect sense. He knew if he showed up at school again bruised and beaten by his drunken father, Miss Jacobs would notify the constable.

It was indisputable; the variables were all there. The hat, the not coming out on the porch, the not being in school, his mother's shop shuttered, his wanting to make sure Petey came fishing, his need to be certain there were witnesses to what he wanted to happen. All led to the same conclusion: His father must have beaten Curly and his mother so severely that the only way Curly could show his battered face without getting his father tossed in jail was if he very publicly lost a fight to someone tougher than he.

If he had asked me, I would have pointed out that there were many less painful ways to do this than taking a thumping from Petey Demers. But he *had* thought it out carefully; fighting Petey guaranteed both a loss and a badly battered face and body.

"Curly!" Hickman yelled. "This is madness!"

Curly stood over Petey with his hands balled and his chest heaving.

Petey slowly pulled himself up. Curly raised his fists and squatted into a defensive posture.

Petey spit blood from his mouth, and then, in a beautifully righteous turning of the other cheek, started back down the road to Chatham.

"What?" Curly yelled at Petey. "You ain't gonna do nothing? You're just a yellow-bellied coward!"

Hickman grabbed Curly again to try to bring this nonsense to an end.

Curly yelled, "You're as worthless as your ma! She didn't even have the decency to stick with her own kind! She couldn't even get a white man to marry her!"

Petey's father was Cree and his mother was Irish. This was a constant source of problems for him. He had beaten those two men so ferociously because they had made rude, unflattering comments about his mother.

I found it hard to imagine their remarks were anywhere near as rude as this!

Hickman turned Curly loose as if he had metamorphosed into a ball of fire and said, "Ooh! You're on your own, chum."

Curly's words caused Petey to freeze in his tracks.

No one breathed.

But instead of coming back and beating Curly to within an inch of his life, Petey continued walking toward Chatham.

Hickman said, "I'd leave town if I were you; once he realizes what you said, he'll be back. I don't think this is over yet."

Curly turned on him. "You think I give a care what a low-down black fool like you has to say? You're the one who needs to leave town and go back to Africa or America, slave boy. Who wants your kind here in Canada anyway?"

Whatever sense of forgiveness had prevented Petey from attacking Curly did not extend to Hickman. His fists flew fast and accurately, and the wounds Curly's father had given him were soon reopened and fresh.

They fought long and hard, battling until they were tired enough that neither resisted when we pulled them apart.

Thus ended the strangest night of fishing I ever hope to be involved with. If I wasn't such a student of science, I would've blamed the shenanigans on the full moon.

CHAPTER 5

The Phoenix Flies!

BENJI

Spencer Alexander and I were standing in the exact same spot we'd stood four and a half days before, and just like then, our heads were thrown back, looking up. The difference was now me and Spence were bruised, cut, sore, and barely speaking to each other. We both looked like we'd fought a tiger.

My left thumbnail was gone and the thumb was probably broken from when I'd hit it with a hammer while trying to put shingles back on upside down. My left shoulder had been wrenched something terrible when the mule bolted and I didn't let go of the reins in time.

Spencer wasn't much better off. He sported a fresh black eye from where he'd been hit by a board, and had seven stitches closing a gash on his leg where the saw had slipped.

We'd worked hard for four and a half days and, even though it looked kind of shaky, the tree house was finally up just as I'd planned, upside down. The ladder now let you into the house through the upside-down roof, where I'd made a trapdoor in some of the shingles.

Making trapdoors looks easy, but take my word, it isn't.

I'd even nailed the chairs back on the porch upside down.

It was a lot of work, and while most times if you work hard at something, you feel a sense of pride when you're done, all I felt was embarrassed.

Spencer didn't look real pleased with himself either.

We'd been avoiding each other's eyes.

He said, "I have to tell you, Benji, this was a lot of work just to make your brother and sister cry and hurt their feelings. Instead of going through all of this . . . this . . ."

He waved one hand at the upside-down tree house. For once the great debater was having trouble finding the right word.

". . . this folderol, it would have been a lot less painful if we had just walked up to Patience and Stubby, punched each of them in their noses, then taken our punishments."

What could I say? The whole adventure *was* ridiculous. We both knew it, but Spencer couldn't stop himself from beating the dead horse even more.

"It reminds me of that old proverb that says the mountain laboured mightily and brought forth a mouse. That's what's happened, Benji. You and I just worked our tails off and gave birth to an upside-down mouse."

He started limping toward the road home. He wasn't through; he had to add, "I used to be sad that I don't have brothers and sisters, but after seeing how strangely siblings act with each other, I see I've actually been blessed."

And even though he now understood how lucky he was to be an only child, his words stung. There had to be more, there had to be a way to make all of our work something more than a mean, pitiful way to make those spoiled brats cry. There must be something to make a phoenix arise from the ashes of my envy.

A smile slowly crept across my face. I had it! Flipping their tree house over might only make Patience and Stubby cry, but if this new plan worked, I'd scare them so much they'd stay out of these woods forever! All of this trouble might be worthwhile after all.

There were silly stories that some of the old folks in Buxton made up about someone they called the Madman of Piney Woods. Even though they talked about him like he was a boogeyman and used him to scare us into doing some things and not doing others, what really made him real to me and the other children was that the original settlers of Buxton wanted to make certain we didn't plague him in any way.

I remember once, Mrs. Solomon had got wind of me and Spencer sneaking off into the woods late at night. She'd told us the Madman had put a spell on rabbits and turned them into vicious killers who hunted when it was dark and ate any children who weren't in bed where they were supposed to be.

Spence had told Mrs. Solomon, "My father's taught me to hunt, and when I go out, I'm taking the shotgun and if I see him, I'm going to put an end to this Madman."

Mrs. Solomon is old and sits mostly in a wheelchair, but right after those words passed Spence's lips, she'd moved like a cat and used her cane to whack him hard in the stomach. He fell over, clutching onto his belly.

She'd stood over him and said, "If you even thank 'bout harming one hair on that man head, you'll be dealing wit' me, boy. Just stay out them woods at night, 'cause if he don't get you when you out there, then I'm-a get you when you gets back."

The stories about him just wouldn't stop, and we'd asked, "Shouldn't the constable be notified about what he's doing?"

Every question like that led to the answer, "He don't bother you and you best not bother him." And they meant it. We weren't sure if he was real or not, but with the old folks getting so upset, it seemed like there had to be something to the stories. Where there's smoke, there's fire.

Stubby was more scared of him than anyone else, and I was going to use that to my advantage!

I ran home to save the four and a half days of hard work me and Spence had put in from the scrap heap.

It's about time the Madman of Piney Woods did some work for young folks!

I'd sold myself short. The looks on Stubby's and Patience's faces made the whole prank worthwhile! And they hadn't even reached the scary part of my plan; that was going to be like the painting of the lily.

They were standing in the same spot where Spencer and I had stood, their mouths open and their eyes locked on their topsy-turvy tree house.

Patience's hand slowly came up to cover her mouth. Stubby's legs gave way and he plopped to the ground, the expression on his face never changing. Pay's hand reached down to him at the same time his hand reached up to her. She stood and he sat, holding hands with the most ridiculous looks on their faces!

Stubby said, "Oh, Patience, what a terrible nightmare this is! It can't be true and yet it seems so real."

In a dead voice, Patience said, "It *is* real. Charming Little Chalet in the Woods has been turned upside down."

I fought not to bust a gut; they'd even given the ridiculous tree house a ridiculous name!

Stubby said, "I *know* we had it braced up the proper way. How could this be?"

Patience said, "I don't know. There's something more to this."

Stubby said, "Do you suppose someone's placed some sort of spell or curse on it?"

I couldn't have asked for anything more! It was as though Stubby was setting everything up just as I wanted.

Patience said, "Spells are just superstitious nonsense."

Stubby said, "How else to explain that?"

He pointed at Charming Little Chalet in the Woods.

"Should we go tell Mother and Father?"

Pay said, "We can't; this is supposed to be our secret. Besides, they'd ask too many questions about where we got the money for the lumber and nails."

"What about Benji? Maybe he'd know what we should do."

Her answer cut me to the quick and made me wish I'd followed my first instinct and smashed their tree house into a million splinters.

Patience snorted and said, "Benji is just a blowhard. I trust that boy as far as I can throw him."

Digging the dagger even deeper into my back, Stubby didn't offer one word on my behalf.

Patience said, "Our tools! We've got to go up and see if they are still there. I don't care about ghosts. I need my tools."

She slowly climbed the ladder. When she got to the trapdoor in the cedar shingles, she called down to Stubby, "It *didn't* just flip over in the wind; someone has cut a door into the shingles. It looks as though a child did it."

Another knife in my back. It was while working on that trapdoor that I'd broken my thumb.

Patience disappeared into the roof and after a moment called out, "The toolboxes are here!"

Her head popped out of the trapdoor and she yelled, "Someone's left a note in my toolbox!"

Stubby said, "A note? Is it just to you or is it to both of us? What does it say?"

"It's too dark in here to read. I'll lower the boxes."

Stubby's toolbox dangled out of the trapdoor from the end of a thick rope as Patience slowly lowered it to the ground. He untied it, and the rope went back up, then her tools came down.

She clambered down the ladder, holding my note.

Now the real fun and confusion were about to begin! Patience read my letter aloud.

"I am watching you! I know where you live! I will put the same upside-down spell on you that I put on this tree house! You will go through the rest of your life walking upside down! Your hands and arms are going to get very tired! This is your only warning!

*These are my new woods and you must leave and
never come back! Play only in your own backyard!
Or else!!!*

   *Sincerely Yours,
   The Madman Of Piney Woods"*

They looked around the woods, sensing they were being
watched. But I'd hidden myself so well in a tree that I
could've lit myself on fire and, except for noticing where
the smoke was coming from and my screams, they probably never would find me!

Patience said, "Let's go home; we can figure out what
to do there. I don't feel good being around here anymore;
it's kind of spooky."

They lugged their tools down the path, occasionally
throwing worried looks over their shoulders at the tree
house until they were out of sight.

I was redeemed! Not only had I given them a fright,
but they no longer felt comfortable in my neck of the
woods! My only regret was that Spencer hadn't been more
mature and wouldn't come with me to watch them discover
our work.

Patience and Stubby didn't say a word about the upside-
down tree house at supper that night nor for the next week.

If I'd built a Charming Little Chalet in the Woods and it got flipped over, I'd've been bursting to tell everybody, but my brother and sister kept their secret like it was hidden gold.

I checked the woods a couple of times and they hadn't been back. The rains had washed away the mule's tracks and the drag marks from the travois they'd used to bring everything in. The wood chips and slivers Spencer and I had made with our work were being slowly carried away by birds or squirrels or ants. The woods were bit by bit healing themselves.

I knew the battle was over and I was victorious when Pay and Stubby started working on some different harebrained project! This one was kept a secret too. Not that I'd want to see it anyway; as long as they stayed away from the woods in the north fifty, all would be peaceful.

Today's headline would read:

THE BEST-LAID PLANS OF MICE AND MEN MIGHT GO WRONG, BUT A WELL-THOUGHT-OUT SCHEME NEVER DOES.

⇥ Chapter 6 ⇤

Curly and Hickman Make Peace

RED

The fight between Curly Bennett and Hickman Holmely was the talk of the school the next day.

"Did you see his face afterward? He probably won't come back to classes at all after taking a pounding as severe as that one."

"He beat him to a bloody pulp!"

"Wait," someone asked, "you mean to say Curly Bennett beat Hickman Holmely?"

Bucky Baylis said, "No! Hickman delivered a great proper thumping to Curly!"

"No!"

Since Hickman and I were considered to be the most intelligent boys in the school, most people believed us to be both unwilling and incapable of fighting. Particularly fighting someone as tough as Curly Bennett.

Buster said, "It's true; ask Red!"

All eyes fell on me.

"Yes," I said, "it was as though Curly's heart was not in the matter at all."

"Why'd they fight?"

"Curly sneaked up behind Petey Demers and . . ."

"Wait. Oh, I see, it was *Petey Demers* who whipped Curly! That makes a whole lot more sense."

"No!" the Baylis boys and I shouted at the same time.

"Then how was Petey Demers involved?"

"If you'd listen quietly, I could explain," Buster said. "Curly punched Petey, and Petey just walked away, so Curly mentioned to Petey that Petey's mother wasn't good enough to get a white man to marry her and . . ."

"Oh, poppycock! Curly said that about Petey's mother and we aren't at Curly's funeral today? Nonsense. There's no way even someone as ill-bred as Curly Bennett would say that."

The Baylis boys and I said, "He *did*!"

We were standing at the side of the school, waiting for the bell, when the whispering suddenly stopped and all eyes went to the bend in the road. Hickman Holmely and Curly Bennett were walking side by side. They were laughing and in such a cheery mood that they might as well have been holding hands!

No one said a word as the odd pair approached.

If one were to look beyond the laughing and high

spirits, their physical appearance suggested they had been caught in the pounding surf at Lake Erie during a gale. Hickman's right eye was swollen shut; a trail of four parallel scratches started on his right cheek and ran over to the left, interrupted only by his nostrils. A plum-sized lump protruded from the centre of his forehead as if he were attempting to become a unicorn.

But Curly had clearly been left with the short end of the stick.

Hickman's fists had found all the same spots on Curly's face that his father had, and several more as well. A tremendous cut on his chin had been stitched closed, but the effort was wasted; flaps of flesh were dangling from the split that had been carelessly joined by green pieces of thread. His chin looked as though a farsighted person had attempted to sew two thickly cut slices of bacon together in a dark room.

In spite of their injuries, Curly and Hickman behaved as if everything was normal, as if their bumps and bruises and cuts were regular features on their faces.

Hickman said, "Hey, fellas, what's everyone talking about?"

We were all too thunderstruck to answer.

Curly said, "You act like you've seen a ghost. I'm sick at home for a week and everything comes apart at the seams?"

I couldn't take my eyes off the gash on his chin and think. Indeed, everything!

Bucky Baylis said, "This is quite peculiar. The last time we saw you, you were each vowing to never rest until the other was dead."

Hickman and Curly looked at each other through their respective one eye that was open and laughed.

Curly said, "Shucks, friends always have disputes. I suppose none of you has ever had an argument with a pal. If you were older and smarter, you'd do like I did and apologize for my unkindness and shake hands and let bygones be bygones."

Buster Baylis said, "Me and Bucky have disputes all the time, but they've never ended in attempted murder or mayhem."

Hickman said, "If we aren't worried about it, why should you be?"

The school bell rang and we lined up.

Buster whispered to me, "Maybe they want to act like there's nothing wrong, but we'll see what Miss Jacobs has to say about the matter."

Miss Jacobs greeted us at the door. "Hello, Kimberly. Please leave Leonard alone and tie your shoe before you sit. Good morning, Leonard. Good morning, Jessica."

Instead of saying anything to Hickman when he got to

the door, she grabbed his arm and pulled him aside. Curly received the same treatment.

"You two. A word."

When the last of us was in, Miss Jacobs put her head in the classroom and said, "Take your seats and no talking. I shan't be long."

Buster cupped his hand to his mouth and whispered what we all knew. "It's a good thing they've become such chums; they'll be duck-squatting in the cloakroom together until the dismissal bell is rung."

Five minutes passed before the classroom door opened and Hickman and Curly walked in. Instead of going to their seats or the cloakroom, they walked to the front of the class and stood side by side. Curly's head was slumped and Hickman stood in perfect speaker's posture, as if he were in the Upper Ontario Forensics Competition again.

Miss Jacobs said, "Mr. Bennett."

Curly said, "I said some unconsiderate and rude things to Mr. Holmely and I . . ."

If Curly thought this was going to be easy, Miss Jacobs had other plans.

She said, "Mr. Bennett, I have never seen a speaker approach his audience with his eyes so tightly clenched. I understand that the swelling has seen to it that your right eye is closed; please respect your audience by looking at them through the left one."

Curly sighed and opened his good eye.

"I spoke with rudeness and unconsideration to Mr. Holmely and I sincerely apologize."

Miss Jacobs said, "Well, I suppose your eye was open even though it was rolled all the way back in your head. You may be seated.

"Mr. Holmely?"

Hickman is by far Miss Jacobs's favourite student. She teaches English, and he has won the Upper Ontario Forensics Competition two of the past three years and sees every chance to speak in public as an opportunity to show off his oratorical skills. He is so talented that it's widely agreed he was cheated the one year he lost.

His face twitched as he tried mightily to open his left eye. He saw that it was too tightly closed, so he looked at each of us in the classroom with his right eye and said, "To my dear gathered fellow students whom are here all together on this special occasion of Mr. Bennett apologizing, I, being the humble and modest soul that all of you have learned to respect, must say that I too have fallen short and that to admit this to such a distinguished group leaves your lowly speaker humiliated and at a loss for words."

Miss Jacobs said, "Hardly, Mr. Holmely. Please limit the verbiage and get to the point."

"Thank you, Miss Jacobs; your most welcomed criticism

is appreciated and warmly taken deeply into the deepest and darkest chambers of my heart."

"Mr. Holmely, would you like me to walk you home after school?"

Hickman saw she was serious and finished quickly. "I apologize to Curly and my family for reacting to words that I should have ignored. Fighting and violence are traits of lower animals, not God-fearing human beings."

"Take your seat. Open your science books, please."

Curly and Hickman had obviously straightened out their difficulties. Somehow I didn't think it was going to be so easy for Curly to get back into Petey Demers's good graces.

CHAPTER 7

Demons Invade the Woods

BENJI

There was a furious pounding on our front door, followed by those hair-raising wails people make when they know their very lives are about to be cruelly snuffed out.

Maybe when I'm older, my newspaperman instinct will take over and I'll want to go investigate. But for now, my instinct was to get behind the couch as quickly as possible and make myself as small as I could.

When the door poundings continued with more and more screaming, I screamed too and peeked out as Mother rushed to open the front door.

The Miller twins nearly knocked her off her feet as they barreled in. They looked devastated, and each one had his cupped hands pressed hard against his ears. They huddled around Mother like startled chicks around a hen.

"Oh, Mrs. Alston," Big Twin wailed, "you must lock all the doors and close every window this minute! The woods are overrun with haints!"

"What?"

Little Twin said, "Haints! They're capturing most of the children and are leading them to who knows where! It's like the pied piper of Hamelin, Mrs. Alston! It's the same dreadful story!"

Big Twin said, "We were walking through the woods and saw hundreds of children that had already been captured; the poor souls had bags tied over their heads and were under some wretched spell! They were laughing as they were being led away, *laughing*, I tell you!"

Little Twin said, "Their hands were tied behind them and they were holding another rope and marching in a long line! There was a tiny ghoul that wasn't more than two feet tall flying in front of them, enchanting them with a magic flute while another was behind beating a drum."

Big Twin cried, "It has to be the Madman of Piney Woods behind this! He's using those demons to get revenge on everyone who's ever lied about him!"

Little Twin said, "Yes, and I'm afraid Big Twin has made up some horrible tales about him!"

Mother grabbed one of each twin's arms, but they kept their hands over their ears.

"Boys! Calm down! Stop all of this exaggerating!"

Big Twin said, "Pardon me, ma'am?"

Mother pulled his hands from his ears, held his arms at his sides, and looked directly into his eyes.

"Philip, Gregory, do not tell me what you imagined, tell me exactly what you saw."

I'd forgotten the Miller twins had real names.

Big Twin said, "It's just as Little Twin said, every horrible moment of it! There are two small demons leading away hundreds of enchanted children who have sacks tied over their heads!"

The second he stopped talking, his hands flew back over his ears.

"Boys!" Mother said. "Calm down!"

She pried Little Twin's hands from his head and said, "There are no demons in the woods. Do not put your hands near your ears again!"

Little Twin said, "Oh, Mrs. Alston, I'll never be able to get the sight out of my eyes! Please, if you don't give us shelter, our deaths will be on your hands! Please don't turn us out into those woods! Please, we beg you!"

They were frantic. They began jumping up and down and their hands once again covered their ears. Their eyes remained squeezed tightly shut.

Mother said, "Benji, get from behind that couch and come help me."

Mother roughly shook each twin and pulled their hands from their ears. They opened their eyes.

Big Twin said, "Please tie us to something so we can't be enchanted and led away, please!"

"Calm down! Why are you covering your ears like this?"

"The music, Mrs. Alston! The dreaded music was what the demons were using to enchant the children. We don't want to hear it and become enchanted too!"

Mother threw her hands up in despair. "I've had enough of this nonsense. Benji, walk them home."

First one, then the other twin darted behind the couch that I had just left.

I couldn't believe my luck. What had started as a dull Tuesday evening was going to end in great fun! I began planning what I'd do as I walked them home.

I could lead the twins through the deepest part of the woods, tear away from them, and once I was sure they couldn't see me, I'd start whistling and banging!

They'd smack full speed into one tree after another! I knew this walk through the woods would produce one of the greatest headlines in the history of newspapers:

ANOTHER MYSTERY IN WOODS!! TWINS FOUND SENSELESS AT FOOT OF NEARLY TOPPLED ELM TREE! OTHER TREES IN FOREST SHOW SAME DAMAGE!

Mother said, "Benji, get those boys from behind that couch and take them home!"

The twins had other plans. They clung to each other and the back of the couch so hard that a team of the strongest draught horses couldn't have pulled them out. All I was able to do was tug the shoe and sock off of one of them and the britches off of the other.

Mother said, "Never mind, Benji. I blame Willie Swan and those foolish Saturday night fright stories of his for this. Run and tell their mother or father that these two are on the brink of losing their minds and need to be taken home."

I was disappointed but had no choice but to follow Mother's orders.

Of course I didn't believe the nonsense the twins were spouting, but I've noticed if a person sounds really sincere when they're telling you something and they even will disobey an adult's orders because they're so scared, you'd have to be daft not to wonder what they'd seen.

I'm not a coward, but I was glad there was a moon so everything was well lit as I walked to get Mr. and Mrs. Miller.

Not far from home, my breath caught when I saw two figures on the road walking toward me.

I was relieved when I recognized my brother and sister. They were coming home from their apprenticeships at the carpentry shop.

The second Stubby saw me, he hid what looked like an empty flour sack behind his back.

His shoulders stiffened and he avoided looking at me.

My spirits started rising again. Maybe this was going to be a fun Tuesday evening after all!

→ CHAPTER 8 ←

"Who, Then, Shall Bell the . . . ?"

RED

I didn't hear her sneak into the kitchen as I stirred the boiling potatoes I'd just peeled and cut into cubes.

My first clue should have been the whooshing sound her weapon made as it cut through the air. Instead, the stars that followed the solid clomp to the back of my head were what made me aware that she'd done it again.

It was simply by the greatest of luck that I didn't fall face-first into the boiling pot of potatoes.

I whipped around with the heavy metal spoon raised above my head like a dripping club. I knew full well it was she, but if I struck her one time quickly, I could tell Father I just blindly reacted and didn't know whom I was hitting.

She glared at me, her cold green eyes filled with anger.

I couldn't do it. I slowly brought the spoon down.

"Grandmother O'Toole! What is wrong with you?"

She cried, "Go ahead, ye little red-haired cur; ye think I don't know what ye've planned for me since your eyes first blinked into mine thirteen years past? Here! Here, black-heart, I'll make it easy for ye! D'not use a spoon; use what it is the divils are telling ye to!"

She picked up the knife I'd used to peel the potatoes and I saw how fortunate I'd been; she had hit me only with her cane. As confused and angry as she becomes, the whooshing sound I'd heard could have just as easily been the knife cutting through the air before she buried it to the hilt in my back.

She clasped the knife's blade and tried to force me to take the handle.

"Go ahead! Go ahead!"

She began unbuttoning her black sweater, showing so much of the skin on her bony chest that I feared I might have to gouge the eyes out of my head if she continued.

She finally stopped unbuttoning and pulled the sweater apart and shouted, "Plunge it in me chest! Finish the deed, filthy assassin! Why don't you just get it over with and mur-der me straight off instead of torturing me *this* way?"

She pointed and I saw what had caused her to become so upset.

The potato peels.

She scooped a handful of them from where they lay on the old newspaper. There was no confusion. Grandmother O'Toole was truly devastated.

"Grandmother, I'm sorry."

"Why do you spit in my face like this? Who are we? Are you the Queen of England? Am I? How can you do this? How dare you after all your great-grandparents went through?"

For being as old as she was, she had a terrific throwing arm. The potato peels hit my face with a splat.

"Are we so bloody wealthy that we can peel half the potato away? Are we so bloody high and mighty that we can throw out perfectly good peels?"

Grandmother O'Toole was absolutely insane when it came to potatoes. She had shown me many times how a potato was to be properly peeled, but I never could get them thin enough for her liking. She had the hands of a surgeon when it came to peeling potatoes; the peels were so thin when she finished that I wouldn't have been surprised if they had floated daintily to the ceiling. They were thinner even than the plant slide specimens I used in the microscope at school.

And she believed I cut them too thick on purpose.

I reached back to feel the spot on my head where she'd struck me. There was no blood, just the beginnings of a swelling.

Grandmother O'Toole said, "Aye! Serves ye right! That's the heavenly Father's punishment on ye for wasting his gifts."

She picked up her cane and limped out of the kitchen.

I looked at the clock. Father was supposed to be home from the courthouse in an hour; I hoped he'd see she'd gone too far. I hoped he would finally understand she really was out to kill me.

Father called from the front door, "Hullo! Another day's work is done and I'm back in the loving embrace of home!"

I went into the parlour to greet him.

"There he is, the handsomest boy in Chatham! And how was your day?"

I turned so he could see the back of my head and the lump Grandmother O'Toole's cane had given me.

Father sighed. "Oh, dear."

He looked carefully, frowned, and said, "My, my, my."

He sat down and patted the spot next to his on the divan.

"Alvin, have a seat."

"Yes, Father."

He put his arm around my shoulders.

I didn't even have to tell him what happened. He pulled me closer and said, "I'll talk to her."

"But, Father . . ."

"Let me finish, Alvin. She's gone too far, I know. But I want you to be aware of what the future holds if we do what we've talked about."

"Sir?"

"We both know the only practical solution is sending your grandmother away."

I was so relieved! "Oh, yes, Father! She could move in with Great-Aunt Margaret in Windsor."

"No, Alvin, your great-aunt can barely fend for herself. We'll have to have Mother O'Toole put in an asylum."

Father paused and I knew it was a time in which I was supposed to reflect on Grandmother O'Toole being forced into an asylum. It was time wasted, though; as far as I was concerned, sending her away was a grand idea.

Father and I each waited for the other to break the silence.

Finally he said, "Do you know what that means?"

"Yes, sir." I'd done my research and paraphrased one of the advertisements, "She would be in a place where she could be lovingly looked after. Where she'd be a hazard neither to herself nor others."

Father smiled. "That's nothing but advertising, son. The reality is much different."

"It is for the best, Father."

"Alvin, me boy . . ."

Those words and the return of his Irish brogue always signaled Father's best efforts to reason with me.

"You're a bright lad, so I'm going to speak to you the same way I'd speak to an adult. I know your grandmother can be difficult, but we *do* have to make certain allowances for her behaviour."

I was willing to hear him out, but I'd be amazed if he changed my mind.

"First, she's an elder to both of us . . . and second, she's kin as well. She is also the mother of the woman you and I loved above all others. Am I right?"

"Yes, Father."

"She's due all the respect in the world for those reasons if for nothing else. Plus, you should ask her about her life before she came to Chatham. Have you ever tried that? You might get an understanding of the crosses she bears."

"Father, it's difficult to talk to someone when they're always trying to slip up on you from behind and bash your skull in."

Father put the crook of his arm around my neck and tapped the top of my head with his fist.

"'Tis a good thing then that ye've a rock-hard Irish skull, is it not, me lad?"

I laughed.

"You owe it to yourself to give it a try, Alvin. If you can get her to tell you about those days, you might have a better understanding, or maybe even a bit of sympathy, for why she is the way she is."

"But, Father . . ."

"No, Alvin, you must talk to her. She's seen times you and I couldn't imagine, in Ireland, on the ship over, and even once she arrived in Chatham. But you need to be patient with her to get her to talk. Just try asking her once." Father smiled. "Remember, lad, 'tis not a tree in heaven higher than the tree of patience. Will ye give it a try? For your poor old father's sake?"

"But, Father, can't we hire someone to come watch over her? She's getting worse every day."

"Hire someone! Son, I'm just a judge; you know we barely get by on my salary."

"I nearly fell into the boiling potatoes, Father. Are we going to wait until she kills me?"

"I don't think it's that bad, Alvin. You've just got to be careful and more watchful when she's around."

"She's as sly as a fox, Father. I only catch her sneaking up on me half the time."

Father laughed. "Well, then, I have the perfect solution. Do you remember your mother's old cat, Paws?"

"No, sir."

"Paws was a true terror. He'd bring back dead animals every day as gifts for your mother. She was mortified! That cat was the scourge of every bird and mouse and even rabbit in the neighbourhood. Do you know what we finally had to do with him?"

I knew that some barbaric people will tie unwanted kittens in bags filled with stones and throw them in the river. But I could see there would be problems with doing that to Grandmother O'Toole. Even though she was extremely old and at times acted as though she was extremely confused, I thought it would be difficult to get her to go to the river's edge, then willingly climb into a bag filled with stones.

She was simply not that confused.

I laughed to myself; the worst asylum would be far better and more humane than that.

"No, sir, I don't know what you did with Paws. But I know Mother would never have harmed an animal."

"And you're right. We put a bell on him and that solved everything! He couldn't sneak up on a sleeping mouse with cotton in its ears with the racket he made."

Father narrowed his eyes and cocked his head to the side as though he was deep in thought.

"There it is! Perhaps we should bell Mother O'Toole! Maybe then she couldn't ambush you."

Father constantly tries to make me laugh. He almost always succeeds. And even though I knew what he was doing, it worked. Regardless of the fact that my head was home to a new bump, my mood lightened.

I said, "But that leads us to the question: Who, then, shall bell the grandmother?"

Father smiled, felt around the silvery crown of his head, and said, "I don't seem to have any lumps on my head, so it seems to me that you have more skin in the game than I. Therefore, the job falls to you."

Father may have been joking, but this wasn't a bad idea. I could buy a necklace with a small bell and give it to her as a gift.

But that would never happen. Grandmother O'Toole would never accept any kind of gift from me.

She would only begrudgingly accept one from Father. She'd had but one pair of shoes since I could remember. Even though Father had bought her several new pairs, they'd sat for years under her bed. She kept them polished but had never worn them. She had her old shoes resoled again and again.

"They're perfectly good for now," she would say.

What could I do but wait as Father asked? For the sake of Mother's memory, I could be patient for another week or two.

→ Chapter 9 ←

Never Trust a Genius

BENJI

The moon didn't need to be out for me to see that Patience and Stubby were up to no good.

I said, "Guess what."

Patience said, "What?"

"You two had better get home fast. Even as we speak, the Madman of Piney Woods has gone berserk in the forest."

Her eyes rolled.

I laughed. "Don't believe me, then. Go home; ask the Miller twins. They're behind the couch, shaking like wet bunnies. I'm walking over to get their folks to take them home."

Stubby said, "They *really* saw the Madman?"

"Not really, they saw a hundred tied-up children with bags over their heads, laughing and being led away by demons. They just guessed the children were being taken to the Madman."

Patience's hand covered her mouth, but it wasn't from fear. They looked at each other, and I sensed that the flour sack behind Stubby's back wasn't the only thing they were hiding.

I put my hand out. "The sack."

Stubby hesitated.

I said, "The twins really did see something, and you two know what it was. Give me the sack or I'll hurt both of you."

Stubby knew I was serious and handed over the sack.

Patience stamped her foot and gave him a dirty look.

Inside the sack were five or six folded pillowcases, a long rope, a hollowed reed flute, a one-foot-by-one-foot piece of tin, and a wooden spoon.

"Explain."

Pay said, "You have to swear not to tell Mother and Father."

"What did the twins see?"

Stubby said, "Promise you won't tell."

I crossed my fingers and said, "I swear."

Pay said, "Give me the sack back."

Neither one of them could be trusted, especially Patience. The looks that Patience gave me could send cold shivers through my heart. And there was the problem of that knife she always had near at hand.

I handed the sack to Stubby. "You show me."

He dug into the sack, then reached into one of the pillowcases. He pulled out a stack of papers and handed one to me. It must have been printed at Miss Cary's shop in Chatham.

THE 9TH WONDER OF THE WORLD!
COME WITH US ON A
JOURNEY OF AMAZEMENT!

SEE IF YOU CAN SOLVE THE MYSTERY OF
CHARMING LITTLE CHALET IN THE WOODS!

WHAT CAUSED THIS TRAGEDY?

WHO PUT SUCH A VILE CURSE ON THE HUMBLE HOME
OF A KINDHEARTED OLD FARMER AND
HIS ORPHAN CHILDREN AND WIDOW WIFE?

YOU MIGHT EVEN GET A CHANCE
TO MEET THE FARMER!

**FOR ONE PENNY YOU CAN SEE
WITH YOUR OWN EYES.
PREPARE TO BE SHOCKED!!!!!!**

FIVE DOLLAR REWARD TO WHO CAN SOLVE THIS
MYSTERY AND EASE THE FAMILYS PAIN!!!

"Explain yourselves."

Stubby said, "Benji, you won't believe it, but we built a tree house in the woods and some way it got turned upside down. It happened when we went to Toronto with Father."

Patience gasped. She'd put one and one together. I could see her getting madder and madder.

"Go on," I said before Pay had a chance to get too worked up.

Stubby said, "We decided the best thing we could do was to try to make something good from all of our work. We charge a penny for anyone to go into our upside-down tree house."

The little crooks! They were inviting all sorts of people into *my* woods! And making money from doing it!

"We only take six people at a time, not a hundred. We can control six real easy."

"But how would they not see where you'd taken them and then just come back with their friends to see it for free?"

Pay said, "That's what those rat twins saw. We put pillowcases over our customers' heads so they can't see, and then, so they won't rip the cases off to get a peek, we tie their hands behind their backs. Then we make them hold on to a rope and follow us."

"People pay you to do this to them?"

"We give them their money back if they don't have fun."

My brother and sister are geniuses! Tricky little geniuses!

Stubby started running his mouth, bragging almost. "We walk them in circles for a while so they don't know what direction we're going in. Once they're confused, we lead them to the tree house, then we take the pillowcases off their heads. We only do it at dusk because it makes everything scarier, and with no sun up, it's impossible for them to tell where they are in the forest."

Pay hissed at him and he shut up.

"And the demons the twins saw?"

"That was us. We do that to make it more mysterious and fun."

"And this flute and this piece of tin were the music you enchanted them with?"

Patience said, "That's nonsense; those twins are idiots."

"How much money do you make doing this?"

They hesitated and I lunged at their ears.

Stubby blurted out, "Twenty-five pence a week."

"*What?*"

"On a good week, thirty or forty pence. Kids have been coming all the way from Chatham to see."

My anger and disappointment at what little crooks my siblings were turned to something else.

"Well, since you are using *my* woods, you need to pay rent."

They whispered back and forth a bit before Patience said, "How much?"

"Fifteen pence a week."

Stubby jumped like he was going to attack me.

Patience said, "Wait, Timothy. You must trust me."

She said to me, "Do you promise not to bother us in any way if we pay?"

"Of course. There are more important things in the life of a newspaperman than childish nonsense like this."

She stuck her hand out. "Ten cents; not a penny more."

I shook her hand. It's sort of frightening that a little girl's hand can be so calloused and rough.

I said, "And I *will* need a week's rent in advance."

Stubby drew back again.

Patience turned her back to me, reached into the pocket of her dress, and turned toward me again. She opened a small pouch and counted out ten pennies!

Being a landlord is great!

I pretended I tipped a hat at them, took a big bow, and said, "It's a pleasure doing business with my two new partners. Give me a hug, you little scalawags! There's something very special about being in business with your own family, isn't there?"

Neither one of them would embrace their new partner.

I put the ten pennies in my pocket and continued my walk to the Miller twins' house. A nagging voice told me I should pay more thought to the angry look on Pay's face.

The night's headline would read:

TWO HEADS BETTER THAN ONE? NOT ALWAYS!!

CHAPTER 10

A Blessing from Northern Ireland

RED

When it comes to Father, I'd learned that all I had to do was wait and even the oddest circumstances would be shown to have a rational explanation.

It had been a week since Grandmother O'Toole caned me in the kitchen, and the small hammer next to Father's plate at supper was definitely an odd circumstance. I'd be like the tallest tree in heaven and patiently wait to find out why it was there. Grandmother O'Toole eyed it suspiciously as well. But both of us held our tongues.

We finished eating and I cleared the table. Father winked at me, then slid a blue-ribboned Hirsh Jewelers box across the table to Grandmother O'Toole.

"Chester Stockard, what in the heavens is this?"

"Something to show a little appreciation for all you do around here, Mother O'Toole. I know it's not easy looking after Alvin and me, and I know at times it may seem we take you for granted, but nothing's further from the truth. Both of us appreciate you from the cockles of our hearts."

I was glad Father didn't ask me to agree with that statement. The cockles of *my* heart agreed with *me*; Grandmother O'Toole needed to go to an asylum.

"Oh, Chester laddie, ye shouldn't've. What have I done to deserve a gift? Spending me every waking hour watching over this lazy chowderhead of a grandson is me duty, and though it fills me with dread each morn when I awake, and even though it's cutting years off me very life, ye've never heard me complain, have ye? Aye, Chester, 'tis me duty to my poor dear departed daughter Mary, not the sort of thing to be given such a grand present for." She turned the small box over and over. "From Hirsh Jewelers no less? How did ye afford this, son?"

Father smiled. "I saw it in their window and knew, regardless of the price, it had been made for my beloved Mother O'Toole and I had to have it. Go ahead, open the box."

Her trembling hands took the blue bow off, then opened the blue clamshell box. She gasped and pulled a large postage-stamp-sized silver bell from the blue felt inside. There was a four-leaf clover and the word *ERIN* fancily engraved on one side of the bell.

"Oh, Chester! 'Tis far too grand for such a poor old woman as I! 'Tis beautiful! And mercy, do me eyes deceive me? 'Tis really Irish?"

"That's what it says. I'm glad you like it, Mother O'Toole."

"But what is it?"

She turned it over and over, studying the bell with great curiosity. "I'm not one to complain, but there's no loop to thread a necklace through. And alas, though 'tis as fine a bell as I've ever beheld, I've never seen any jewelry with a nail at the end where ye'd be expecting to see a loop."

She looked at Father and asked, "'Tis some new fashion one of these wretched Canadians has started?"

Father said, "No. Word is it's from the north of Ireland, Mother O'Toole. They call it a cane bell. They say every time it rings, another sin is washed clean away from the soul of a poor Irishman."

"No! And you say in the north 'tis known as a cane bell?"

"Truly."

Father took her cane and picked up the small hammer he'd brought to the table. After a few taps, the bell dangled from the end of the cane's handle.

Father shook the cane, and the light tinkling sound assured us that a whole gaggle of Irishmen had gotten away with something.

Grandmother O'Toole hugged the cane with its new bell to her chest.

"'Tis is the most glorious gift I've ever been given, son. Thank ye from the bottom of me heart. Every time it rings, 'twill remind me of what a grand decision me Mary made in choosing ye for her spouse."

She looked at me and snarled, "Do ye see how a true gentleman behaves, ye little redhead hooligan? Do ye?"

I smiled and looked at my father.

"Yes, Grandmother O'Toole, I do see. And I'll be praying every night that someday I can be as grand a gent as he."

→ CHAPTER II ←

The Sad End of Charming Little Chalet in the Woods

BENJI

Two mornings after I became a landlord, I walked into the kitchen and knew trouble was in the air. Mother, Father, Pay, and Stubby sat at the kitchen table without speaking. No one returned my good-morning greetings.

Like any good newspaperman, I surveyed the scene. One of the oddest things was the opened cookie jar sitting in the middle of the table.

Father pointed at my chair. "Sit."

This wasn't good. Mother and Father were very tense. Patience and Stubby had their eyes cast down, traces of something I couldn't read on their faces. I wondered if they'd snitched on me for charging them rent.

But no, this had to be about some mischief that involved the cookie jar. My fears eased when I realized I had no worries; it had been months since I'd last taken a cookie without permission. Well, maybe it had been weeks. But it had been long enough ago to have been noticed before now.

These were turning out to be really bad days for Stubby and Patience! Not only did they have an upside-down tree house and a new partner they didn't want, they were also about to face Mother and Father's anger for stealing cookies. I hoped they would deny doing it. That would make their punishment all the more severe!

I was surprised when Mother said, "Patience and Timothy, you are excused."

As she rose from the table, with her back to Mother and Father, Pay fought to keep her face straight. She widened her eyes and pursed her lips in a long silent whistle directed at me. Stubby wiggled his eyebrows.

I was confused.

Mother said, "Well, Benjamin?"

"How many did they steal, Mother? I *thought* I saw crumbs on their pyjamas the other night before they went to bed and wondered what nonsense they'd been up to. I'm shocked! Who would have thought they'd —"

Father's hand slammed on the table. Me, the cookie jar, and the silverware all jumped.

He said, "You wanna know what that's good for? That's good for a week in the Amen Corner!"

I was thrilled! Even though they called it a time for learning, the Amen Corner was the worst punishment Mother and Father could give. Patience and Stubby would have to spend their every spare minute for a whole week sitting in the corner of the parlour with their backs turned to us while they read the Bible!

We only have one Bible, but that shouldn't be a problem. I could run over to the Alexanders' home. I'm sure they wouldn't mind letting us borrow theirs for a week.

I decided then and there that even though Stubby and Patience weren't going to be giving expeditions to our Charming Little Chalet in the Woods for a week, they would not be excused from paying their rent. I hoped they'd saved some cash.

I tried not to sound too excited when I told Father, "A whole week? That seems a bit on the harsh side, Father?"

The cookie jar, me, and the silverware jumped a second time when *Mother's* hand slammed on the table! She said, "Enough, Benjamin! You deserve every minute of this punishment and even more!"

What?

"*Me?*"

There was a terrible mistake being made here.

"Mother, what do you mean? I didn't take any cookies, I swear!"

Father said, "One more word out of you and . . ."

I'd always told myself that one day I was going to be brave enough to find out what the *and* means that Father always dangles at the end of a threat.

Today was not that day.

Mother said, "I found three of the cookies under *your* clothes hidden in *your* chiffonier, Benjamin. And crumbs all over your pillow and sheets. We will tolerate neither thievery nor lying in this house. Two dozen cookies? Shame on you. Did you take them and give them to your friends?"

"What? Of course not!"

Father said, "Then you've committed the mortal sin of gluttony as well. Ten days!"

There is no feeling as rotten as being convicted of a crime that you had nothing to do with. Later, once the bitter anguish began to fade and I sat in the Amen Corner with the Bible in my lap, I started to understand what had happened.

Patience!

This was her doing. This was the price she was making me pay for becoming their landlord.

Well, she and Stubby were about to get a very unpleasant surprise. When my ten days of Bible reading were done, I was going to smash Charming Little Chalet in the Woods into enough kindling to set the world on fire!

The Amen Corner lasted for two weeks instead of ten days.

On the eighth day, Mother was making dinner when Patience walked past me into the kitchen.

I heard her say, "Mother, may I ask you a question about the Bible?"

"Of course, sweetheart."

"Is the chapter in the Bible called *Cowboys of the Wild West* about Moses or Goliath?"

"Patience, don't be silly." Mother paused for a second, then said, "Why do you ask?"

Pay said, "No real reason; just curious."

It took Mother two seconds to come into the Amen Corner and snatch my Western novel from under the Bible.

It didn't take her that long to add four more days to my sentence.

On the fifteenth morning, the day I finally got out, I have to admit I felt more holy and kind from my weeks of reading the Bible. I stumbled into the sunshine and stretched to celebrate.

My first stop was at the shed, where I got a crowbar, a hammer, and an ax. Within an hour or two, there'd be no more Charming Little Chalet in the Woods; there'd be a Charming Huge Pile of Toothpicks at the Base of a Maple!

I put the tools in a wheelbarrow and went to fetch Spencer so he could help me. Even he would see that this was the right thing to do.

*   *   *

Spencer Alexander is no longer my friend. For the second time, he refused to help tear the tree house down. I went into the woods of the north fifty on my own.

When I got to where the tree house was, it was my turn to slap my hand over my mouth in shock.

It was gone! There wasn't a scrap of wood or even a nail left. The only proof it had ever been there were the scars on the tree.

I noticed a group of mule tracks and travois drag marks leading from the back of where the tree house used to be to the road.

I understood.

Patience and Stubby must have known that once my time in the Amen Corner was done, I'd look for revenge. They'd come up with the cookie jar scheme to give them enough time to take the tree house down and move it away.

They knew that once they got to the road, I wouldn't be able to track where in the woods they'd rebuilt it.

It didn't take me long to know the day's headline would read:

EVIL WINS A BATTLE! WAR MAY NOT BE LOST, BUT THINGS NOT LOOKING GOOD!

→ Chapter 12 ←

The South Woods Lion Man

RED

The Baylis brothers, Curly Bennett, Hickman Holmely, Petey Demers, and I were on the bank of the Thames River with a considerable good haul of fish. As so often happens when things are slow and the sun is warm and the fish have tired of our night crawlers and minnows and have moved to deeper waters, the conversation turned to one of our favourite subjects: the South Woods Lion Man.

If, on a Thursday morning, one were to start relating all of the rumours about him, the tales would not be exhausted until the following Wednesday afternoon.

There were as many theories and stories about who or what he was as there were different bolts of cloth in Curly's mother's shop. And the tales were just as colourful.

The only things that all those rumours and legends had in common were that the Lion Man was over a century old, escaped from slavery in the southern United States of America, spoke no English or other civilized tongue, wanted nothing to do with other human beings, was or soon would be a vicious murderer, was as mad as a hatter, and should be avoided at all costs.

The Baylis boys were the authority on the subject. They were the only ones to have actually laid eyes upon this mystery man of the pine forest that lies south between Chatham and Buxton.

Buster stretched the huge perch he had caught between his upheld hands.

"So, lads, the fish have quit biting and you need to line up to take your punishment. There's no doubt that this little beauty makes me the winner today!"

Whoever caught the day's biggest fish was allowed to punch each of the rest of us once in the arm as hard as he chose to. Buster hadn't won in quite a while, so we all knew he was sorely excited about getting revenge. His punches would be harsh.

Hickman said, "Not so fast. Yours is longer, but my bass is heavier."

Buster said, "This isn't a forensics competition, Hickman. You can't talk your way into having the biggest fish. Fellows, tell him."

After hefting each of the fishes, I felt that not only was the perch longer, it was heavier; plus, even though it had already died, it was a much more impressive fish than the bass that wiggled weakly on Hickman's stringer.

I passed both fish to Bucky and said, "Sorry, Hickman, Buster's is bigger."

Bucky said, "I don't think so. This bass weighs a bit more; it's the biggest," and passed the fish to Curly.

Curly opined, "Naw, the perch is heaviest."

Buster smiled. "Ha! Two to three. Line up and take your punches like the men you boys pretend to be."

Hickman said, "Wait. We haven't asked Petey. Let's wake him up; his vote could make a draw."

Petey said from under his straw hat, "I'm not asleep."

He propped himself on one elbow, squinted to look at the fish, then stood.

Hickman handed the bass to Petey.

Instead of giving his opinion, Petey took the fish to the water, squatted down, pulled the groggy fish off the stringer, gently put it in the river, and kept his hand underneath until it regained enough strength to swim sadly away from the bank.

Hickman wanted to complain, but this *was* Petey, and no one was certain how long his new peaceful attitude was going to last, so Hickman's silence was a wise choice.

Bucky asked, "Uh, why'd you let him go, Petey?"

"*Her,*" Petey said. "She was heaviest because she's full of eggs. Leave her be until she lays 'em."

Curly said, "You're getting to be more of a wild

woodsman every day, Petey. I bet if the South Woods Lion Man ever retires, you'll apply to take over his job."

Petey smiled before he pulled the straw hat over his face and stretched back out. We all laughed.

Bucky said, "Petey wouldn't get the position. He's too young, too short, and nowhere near crazy enough."

Curly said, "Plus, Petey's got white blood in him!"

All eyes went to Petey. Petey never encourages any conversations about his ancestry, but there are times when he's more sensitive than others. We gave Curly quizzical looks that he'd risk riling Petey. He'd apologized for his previous rude remarks and the newly kind Petey had accepted, but perhaps this was too much. It appeared Curly wouldn't be content until he'd poked the sleeping bear into a rage.

Curly said, "What? I ain't said nothing wrong, did I, Petey? Saying that somebody's got white blood in 'em is the highest compliment you can give."

Hickman said, "So what does that make me, Curly Bennett?"

Curly said, "Aw, come on, Hicks, half the time I don't even notice you're a black boy. You're just like the rest of us to me."

Hickman said, "You're all kinds of ignorant, Curly. You best tread lightly what you talk about or I'll give you a second thumping."

I tried to direct the conversation to subjects less explosive. "Buster, that's not true, is it? Petey is larger than most full-grown men. It seems impossible that the South Woods Lion Man is bigger than he."

Both Baylis boys blurted, "The Lion Man's a whole lot bigger!"

None of us believed everything Buster and Bucky said about their encounter with the South Woods Lion Man, but the absolute sincerity and panicked air that overtook them when they talked about the meeting showed they had indeed seen something horrifying in the woods one evening last September.

Hickman saw where this conversation was now heading and said, "Here we go again."

Buster said, "You can act scornful only because you haven't seen him. Tell 'im, Bucky."

"He's right. If you saw what he really looks like, you wouldn't be so bold."

I fanned the flames. "But come on now. Snakes? For his hair?"

They had told us the stories were true; the Lion Man had snakes where his hair should have been.

Buster said, "Scoff if you must, but he is a modern-day Medusa."

Hickman said, "If that's true and he does have

Medusa's hair, why weren't the two of you turned to stone when you saw him?"

Bucky and Buster exchanged a glance. Perhaps they'd already given that question a great deal of thought. Or maybe not.

Bucky said, "Well, we figure it's 'cause we had the good sense not to look for long. We each took a quick glance before we ran. I bet you only get turned to stone if you look at him and stare."

Buster said, "Bucky's right. I looked a little longer than he did and I swear my left big toe started stiffening and hasn't been able to bend at the joint since that day!"

Curly said, "I heard that he carries a hundred-year-old oak tree for a club, and he's fast enough to run a deer down and rip the throat out of its neck with his teeth!"

Hickman said, "I heard that too, and that if the deer is dead before it hits the ground, he won't eat it. He won't eat anything that's not screaming and fighting for its life. He steals the animal's spirit that way and becomes more like it. That's why he can walk through the forest like a ghost."

Buster said, "And he's about eight feet tall! And I know it's true that he's an escaped slave from the United States of America. He's still toting the chains 'round with him! They're thick as the chains that hold the elephants down at the circus."

Bucky said, "Yup, and the chains are made out of the gold the Lion Man stole from his old master before he slit his throat! His master put a curse on him just before he died and now the Lion Man can't spend the gold but has to wear it around his waist and ankles forever!"

Hickman said, "Pshaw!"

Bucky said, "No! I swear! Why else would he still be carrying those chains?"

I am not a coward and like instead to think of myself as sensible. Some of the stories seemed far-fetched, but Father said that, twenty years ago, nothing was more far-fetched than imagining there would be carriages that raced down roads without horses or oxen or any other type of animal pulling them. One has to keep an open mind until the truth unfolds.

Since he is the wisest man I know, I'd asked Father about the stories the Baylis boys told right after they met the Lion Man.

Father had said, "Alvin, it's human nature to embellish. Don't blame the Baylis boys. That's what naturally happens to any story over time, especially an eyewitness story. I had a professor in law school who lectured us on eyewitnesses and told us that ninety-nine percent of the time, they are worse than worthless."

"But how is that possible, Father? They actually saw him. With their own eyes."

"Their observations, like all people's, evolve and change with time. Memory is imperfect."

Father went on, "For example, will you have a better recollection of this conversation tomorrow or six months from now?"

"Tomorrow, of course."

"Right, our memories are always in the process of falling apart; they're constantly fading. Keep that in mind when people tell you about the past. Your friends aren't necessarily being malicious or trying to frighten or deceive you. They're probably doing their best to recall, but even the sharpest memory becomes more unreliable with the passage of time."

→ CHAPTER 13 ←

Face-to-Face!

BENJI

There are only seven of the original thirteen settlers of Buxton still living here, and they're different from the rest of us. And not just because they're tired and move slow.

Those who escaped from slavery have this way of always looking over their shoulders, and if you believe even half of their stories about the southern United States, that's easy to understand.

What I *can't* understand is why, after more than thirty-five years of being free, they can't seem to relax. There haven't been any slave catchers around here since Hector was a pup, and slavery was outlawed down in America after the rebs got whipped, so the old-timers really don't have anything to worry about. But even knowing that, the hardest thing for them to do is take an easy breath.

I don't know if that same uneasiness is in my blood or if I picked up the watched feeling by being raised in a town full of nervous old people, 'cause many times I feel the same way. Lots of times, I feel itchy that someone is watching me, mostly when I'm in the woods.

It was happening again.

Some of the time when I'm in the forest and this feeling comes over me, I'll look up into the boughs of a tree and I'm relieved to spot an owl. I tell myself that the owl was what was causing my nervousness.

Owls have a way of looking at you that makes you feel they're thinking, "Not only do I know what you just thought, I also know what you're about to say," and that can't help but make your stomach jumpy.

It's bad enough when it seems like there's a person reading your mind; it's even worse when the thing that's staying two or three thoughts ahead of you is doing it with a bird's brain.

I slowly looked at the trees from top to bottom. No owls.

The feeling wouldn't leave. I *was* being watched.

I noticed one branch of a tree, maybe twenty paces off to my left, sway one time to the right and one time to the left. It was such a tiny movement that I wasn't sure I'd seen it at all.

A good woodsman learns to trust what he's seen, so I had to look away from the branch before I talked myself into believing it hadn't moved after all. The branch *had* moved and whatever had brushed against it was still close, maybe watching from right behind the tree.

I was going to figure out who or what this was. The woods are like a pond: Nothing can go through them without leaving ripples; you only have to be able to read the ripples to know what has moved.

There was no breeze and this wasn't a wild animal. The only animal left in these woods bold enough to follow and watch a human being is another human being.

That was one ripple.

I didn't let on I knew I was being spied on. I poked the stick I was carrying into the ground and dropped my head, as if I were interested in a stone I'd overturned. But my eyes stayed locked upon the area around the branch that had swayed.

Higher up in the same tree, a pair of mourning doves lighted in the branches and, just as quick, squawking like they were being squeezed, they took off.

Another ripple.

Mourning doves are the stupidest birds on the face of the earth; about the only time one will move is if you step right on top of it. Plus, one had flown east and one had flown west, a sure sign something at the base of the tree had startled them.

A third ripple.

My pride was pinched. This person was good. I'd prove I was better.

It wasn't Spence or any of my other chums. The words that describe the way they move in the forest are trounce, stomp, and break. No, this was someone who was just as at home in the woods as me.

This was a hunter.

Which meant there was a good chance they would be armed.

I went from wanting to play a game to knowing I'd better protect myself by losing whoever was trying so hard to keep an eye on me.

Then, like a rock to the head, an idea hit me and made me want to leave the woods as quick as I could. What if this was the Madman of Piney Woods? It was silly, but what if it really was true?

Just in case, I picked up a large stone.

I slowly kept going to my right, my head down, moving away from that tree, putting many, many other trees between me and the one I thought my spy was behind. As soon as I knew they couldn't see me, I changed directions and darted to the left, making a huge circle to come up behind whoever this was.

I'd moved with perfect silence; they'd be just ahead of me.

I held the stone over my head ready to throw, held my breath, then jumped out to see who was behind the mourning dove tree.

All that was there was the back of the tree.

Even though I was positive the person had been here, there were no tracks or no disturbed ground to prove it.

Whoever had been there was *very* good.

I stood stock-still to hear anything unusual.

I felt as though I'd been hit by a bolt of lightning when I heard, "You ain't half bad, boy. Nope, and you getting better."

I dropped my rock and whirled toward the voice.

Mother and Father always tell us we must be grateful for the little things, and this was a time I was. I was very grateful there were no other reporters around to describe the way I looked when I saw the face of the person who'd spoken to me and stood just five feet away.

I'm not entirely sure how much showed, but I felt everything in my face go loose and saggy whilst my jaw quivered. If those reporters had written there was drooling involved, I couldn't honestly say they were lying.

But who can blame me?

How many times had somebody's mother or father told us that this very man had gone down into the devil's own house and slapped him in his face?

How many times had one of the originals warned, "If y'all stay out too late or wander too far and *he* snatch ahold of you, leave a trail of bread crumbs or a note telling which direction you got dragged off in so's we can find your corpse and give it a proper burial"?

How many times had we heard that anything that went wrong or went missing in Buxton was because of this man?

The boy in me was terrified while the newspaperman in me thought, *This is great! In all the stories told about this man, there has never been one of a person ever coming face-to-face with him and actually hearing his voice! I'm the first person he ever spoke to!*

Or maybe not. Maybe there *were* other people he'd spoken to . . . but maybe they hadn't *lived* to tell the story!

The Madman of Piney Woods said, "Wanna know how I got behind you?"

All I could do was nod.

He smiled. "'Tain't none your business, boy."

I took a deep breath.

He shut his eyes and threw his head back to laugh. It was the exact kind of laugh you'd expect from a madman, except it wasn't mean. It wasn't as though he was laughing at me; it was more as though he was one of those irksome people who think their own jokes are really funny.

It gave me a chance to look at his face.

His open mouth showed that his gums were home to only one tooth on the top and two or three on the bottom.

I saw that the hat everyone said he never took off wasn't a hat at all — it was hair. Thick, tangled, long hair with a rainbow of blacks and silvers and oranges winding from one end to the other.

It's odd where your brain goes when part of you wants to be terrified and another part wants to take notes. As I looked at his hair, I thought what a nightmare it would be for the Madman of Piney Woods if he was forced to sit like Patience does whilst Mother wrestled a comb through his tangled, twisted hair.

That fight would go on for days.

The Madman's laugh ended and my eyes were captured by his again.

"I seent you 'bout these woods for years, boy. Don't you never go to school?"

"Uh . . . school, sir? School's out for the summer."

The Madman said, "Oh, that's right. Who your people, boy?"

"My father's Timothy Alston, Senior, sir, and my mother's —"

"Timmy Alston? Whoo-ha! I thought so. That mean you's TooToo's boy!"

I'd been brave up to this point, but those words frightened me. How was this possible? How in the world could the Madman of Piney Woods know Mother's nickname?

Most folk used her proper name. Only Father and some of the really old people in Buxton called her TooToo.

"Yes, sir! But how do you know her other name?"

Was he spying on me at home too?

"What you mean how I know your momma's name?"

"I just thought you were too . . . I mean, how could someone who's . . . um . . ."

He laughed again.

"Oh, I see. What you wanna say is how come some crazy old man who lost his mind and been chasing 'round for his soul in the forest know all this 'bout your momma?"

"No, sir," I lied, "it just seems odd to me that you know something about my mother that not many people do."

The Madman said, "I been watching over everything what go on in these woods for more years than you been born, boy."

He *had* been watching me!

"But that don't mean my ma birthed me under no rock out here."

Only every once in a while did his eyes lock on mine. Most times they watched the woods. The peculiar thing was that, even though his eyes were darting from side to side and up and down, rolling 'bout like a couple of dark brown marbles in a pot of boiling, yellowy milk, his head never moved. Just like an owl.

It wouldn't have surprised me if he flew into a tree and started asking, "Whoo-whoo? Whoo-whoo?"

He said, "Not to change no subjects, boy, but from what I seent and what I heard, there's something in you what call to mind myself."

"*Really?*"

He threw his head back and laughed again, giving me the chance to look him up and down.

He wore a buckskin shirt and trousers. Around his waist was a chain attached to a couple of muskrat traps. There was something odd about the chain's and traps' colour, but before I could tell what it was, his eyes came back to me and I had to look up.

"It look like that shock you, boy. Don't you know any-time someone tell you you remind them of themselves, it the highest compliment they can give? 'Stead of looking like you just got chunked in the head with a rock, you should be thanking me."

I mumbled, "Uh . . . thank you, sir?"

I wasn't slow to answer because I didn't agree; it was because what he said was something I'd thought of too. No one would ever say to a liar or a thief or a complete idiot, "There's a lot about you that reminds me of me," would they?

"Pay attention, boy. I knowed your ma when she waren't nothing but a babe. I knowed her when she first come to Buxton."

His eyes began jumping even more. I could tell he was done talking to me. Without another word, he took two steps back and quickly started walking away.

I had to act fast. If I lost sight of him, he'd be able to disappear and I might never have this chance again.

I yelled, "Sir, wait, please!"

He looked back at me but kept walking. I ran after him. There were a thousand questions I wanted to ask.

The newspaperman in me jumped up and down in glee when he stopped.

I could have asked him anything.

Such as why he stayed in the woods when he could have easily come live in Buxton.

Such as didn't he ever get sad or scared or lonely being out here all alone?

Such as how he knows so much about my mother.

I was sore disappointed in myself when the first thing I asked was, "What is it about me that reminds you of yourself?"

His eyes calmed as he smiled.

"It's these woods, boy. You's more comforted being out here than anywhere else, huh?"

"Why, yes, sir."

"So's I. That one the things we got in common. You get feelings out here just like me 'cause these woods is constant talking to you."

He swiped his hand at the hair on the side of his head over and over, as though a fly or skeeter was buzzing 'round his ear. If there was, I couldn't see or hear it.

"I know how it is," he said. "If you knows how to listen, the woods is constant gibber-jabbering at you. They been telling you all along you being watched. I seent how you gets all tetchity when, even though you ain't never seent me watching, you feels it. It's these woods what's telling you I'm there. They's talking to you near's much they talks to me; it won't be long afore you understand what they saying near's good as me."

He was right again! In a strange kind of way, I did feel like the woods and everything in the forest talked to me.

He said, "I seent how whilst no one, 'cluding that pack of mo-ron boys you be leading out here, ain't got no idea they's being spied on, you do. And you got the good sense not to tell 'em what you feeling. You been keeping the woods' secrets to yourself."

He called Spence and the boys "mo-rons"!

"I also seent how it been harder and harder for me to stay hid from you and that mean the woods is pulling you in too, drawing you closer to they boo-sum. You showed 'em you's worthy of trust; you getting that good."

"Thank you, sir."

"But truth be told, boy, I envies you."

He looked straight in my eyes. "You and me traveled

different roads to reach this here point. I envies you 'cause the journey here come natural and easy for you. Ain't no big price been paid by you.

"Me? Shoot, boy, to get here, I had to go through trials and fire and pain you caint come up with in your worse nightmare. Umm-hmm, I envies you most of all for the things you ain't seen. But that don't matter. The woods is the judge, and if they say you and me's one in the same, who's I to be thinking elsewise?"

He was quiet for a moment, then said, "Everything's a circle, boy. Just like I'm where I'm at, you gonna come 'round this way 'fore long. Just like I been watching you, there's something out here what watching me. And just like you fount me, I ain't resting till I find them. 'Round and 'round and 'round we go, and I ain't gonna stop till I find them monsters."

A chill brushed over me.

"Monsters?"

"That's what I said. Monsters is watching me all the time and I ain't gonna rest till I fount out why. These woods is talking to them too, but the monsters get the messages from the forest on the tips of the wings of crows."

I must not have done a good job of hiding what I felt.

The Madman of Piney Woods laughed again and said, "Oh-ho! Now you gonna look at me like *I'm* the one who crazy. But you got me worried, boy. Maybe them rumours is true; could be that I lost my mind. 'Cause me getting told I's crazy by someone who durn near kilt hisself tearing a tree house out a tree, only to put it back upside down, is pretty good proof I might for sure be gone mad. 'Cause like they say, it take one to know one, and when it come to crazy, all signs point to you knowing what you talking 'bout."

With that he folded himself back into the curtain of the forest.

I blinked and stood there shocked.

It wasn't until I was home that I realized I was probably the only person in the world to get insulted by the Madman of Piney Woods and live to tell the story.

But I wasn't going to let anyone know about this meeting. He'd given me a lot to think about and even though it would near kill me not to tell Spencer and the boys what the Madman had said about them, I wouldn't.

But that didn't mean it couldn't be in today's headline:

PROOF FINALLY IN! MADMAN OF PINEY WOODS
AGREES SPENCER ALEXANDER AND THE REST OF
MY CHUMS *ARE* A PACK OF
MO-RONS!

Just like the forest's other secrets, and the Madman of Piney Woods and me meeting up, I was keeping this to myself.

CHAPTER 14

Cornered!

RED

Since I am a scientist, I am loath to believe in anything superstitious or otherworldly. Yet Grandmother O'Toole's old saying "Speak of the divil and surely he shall come a-knocking" was all I thought of.

Mere hours after the lads and I had debated whose fish was larger, I climbed one of the trees near the creek and found myself dozing. I have no idea how long I napped before a movement or sound from below roused me. I rolled my head in the direction of the disturbance and suffered a searing moment of white-hot terror.

Below, not fifty yards away, an odd, human-seeming figure materialized from between the trees of the forest. This apparition before me, which seemed to slip in like a fog, could be only one person: I had the dire misfortune of awakening and having my eyes fall on the South Woods Lion Man!

The drumbeat of my heart filled my ears as the realization of what a horrible plight I was in dawned on me. My

105

mind became confused and took flight. It danced and flitted much as would a sparrow being pursued by a hawk. The only parts of me that seemed capable of movement were my eyes. And what a dreadful sight they beheld! I didn't know whether to laugh or cry. This wasn't possible, but as I saw the Lion Man, I realized every story about this half-human creature's appearance was true!

Even from a distance he was huge, much larger than any of the unfortunate giants who come to Chatham with the summer circus. Maybe not eight feet tall, but at least seven and a half, and he weighed four hundred pounds if he weighed an ounce!

His head *was* covered with a thick tangle of black and red and white snakes, which waved and bobbed through the air around his shoulders! And there *were* golden slave shackles hanging from his waist. Even more confusing was that he walked without making a sound; the chains that held his slave shackles in place were silent. Had I been struck deaf? Was this some horrible nightmare?

He seemed to be homing in on where I had unfortunately chosen to nap, forcing me to study this ghastly vision even more closely.

As he drew closer, it appeared his head was covered by a hood, something you would wear to keep your ears safe from the deepest winter's bite. As his head turned this way and that, I saw it was not a hood; it was more like a lion's mane, a thick, dense mass of fur. Soon I could make out a confused mixture of silvers and blacks near his dark brown forehead fanning out into orangish reds as the mane spread down his shoulders and back like a short cloak.

I was close enough to see it was hair, a massive clump of snarled hair fanning out in thick, snakelike tendrils that were tangled and woven in the manner of the most impenetrable bramble one could imagine.

The more I studied him, the more quickly I began to doubt the other stories and my own first impressions. Particularly the ones proclaiming how he fed himself by running down full-sized deer, clubbing them with the trunk of a tree before he bloodily used his teeth to tear the animal's organs from its still-kicking body.

The Lion Man appeared to be too old for such feats. Even though his dark brown face was smooth and unwrinkled, the way his lower jaw and chin seemed collapsed showed he had suffered the same malady many of the older people in Chatham had — he'd lost most of his teeth. And if he actually did run game to ground, why would he need what he was carrying, a very old musket, not the entire trunk of a centuries-old tree?

My eyes moved down. His clothes were much like what the Cree and Ojibwa, who occasionally came through the woods, wore. They were made from the tanned hides of some animal.

Chains *did* hang from his waist, but they didn't terminate in slave shackles; at their ends were spring traps for small game. And he'd wrapped each link of the chain with some type of yellowed reed or dried grass, which stopped them from rattling as he walked.

Despite all of these normal explanations for the mysteries told about him, each step he took in my direction made him seem even more terrifying! He finally stopped right below my tree, and I knew he'd run me to ground and wasn't allowing me to know I'd been spotted. His next actions would probably be to scamper up the tree in the manner of a giant rabid squirrel and dispose of me in a most horrible and painful way.

I prayed it would be quick.

In those final seconds before I was to be eaten, I hoped this beast wouldn't leave my body tangled in the high branches of this oak. If he did, my loving father would never know what a cruel end befell his only child. I imagined him walking by the tree time and time again calling out to me, not knowing my rotting, disemboweled corpse was a mere twenty feet above his head.

The final sliver of hope I held, that perhaps it was a coincidence that he'd come in this direction, that he hadn't noticed me, vanished when the Lion Man leaned his musket against my tree and lingered there.

With a sound that reminded me of the puffing snort a horse gives after a strenuous race, he closed his eyes, threw back his head, and released a long sigh, no doubt gathering his strength to better scamper up the tree and kill me.

As I prayed for forgiveness, my confused ears imagined the sound of splashing water. I nearly passed out in fear before I realized what was happening.

The South Woods Lion Man was peeing on my tree!

Perhaps I too gave a sigh, one of relief; perhaps even though he was old, he still possessed those unnaturally sharp senses. For a hummingbird's wings could not have completed one beat in the time it took his eyes to shoot up and lock on mine!

My terror, which had seconds before begun to leave me, came home to roost with a glowing, red-hot intensity.

We stared at each other for the longest time; I was extremely confused. His eyes were soft and, it's odd to say, there was kindness in them. His face slowly dissolved into a mostly toothless smile. Then, with a look that was shy or almost embarrassed, he put his hand to his head as if tipping a hat and said, in clearly spoken English, "I do apologize, boy. If I'd-a knowed this here tree was occ-a-pied, I'd-a sure u-ro-nated elsewhere."

And with those words, he picked up his musket and disappeared back into the woods.

While I remember clinging to the tree's branch, I don't recall how I got home. I'm fairly certain I would've remembered if I had run in screaming horror as the Baylis boys had done after their encounter with the South Woods Lion Man. I'm almost certain I behaved in a more dignified manner. But honesty forces me to say it wasn't because I'm braver than those lads; it was the fact that I was in shock.

My first actual memory after coming face-to-face with the ghost of the woods was being in bed at home with the covers pulled tight under my chin, staring at the ceiling, trying to make sense of what had just happened.

When dawn came, after a night of pondering and sweating and examining, I came to the conclusion that if one reaches a point where one is absolutely convinced life is about to come to an end, God works to cushion the blow. He reveals that death is normal, that everyone who has lived, everyone who is living, and everyone who will someday live has to walk this same path.

One reaches a point of accepting that one's allotted time on earth is at an end. Whether the end comes because of having carelessly chosen to cross a road just as a runaway team of horses hauling lumber to the mill is barreling by, or after fighting some dis-ease of the body for months and understanding the point has been reached where there's no more fight to give, or waking to the chilling sight of a murderous, half-human, half-lion beast, God leads one to accept and surrender to the circumstances.

It's similar to playing chess with Father. There's a point when the checkmate is inevitable and any further wiggling is senseless. The wise person uses what dignity he has left to tip his king and resign.

There comes an epiphany that fighting is useless, and once that point is reached, there is relaxation, there is calmness, there is almost light-headed happiness. A sense of coolness and relief had come over me in that tree, much as though I'd stepped into the icehouse in the midst of a brutal July heat wave.

But if something happens and the runaway team of horses is somehow diverted, or the illness disappears, or the South Woods Lion Man chooses at the last second only to pee on your oak tree and then acts embarrassed about it, one is left in a bit of a quandary.

Something has been drained. Life can never be the same. I'm not certain if that's good or bad. I do know I will not be visiting the forest any time soon.

CHAPTER 15

Twenty-Six Letters

BENJI

A week after I was pardoned from the Amen Corner, Mother and Father called me to the kitchen table.

It was a real relief when I saw they didn't have any other pieces of fake evidence that Patience had come up with. This meeting was about something other than a bunch of lies told about me.

Father said, "Benjamin, your mother and I have decided that it's far past the time you learned the value of money."

"Sir?"

"Some of your actions show you don't have no real 'preciation of the cost of getting by from day to day. You needs to start getting paid so you can understand how rough it is to get a dime. You've got to learn the only things that come cheap or easy is cheap and easy things."

"Does that mean I'm going to get an allowance like Spencer does?"

Mother said, "No! Whoever heard of paying a child to do what they're supposed to do? That's nonsense. What it means is we think you're old enough to start working outside of the home."

"*Really?*"

This was great news!

Patience and Stubby had been working as apprentices for Mr. Craig the carpenter for almost a year now, and while it's true that everyone said they were geniuses with wood and the sooner they got started the better, I'm older and Mother and Father still wouldn't let me do anything but chores and schoolwork.

"Really." Mother reached across the table to hold my hand and said, "But that's not the good part of the news."

"Oh, Mother, what could be better news than that?"

"It's where you're going to be working!"

She looked at Father and said, "Do you want to tell him or should I?"

Father cleared his throat and said, "Benjamin, what is it you're always going on and on about wanting to be one day?"

"A hermit?"

"The other job."

"A newspaperman?"

"That's the one."

"You know who Mary Ann Shadd was?"

"Yes, sir, she was the editor of the *Provincial Freeman* a long time ago."

Mother said, "Correct. And you know the Creator has a master plan, so it's no coincidence that Miss Shadd and your Gramma Alston knew each other back in Wilmington, Delaware, in the States. Well, when I heard that her daughter, Sarah Cary, had moved back to Chatham and is starting up a paper of her own, I knew it was time I paid her a visit."

Mother squeezed my hand. "Benjamin, she's agreed to take you on as an apprentice! Twice a week after school, you'll go to Chatham and work with her and learn about publishing and writing a newspaper!"

I was too overjoyed to speak.

"You know of course that you won't be writing any articles at first. In between cleaning and etching, you'll learn about typesetting and inking and such."

Father said, "Be truthful with him, TooToo. You're gonna be a errand boy at the start."

"I don't care! Any job working on a paper will be great!"

Mother said, "We have to tell you the same thing we told Patience and Timothy when they started working with Mr. Craig. We are sending you out into the world as a representative of the Alstons now. Every action you take, every word you say, every way you come in contact with neighbours and friends will be a reflection on this family. Don't say or do anything that you wouldn't say or do in front of me and your father."

Father said, "You been raised proper; you know what's expected of you."

He began counting a list on his fingers. "You must work hard, you must never be late, you must be courteous, you must stay busy, you must keep your eyes open for work that ain't expected of you and dash to do it. Your goal gotta be to make Miss Cary feel by hiring you she's the luckiest person in the world. If you always keep that in mind, you'll make us proud."

"Oh, Mother, Father, you have no idea how happy I am! I'll make you very proud!"

Mother said, "We know you'll do a good job, son. Now, Miss Cary's a substantial woman, Benji; she wouldn't just take you on because her mother and your grandmother were friends, no, sir. We've been working on this for weeks. She even had me bring some of your school writings over, and it wasn't until after she read them that she agreed to take you on."

"Her exact words were, 'Real talent and potential!'"

Father said, "This ain't something you getting handed, son. You got your foot in the door and now it's up to you."

Mother said, "That's right, Benjamin, and we're expecting you to *kick* that door down! And to help you out . . ."

She pulled a large cardboard box from under the table and slid it toward me.

Written across the box were the words CLARK STEEL-TOED REINFORCED BOOTS.

When I pulled the top off the box, that sweet strong smell of freshly tanned leather filled the room! The boots were black with high tops and laces. I picked one up. It weighed a ton!

"Oh, Mother, Father, thank you so much!"

I laced them on. A perfect fit.

Mother was just as excited as I was. She said, "Timothy, your turn!"

Father reached under his side of the table and pulled out a brand-new pair of heavy leather gloves. I put them on.

Mother handed me a square pencil and said, "Everyone in Miss Cary's office has one of these behind their ear. Let's see how it looks on you."

I didn't have a mirror, but by Mother and Father's grins, I knew it looked great.

"Timothy? Stop slowing this down!"

There was more!

Father handed me what looked like a strange-shaped boat made out of folded newspapers.

Mother said, "Everyone there wore one of these to keep ink and dust out of their hair!"

Another perfect fit.

Next she handed me a gift-wrapped package.

I pulled the ribbon and paper away to see a beautiful folded apron made out of blue jean material. Best of all, Mother had embroidered *BENJAMIN* in bright gold letters across the top middle pocket.

"Oh, Mother!" was all I could say.

She said, "Now, Benji, when I ordered this, they told me it was the John Deere of printing aprons, but there's one thing I'm embarrassed to have to tell you. But it can be fixed."

Father laughed. "One *minor* detail."

I unfolded the apron. It had more pockets than I could count and so many snaps and flaps, it would take days to figure out what they were used for.

I slipped the top strap over my head and tied the two strings behind me. When I looked down, I saw the minor detail Father was laughing at.

Mother said, "Now, I did that late last night. That's no excuse, but I was dead tired and should have waited, but I was too excited to give this to you! Don't worry, I can fix it later."

When Mother had embroidered my name on, she'd done it upside down.

"Oh, Mother, it's perfect like it is. I'll be the only person in the world with one like this. May I run over and tell Spencer?"

I fought the tears that for some reason were trying to pop out of my eyes, hugged my parents, and headed over to Spence's home to share the news.

Patience and Stubby were coming in the door just as I was going out.

I grabbed Stubby and twirled him around. I gave Pay a big kiss on her forehead. As I closed the door to run to Spence's, Stubby looked worried and Patience looked disgusted.

This was the start of something big for me, and Spencer was the first person I wanted to share it with.

Everyone in Buxton thought and hoped this would be Spencer's year to win the public speaking contest, and I had always been sort of jealous. Even though we were best friends, it seemed like he was doing so much better than me, like he was getting noticed and appreciated and I wasn't. I know it's silly, but it's what I couldn't help feeling.

But now that was going to change! Now we'd be moving up together! It wouldn't be long before he was Canada's greatest lawyer and I was Canada's greatest newspaperman!

And the strange thing was we both were doing it because we loved what words could do.

We both wanted to be like those people who can magi-cally make words do all sorts of things. In the right hands, words can move more bricks than the strongest team of mules. And what I don't get is that while most of us can talk and a whole bunch of us can write, there are only the teeny-weenyest number of people who know how to make words do magic.

I mean, words are made up of letters, nothing more. And there are only twenty-six of them and they're there for all of us to use. There's no one saying, "No, you can't use these letters; they're saved only for that certain group." It's the same twenty-six letters, taught to most of us, but only a few can make those letters fall into words and do tricks and lift bricks and move mountains.

There's no denying that some people can make words do miracles.

Take making someone laugh.

How is it possible that one person can use only words to make another person laugh? Without tickling them, without making a silly face, without doing something fool-ish, they just make those twenty-six letters fall in a certain order, and for no good reason, I can see your eyes narrow, your cheeks get pulled up, your lips separate, your teeth show, and before you know what's hit you, those twenty-six letters have you doubled over laughing.

Now that's magic.

Now that's power.

If I could get the letters to behave properly for me, I was going to use them to explain to my best friend why writing words is better than speaking them.

I knew it would be hard to do. Maybe I should write it to him instead of telling him.

When I ran up on Spencer's porch, today's headline didn't need any thought:

SHOCKING DISCOVERY! NEWSPAPERMAN STUNNED TO LEARN PARENTS HAVE CHANGED INTO SUCH WONDERFUL PEOPLE!

CHAPTER 16

An Gorta Mór

RED

"Grandmother O'Toole, do you actually remember Ireland?"

"Faith and begorra! What type of question is that? How old are you now? Thirty-two, thirty-three?"

"Grandmother, I'm thirteen."

"Then do you actually remember Canada?"

"Of course I do. We live here."

"Oh, I see! Ye've pulled the bloody caul from me eyes, Your Majesty. Oh, thank ye! Thank ye so much! Ye're so much smarter at thirteen than I was! Here ye are blessed with a perfect, clear recollection of everything whilst poor, unschooled, dirty little street urchin that I am remembers naught. How fortunate I am to be in your presence, m'lord! How noble of you it is to lower yourself to be in the company of a poor beggar girl such as I. Which of your boots should I lick first, m'grace?"

"Grandmother, I didn't mean it in that manner."

Her eyes narrowed and I prepared to leave the room rather than be greatly abused. She stopped, though.

"Of course I remember Ireland."

She paused.

"Parts of it anyway."

If I wanted this conversation to go on, I knew this was not the time to speak.

"But those ships," she continued, "I'll never forget those ships. As long as I live, I'll remember the ships that these vile Canadians kept us on for all that time."

This was quite the surprise. Even without Father's prompting, I'd always wanted to know more about her time coming to Canada, but other than an odd hate-filled mention or two, she'd never spoken with me about it. She'd never spoken with me on any subject other than what a grand and glorious fool I was and how the only way she could explain my being in her family was that I was a changeling, that a spite-filled troll had switched me with her real grandson at birth.

She believed this so sincerely that she even claimed to know the name of her real, switched grandson. He was living under the name of little Jimmy McElroy. And, due to the switch, my life was one of meat for supper every evening and feathered pillows for my head every night, while poor little Jimmy McElroy's life was one of suffering, pain, and constant hunger.

"Why do you remember the boat, Grandmother O'Toole? What was wrong with it?"

"Oh, laddie, 'twas nary a thing wrong with the ship. At first. She was called the *Shenandoah* and a fine ship she was. No, 'twas the sickness that was aboard that turned her into a place fit for neither man nor beast."

"People became seasick?"

"*Seasick?* Pshh! A queasy stomach would have been nothing. No, boy, someone got onboard with the jail fever whilst we were escaping the claws of *an Gorta Mór.*"

"Grandmother, you know I don't speak Gaelic. What were you escaping?"

"*An Gorta Mór.* The Great Hunger. Starvation. The potatoes in the ground had rotted overnight. We went to sleep with healthy green fields and woke up the next day with all of them as withered and black and useless as those runaway slaves over in Buxton."

I grimaced.

She snapped her twisted fingers.

"Just like that, all the crops were dead."

She breathed deeply, closed her eyes, and whispered, *"And the smell!"*

Grandmother O'Toole moaned.

"'Twas as though a mighty curse had fallen on the land. Everywhere in Connemara and, we found out, every-where in Erin, the reeking smell of death clung to the earth. 'Twas as though the very bowels of the earth had been ripped open and spilled across the fields. I would've sworn to the heavens that there couldn't have been a smell anywhere to match the stench of those rotting potatoes."

The wrinkles that crowd the corners of her mouth pulled themselves up in a weak smile.

"Little did I know how soon our heavenly Father would show me otherwise."

She crossed herself and stared out the picture window.

I didn't want her to stop. I took a chance and said, "Since the potatoes were gone, couldn't you eat something else? Weren't there chickens or cows or pigs or corn, *something*?"

After the longest time, she said, "Ye'd not understand, laddie. 'Tis not your fault, but ye've been to the manor born here in Canada, ye've been blessed and don't even know it. 'Twas very different for us back then."

Grandmother O'Toole stood and walked toward the window. I thought I'd ruined my chance to hear her story, but instead of going into the other room, she stopped at the window and stared out.

"Your poor mother died before she was able to give ye brothers and sisters, so ye have no way of understanding. I know ye and your father believe for sure that ye're the cleverest lad to ever have walked the earth, but even with all of your brains and books and studying, ye c'not understand what I'm talking about."

I waited.

"Ye c'not imagine what it's like to watch *an Gorta Mór* snatch away half of your siblings within a fortnight. No one could.

"All your books and lectures and studying won't let you come within a country mile of knowing what 'tis like to watch three of your loving brothers and two of your dearest sisters become living skeletons who weaken to the point of not being able to raise their heads."

She brought her hand to her mouth.

"How the oldest insisted that any scrap of food tha' 'twas to be given to them went to the youngest of us. How we didn't understand till years later, much too late, the sacrifice they were making to keep us alive."

Her hands began trembling.

"Aye. Ye soon learn the true meaning of guilt."

She collapsed onto the divan.

"Even me oldest brother, who'd been a big strapping lad weighing nearly thirteen stone afore he starved to death, was light enough at the end that 'twas I who dragged him to the door, then to the curb where he'd be collected for burial in the pits. That'll ne'er be in one of your books. That ye'll ne'er understand. That no studying in the world will open your eyes to.

"Aye, to truly know that, ye must have twirled the cat."

It had to be another Irish saying, but I had no idea what it meant.

"Twirled the cat?"

"Aye. If ye twirl a cat by its tail, once it's done clawing and shredding and peeling the very skin off your face and arms, you'll have learned things you c'not learn any other way."

The sadness in her voice and on her face made me not want to hear more of this. It appeared as though she began to shrink, as though each word took something from her that made her smaller and smaller. I wished I hadn't brought up Ireland.

Her voice changed in a most unusual manner. While she was normally very expressive in everything she had to say and prone to exaggerations and bluster and a great waving of her arms and fluttering of her hands, she now became very still and began speaking in the most eerie and cutting monotone.

She stared at her hands, which rested withered and tired in her lap.

"'Twasn't long after the potatoes died, people started dying too. In droves, I tell ye. First 'twas the poorest, then the city folk, then even the farmers. So many died, the priests closed all the cemeteries. Said there was no room for even one more soul. People were thrown in pits and buried like diseased cattle. That's when the landlords decided to kick us all off the land."

Grandmother O'Toole began worrying the wedding band on her finger.

"Father and the landlord had already once come to blows. Perkins wanted us off the land, the same land that six generations of our family had farmed and called home, and now the cur had false papers showing 'twas his all along.

"The last thing Father had said to the landlord after he'd knocked the bugger down with a proper good left cross was the only way Perkins could get us to leave our home was to kill him dead as a stone. I think that's what Father wanted.

"And that's exactly what we expected to happen later when the landlord pounded on the back door with Jim Hawkins and Frank Cooper, both huge as bulls and just as stupid, standing at his side. Father looked through the rag of curtain at the back door, kissed each of us, said he was sorry for what had happened and what was going to happen, that he was only one man and had done all he could.

"As the pounding on the door got louder, Father asked my mother to pray for his soul, then took the carving knife from the drawer and slipped it into his pocket. When he went out the door . . . when it closed . . . we knew that would be the last we'd see him alive. I knew the next body I'd be dragging to the curb for the pits would be that of me beloved father.

"Those of us who still had strength to do so stood huddled at the door, waiting for the gunshot or a quick scuffle and scream or the sounds of cudgels battering Father's head and spilling his blood into the dead soil.

"But there was nothing. Only voices.

"After forever, the door opened again and Father staggered in with papers in his clenched fists and tears pouring from his eyes. Me mother told me later she'd known the man for fifty-two years and had never seen him cry. Said in a long life full of sad sights that his tears were the worst thing she'd seen by far.

"Father dropped his head into me mother's lap and said, 'Oh, Judith, our prayers have been answered! The heavenly Father has softened the wretch's heart to the point that he has bought all of us passage to Canada! In four days, we're off to Belfast, then on to Liverpool, and we'll leave this forsaken land behind! We'll be boarding a ship called the *Shenandoah*! Saints be praised! Canada!'

"Mother said, 'Tis this is but a cruel joke? It c'not be true!'

"She handed me the papers and told me to read them.

"'Twas true indeed. In four days, we had to leave for Belfast to board a ship."

Grandmother O'Toole whispered, "'Twas four days too long for me older siblings, Sheila and Daniel, though.

"Aye. Bitter did we weep only three days later as we kissed and shrouded the poor souls farewell and set them out, but we should've saved our tears. They were the lucky ones. The dream of escaping had burned in them for three days and they never knew the pain of having that dream snuffed out. I was now the oldest living child and knew what that meant."

Grandmother O'Toole laced her fingers and kept staring at them.

"To this day, I've not had much to be grateful for. But I am forever thankful for the joy and hope Sheila and Daniel had in their eyes when they slept that final time. I'm grateful indeed for the lovely stories about Canada we told each other that filled those precious angels' final three days.

"Alas, 'twould've been wise if we'd held on to our tears. Those of us who got on that ship were the ones who should've been wept over."

I'd been so transfixed that Father's voice startled me.

"Hullo! Another day's work is done and I'm back in the loving embrace of home."

Grandmother O'Toole sprang from the divan, her cane bell jingling softly.

"Oh, Chester, welcome home. Your supper's but a minute away."

I felt so cheated.

Of course I was happy that Father was home, but why couldn't this have been one of those evenings when business at the courthouse kept him until nine or ten o'clock? Who knew the next time Grandmother O'Toole would be in such a talkative mood?

Before she went into the kitchen, Grandmother O'Toole had one more surprise for me. She turned and said, "Chester's right, as usual. 'Tis important ye know this. Ye're getting to the age where your smartness might not interfere with you learning something. We'll talk again tomorrow. Well before your father comes home."

Though a sense of dread filled me, I began counting the hours.

→ Chapter 17 ←

Off to Work

BENJI

It was going to be my first day of work, and the train to Chatham didn't leave until after three, but I knew something was suspicious when Mother told us we had to be ready to walk to the station by noon.

Right before we left home, Mother held my shoulders, kissed my cheek, and said, "The apron and the cap and the boots and the pencil behind your ear are fine, Benji, but don't you think wearing the gloves on a beautiful day like today is a bit much?"

Maybe she was right. I took the gloves off and hung them from one of the snaps on my apron.

Stubby said, "Momma, why's Benji's name wrote out upside down like that?"

Mother said, "Have you got matching socks on, Timothy?"

Stubby quit asking embarrassing questions and went to our room. He had *no* socks on.

131

Patience said, "I know why it's upside down. It's because it's not there for other people to read; it's there for Benji. Mother was very kind because this way if Benji forgets who he is again and starts wandering around lost, all he has to do is look down to read his name and he'll be able to remember!"

Only Father and Pay thought that was funny.

Even with an upside-down name, I felt great!

Father always tells about how proud he had been to put on his uniform when he enlisted in the United States Colored Troops in Detroit, but there wasn't any possibility that he felt prouder than I did in *my* uniform. I couldn't help standing tall, with my shoulders back and my chest poked out. I felt like a soldier too.

We left home, and on the way to the station, there wasn't one single person to say hello or ask how we were doing. That was very suspicious. That could only mean one thing.

It was no surprise at all when we got to the station and all our neighbours and friends and half of Buxton was sitting in the park by the station on blankets, waiting with dishes and wishes to see me off.

Father said to Mother, "I ain't complaining, but it sure don't take much for you Buxton folk to turn something as simple as a 'fare thee well' into a excuse to have a big pot-luck picnic."

A great cheer went up when we walked into the crowd.

I don't know how it's possible to feel embarrassed and happy at the same time, but after a few minutes of being the centre of attention, I was.

Everyone wanted to pat my back and shake my hand.

Mother whispered to me, "Benjamin Alston, quit standing so stiff!"

Mrs. Stanley said, "My, my, my, Benjamin! Aren't you something? Standing like a soldier going off to fight the war. You sure do look handsome in that get-up, sweetheart. Look like a full-grown man! Congratulations on your new job. I know you'll do us all proud."

"Thank you, ma'am."

I was tempted to give her a salute, but didn't.

Mr. Wesley said to Father, "Timothy, the boy's the spit and image of you."

He slapped my back and said, "We're all behind you, Benji. You take care of business in Chatham for us."

"Yes, sir. I will, sir."

Mr. Craig the carpenter shook my hand and said, "If you do half as good as your siblings, Miss Cary's hired herself a good worker."

Pay and Stubby smiled and thanked him along with me.

All of the food looked great, but I had no appetite. I wasn't even interested in the singing and dancing that started.

When I finally got on the train and it started to pull away from Buxton, I stuck my head out the window and waved at our beautiful friends and neighbours.

People cheered and called out as many "Good lucks" as "Make us prouds!"

I couldn't help it; it seemed like the right thing to do. I felt so much like a hero that I stopped waving and started saluting.

About a minute and a half outside of Buxton, I ignored Mother's advice about my gloves.

I'd pulled them off for her, but now that I was on the train, I unsnapped them and put them back on.

Now I was complete! Today's headline was going to read:

CHATHAM ATWITTER AS GENUINE NEWSPAPERMAN
SPOTTED ON TRAIN FROM BUXTON!!!

CHAPTER 18

The Coffin Ship

RED

The next day, after Father left for the courthouse, Grandmother O'Toole was on the divan again and I took the chair across from her. I sat on the edge of the seat and was stunned when she shook her head and patted a spot on the divan for me to sit at her side.

I cautiously moved next to her and prayed to any saint who would listen that her newly discovered friendliness wouldn't lead to a hug. I wasn't sure how I'd react to that if it happened now, but I was positive there would be nightmares later.

But not to worry. Apparently, I sat too close; with a shooing motion, she let me know I should slide a bit farther away.

"What was I talking of the last time?"

"The ship, Grandmother O'Toole."

"Aye, the *Shenandoah*. She was a grand ship. We were told the crossing of the Atlantic would take anywhere from six weeks to two months, depending on the winds. But

135

thirty-two days? The sailors had never seen the likes of it before.

"They had no idea 'twas the prayers of all those good Irish souls and the hopes we carried that kept those sails full and the *Shenandoah* cutting through the waves like a sharp plow tilling dry soil. And though the sailors apologized for what they called tight rations, 'twas more than we'd had back home. After three and a half weeks, they saw how far ahead of schedule we were and the captain ordered that the stores be opened and we were allowed to eat as much as we could.

"He was a good man, God rest his soul. He told us, 'By thunder, they were a scrawny, scabby lot when they boarded my ship, but I'll not have anyone think Captain John Valentich doesn't feed his passengers.'

"By the time we finally saw land-birds and leaves in the water and knew we were close, we were heavier and happier than we'd been in years. No one else in the family had died. 'Tis amazing how quickly we began taking things for granted. Things like food and water; things like when we'd awaken, we all would still be alive. Things we had no business clinging to so quickly.

"A day before we sighted land, the sailors called everyone on deck and told us to breathe deep.

"Ah! 'Twas the sweetest perfume! I'd never smelt anything in Eire to match the green and brown and blue smell of Canada. It appeared all the stories were true. If it smelled this rich and alive a full day out, imagine what the smell would be on shore.

"No one slept that last night. We came upon Canada in the dark. Sailed into the Saint Lawrence River toward an island called Grosse Ile near Montreal.

"In the middle of the night, the beautiful scent of trees and fresh water and life began to fade. My younger brother, Kyle, and I were on deck that night when another smell rode in on the coattails of the glorious scent of green.

"Kyle grabbed me, raised my arm over my head, leaned in to sniff me armpit, raised his own arm, sniffed again, and said, ''Tis neither me nor ye, Sinead, but something's rotted bad.'

"The farther we went up the river, the stronger the smell became until finally it drove every one belowdecks.

"Some of the sailors told us they'd sailed the world over and never smelt the likes of this before. 'Twas a total mystery to them.

"Captain Valentich shook his head. Said he knew the smell from when he was a cabin boy. Said he'd worked a slave ship and this was as close to that foul odour as he'd ever smelt.

"The next day, like a warning, the first body floated by our ship. The captain sent a crew out to retrieve it for proper burial, but before it could be dragged to land, three more appeared. Then five on top of that. Then another three. The captain ordered the men to let the first body go.

"He weighed anchor and a great debate raged. Oh, did those English officers quarrel! Some wanted to land a scouting party to travel up the river to find out what the trouble was; some wanted to abandon Canada and head to Philadelphia or another port in America.

"Captain Valentich finally decided we must sail on, something that cost him his ship and so many of us passengers our lives. But almost as soon as he gave that order, the winds shifted and the breeze sweetened again.

"We all took it as a sign he'd done the right thing.

"The farther inland we went, though, bodies began appearing again. The odour returned with even more fierceness, and I knew the heavens were showing me that I'd been wrong about the fields being the worst smell ever. I knew this river in Canada had no place to compare for its stench."

She smiled.

"Sixteen days. That's how long it took ere I was shown to be wrong again."

Grandmother O'Toole stopped talking. Rather, she stopped talking in the manner she usually does.

She became very still and the grating monotone from yesterday returned.

"We knew there had been people onboard who were sick. They were moved away from us, but the smell of their sickness still hung in the ship's hold. Stories were told that there was a cabin stacked with the dead, waiting to be given a proper burial on land.

"We ignored the stories. Everyone in our family was doing better than we'd done in years; everyone was too lifted by full bellies and the dream of Canada to have much fear.

"The first clue we had that something was wrong was the man-o'-war ship that sat in the river. They hailed the captain to and sent a small skiff over to us. The captain dropped a rope for them to board and they refused. Shouted to the captain that we were to sail on until we came to a ship that was docked in the river. Said we should drop anchor behind that ship and await orders.

"Captain Valentich said no, that rather than go ahead, he was going to turn the ship around and head to America.

"The man in the rowboat said if he did, they had orders to commandeer the ship, and if the captain resisted, they were to sink him. Told the captain there was no turning back, that all the ships from Ireland were carrying typhus and were ordered to fall into the quarantine line ahead.

"'Line?' the captain asked, but the man in the skiff d'not answer; he ordered the rowboat back to the man-o'-war.

"There were soldiers along the shore, posted every hundred feet or so and looking out at the river. The captain followed orders and we turned a bend in the strait and saw we'd sailed into the divil's own home.

"There was a line of ships as far as the eye could behold. Each one anchored in place and each one flying a blue flag. We soon learned why they, and now the *Shenandoah*, were called the coffin ships."

Grandmother O'Toole's eyes fell upon her folded hands.

"We also learned whence the horrible odour came. The river ran thick with the foulness of those ships, with the stench of diarrhea and fever and death. By this time, I knew better than to think there c'not be a smell anywhere worse on God's green earth, for if there was, I d'not want to be so arrogant to say that and have the heavenly Father prove me wrong again.

"The Canadians told us we c'not leave the ship for fifteen days since there were cases of typhus aboard. Quarantine, they called it. All it did was make certain that those who hadn't arrived with typhus soon got it. They killed Father and most of the rest of me siblings in that fifteen days. Only Mother, me, Kyle, and your great-aunt Margaret lived.

"'Twasn't long ere the food and fresh water were gone. And *an Gorta Mór* found us ten thousand miles from home on a boat in the middle of the Saint Lawrence River."

I said, "Grandmother O'Toole, no one brought you food? They made you stay on the boat and didn't feed you?"

"Of course they d'not feed us. There were too many of us. We found out that the line of ships stretched over two miles up the river. And the farther you went up the line, the worse shape the people were in. That's why the ships were called coffin ships. The ones up front held nothing but bodies. Those who d'not die of typhus or starvation died of dehydration."

I said, "Dehydration? You were in a river! Couldn't they lower buckets?"

"I told ye this wasn't something ye could imagine. The river was too fouled with bodies and death to drink the water."

She was right. I couldn't imagine what that would have been like.

Grandmother O'Toole's right hand scratched her left arm as she said, "And the fleas and lice! Ye'd move the little rag of a cloth pallet you slept on and it looked as if the underneath was painted black afore the fleas scattered.

"After we sat in the water for a week, we noticed there were no more rats. The fleas had plagued them so divilishly that they'd jumped into the water and swam for shore.

"But I believe 'twas that which kept us alive. With the little bit of gruel the ship provided, Mother would mix a paste and I believe that made all the difference."

"A paste?"

"Kyle and I figured it out later. When you're tired and

hungry and sick and disgusted, ye don't ask questions, or maybe 'tis that ye know but don't want to believe. We were just grateful for the paste. It didn't have much flavour, but it did add something to the near-water those detestable Canadians gave us."

"What was it, Grandmother O'Toole?"

"While we slept, Mother was busy going throughout the ship with her pot and lid. 'Twas the fleas and lice and maggots. She'd catch a half a pot full, then grind them into a paste and add it to the gruel."

I gagged.

She said, "D'ye see? D'ye now understand what it means to twirl the cat?"

CHAPTER 19

A Dirty Job

BENJI

Being a set-up boy at a print shop is a lot dirtier than it seems it should be. And it's nowhere as easy or fun as it looks.

I'd been working for Miss Cary for nearly a month, and I was still trying to learn the strange new language of printers' speak.

Mr. Withers, the manager of the shop, spent the weeks teaching me how to set print, what a forme is, and how it fit into a coffin, how to ink sheep's wool and put it on text, how to get the paper we were printing on damp but not wet before we used it, what a tympan and frisket do, how to use a windlass to get a bed under a platen, how to rotate the rounce, and when to use the devil's tail.

I was most grateful to him because when Miss Cary introduced us on my first day, he took me to a closet where three or four aprons hung and said, "Choose yourself one."

I said, "But, sir, I've already got an apron."

He said, "First off, don't never call me sir ever again. Call me Wimpy. And second off, did your ma make that apron for you?"

"She didn't make it; she just embroidered my name."

"She's a kind lady. Do her a favour and take it off and put one of these on. By the end of the day, your whole apron's gonna be black and won't no one be able to see your ma's hard work. Unusual as it is."

And he was right. Ink got to be everywhere and if I had to wear a dirty apron, people might think I was just a dirty kid and not a newspaperman when I rode the train home.

I hung the John Deere of aprons in the closet and picked a dirty one.

I would wear Mother's apron to and from work just so people wouldn't mistake me for not being a newspaperman.

I'd swept the entire shop and was preparing to clean the printer when Miss Cary's voice came barreling at me like a thunderclap.

"Ooh, Ben-jamin."

I put the broom down and tapped on her office door.

"Come in."

"You called me, ma'am?"

"I've asked you to keep your ears and eyes sharp for anything new and interesting happening in Buxton, no-o-o-o?"

This didn't sound good. I right away started wondering what I could have missed.

I'd told her about the Johnsons' two-headed calf, about Pa Dale getting his arm broken in the thrasher, about the Upper Ontario Forensics Competition that was going to be held in Buxton next month, about the Marxes' prize hog going missing and how everyone was sure the Madman of Piney Woods had a hand in it. That was about it. But it was easy to see I'd missed something or she wouldn't have called me in.

"Yes, Miss Cary, I think I told you everything."

"Oh. Reeeallly?"

Come on Benji, think, what had you missed?

"Yes, ma'am?"

"Then what is this?"

It was one of the yellow flyers that had popped up like dandelions all over Buxton. The constable had taken them down soon after they were put up.

ACHING?
SLOWING DOWN?
DID YOUR GIDDY-UP GO AWAY?

COME TO THE CLEARING AND FIND OUT WHY.

OUR CERTIFIABLE MEDICAL DOCTOR
SWAMI HAWLEY
CAN PUT THE SPRING BACK IN YOUR STEP.

MEET THE SEVENTY-FIVE-YEAR-OLD FATHER OF
THREE-MONTH-OLD TWINS!

MEET THEIR SIXTY-FIVE-YEAR-OLD MOTHER!

MEET THEIR ONE-HUNDRED-AND-FIVE-YEAR-OLD
GRANDMOTHER!

MEET THEIR GRANDMOTHER'S
TWENTY-FIVE-YEAR-OLD PARAMOUR!

SWAMI HAWLEY SAYS,
"IF THE GOOD LORD HAD WANTED YOU
TO BE OLD AND FEEBLE, YOU WOULD OF
BEEN BORN THAT WAY."

LET SWAMI HAWLEY GET YOU RIGHT
WITH JESUS AGAIN AND REJUVENATE YOU
AT THE SAME TIME!

"You hadn't seen one of these?"

"I had, ma'am, but I didn't think this was important enough to report about in the paper."

"No?"

"No, ma'am."

"Well, maybe not. But this *is* going to be your first assignment in reporting from the field. I want you to go to this snake-oil meeting and write an article describing what you see."

"*Really?*"

"Really."

"Oh, thank you, Miss Cary! I'll write the best article I can!"

"I would expect nothing less. Don't for one moment harbour the notion that your work will be published in my paper. If that does ever happen, it won't be for a very long time, but you must start somewhere. You've worked diligently and faithfully these past few weeks and you are a capable writer. I believe it's time you took the next step on the long road of learning more about the real work of a newspaper.

"Your deadline is Monday morning at nine."

She looked sharply at me. "You do know why they call it a deadline, don't you?"

"Not really, ma'am."

"It's because if your article isn't in the IN box by nine

147

o'clock, your chances of being anything more than a cleaner and set-up boy in this office are officially dead."

"Yes, ma'am."

"I'm going to give you two hundred words, so use them wisely."

I wondered how she knew she was going to say exactly two hundred words. I took out my pen and pencil to take notes.

She looked at me, wrinkled her brow, then almost smiled before her normal scowl came back.

"No, Ben-jamin, I mean you have two hundred words to complete your article."

"Oh! Thank you, ma'am, thank you so much!"

Some of the time, if you do something embarrassing, it's best to hope no one noticed and act like you don't know.

I closed her door behind me and made myself a promise.

Miss Cary didn't know it, but she *was* going to publish my article. I was going to make sure. After she read *my* writing, she might even think about hiring me full-time as a reporter! She might even retire and let me start running this place like it should be run.

When this was over, Mother and Father will have no choice but to give *me* the same looks of amazement they give Pay and Stubby. This time, they were going to gasp in surprise at something *I'd* done!

Well, this time they'd be gasping about something I'd done that was *good*.

I'd debated with myself for much of the night about how I should act when I went to the snake-oil show. Should I try to be like a normal thirteen-year-old boy or should I put on my newsprint cap and apron so they'd know I was a reporter and take me serious?

When I arrived at the Clearing, I was glad I'd decided not to do either of those things and just went as myself.

I was in the third row of seats in the Clearing. There were chairs in the first two rows, but I didn't want to draw attention to myself. There wasn't a whole lot of excitement from the people who were sitting with me or from any of the people who worked for this Swami Hawley.

Most of the people were men from Chatham, but there were some Buxton men here too.

A white man and woman in front of me kept look-ing back at the white man two rows behind who was singing and laughing and taking long pulls from one of the bottles of elixir that were for sale at a booth behind the platform.

The man said to the woman, loud enough so everyone could hear, "Scandalous! Used to be he was one of the best lawyers in Toronto but got run outta town and told he could never work in another court for the rest of his life. So he come down to Chatham and changed his name but botched that too. Now he's living in the bottom of a bottle. Absolutely scandalous!"

The woman snorted and they both turned away from the happy singing man.

Mother had been concerned that I would see something at the sideshow that would disturb my sleep, but her concerns were wasted. The only thing that was disturbed was my appetite. And that was done by the man whose mother was an alligator from Eatonville, Florida, and whose father, the barker with the megaphone told us, was a poor, lonely dirt farmer from Tupelo, Mississippi.

The alligator and the farmer named their child Gator-O.

Gator-O was in the centre of the little platform that had been put up in the Clearing, his entire body covered by a long cloak and hood. Only two glowing little alligator eyes could be seen peeking out from under the hood.

Standing behind him was a white man with no shirt, big muscles, and a little whip.

The barker sounded very bored when he said, "Behold the tragic offspring of a alligator and a farmer. He inherited his father's hair and eyes and his mother's skin and nasty disposition."

"Here, for all to behold, is Gator-O, the half-human, half-reptilian horror."

The strongman pulled the cloak off Gator-O, and people gasped and looked horrified.

He was a skinny, bright-red white man who turned his back to the audience. He wasn't wearing a shirt and his back was covered from his neck down to his trousers with light-brown and red-and-gray patchy scales.

To my eye they had more of the look of sores than scales, but since he was part alligator, I'm pretty sure they were supposed to be scales. Dragging behind him was a very light chain attached on one end to his ankle and on the other end to nothing.

The barker sounded half-asleep when he said, "Oooh, fear not, ladies and gentlemen, he is securely bound and the animal side of his nature rears its ugly head only rarely. Do not make eye contact with him and, please, I implore you, try not to provoke him by screaming so loud."

I didn't hear any loud screams, just low, disgusted groans.

The barker pointed to the muscleman who was on the side of the platform and said, "Don't worry. If Gator-O becomes too riled, we have the world's strongest man here to restrain the beast in him."

He patted the empty holster at his side and said, "And if Slugger can't stop him, I won't hesitate using this fully loaded pistol."

Something about those words made Gator-O's animal side show up. He turned around and waved long, pointy, dirty fingernails at us while snarling and stomping from one end of the platform to the other. The front of his body was covered in scaly sores too.

Not only had he gotten his mother's skin and disposition, he got her teeth too. There were fangs hanging down from each side of his lips. But when he opened his mouth too wide, the fangs started falling out, so he mostly just stomped around looking angry and g-r-r-ing at us.

Gator-O came to the front of the platform and brushed his right hand back and forth across his left arm. A little blizzard of scales and grayish dust rose up from his arm like snow off a dune on Lake Erie.

He huffed and puffed and blew the scales out into the first two rows of chairs.

The people sitting that close quickly filed out of the rows.

The man who used to be a lawyer stood up, holding on to his half-empty bottle of Swami Hawley's Magical Youth Elixir, and screamed, "By Jiminy, that's got to be the worst case of so-rye-uh-sus in all of Canada!"

People must've felt cheated by Gator-O because the seats started emptying really quick. But another man walked onto the platform, wearing a turban and a white doctor's coat. There was a stethoscope around his neck and a black bag in his right hand. He'd taken the megaphone from the barker and shouted, "Wait!"

The strongman came onto the platform and put Gator-O's cloak back on him and took him away.

People began coming back.

The man with the doctor's bag said, "I know why you've come! I too once was tired and lacked vigour. I too once wondered how I'd make it from one day to the next. But today! Today, three weeks after my eightieth birthday, I have the strength and stamina of a twenty-year-old!"

The swami did look a lot younger than eighty.

"And what gave me my youth back? What makes me get up every morning at the crack of dawn and crow like a rooster?"

The happy drunk lawyer hollered, "Whatever it is, I bet your neigbours find it really annoying!"

The swami winked and said, "What, you may wonder, keeps my twenty-five-year-old wife so happy and cheery?"

The lawyer yelled, "I don't know, but if I were you, I'd keep my eye on old Gator-O. He looks like he might be a real ladies' man!"

The swami nodded at the strongman, who went and sat down next to the happy lawyer.

"I'll tell you what it is. It's the secret elixir formula I was given by a dying mystic from Timbuktu many years ago."

The lawyer stood up and said, "What killed him, was it —" Then, looking as though he'd been dropped from twenty feet, he plopped back down in his seat, leaned his head against the strongman, and was very quiet.

Swami Hawley said, "And now, even though the ingredients cost us five dollars a bottle to make and are clearly marked so on the bottle, if you get in line and tell my aide, 'I too want to be young again,' we will sell it to you for two dollars! Or three bottles for five dollars! Or a case of twelve for fifteen dollars."

He added, "Hurry, hurry, hurry, the supplies are limited. Don't forget the magic words 'I too want to be young again.'"

And with that, the show was over.

I was shocked at how quickly the seats emptied as people lined up to buy the elixir.

The lawyer stumbled out, held up by the strongman. I picked up the empty bottle he'd been drinking from and put it in my pocket.

It would be the proof I needed to write my article.

I couldn't wait to see the look on Miss Cary's face when she saw my work.

Deadlines are terrible. Terrible and unfair.

I don't know how Miss Cary can expect a writer to get

something done by a certain time. I was finding out it's a lot of work to create an article and, doggone it all, the words didn't want to cooperate.

But I worked and worked and worried and worried and finally got my article finished.

I put it in the IN box outside of Miss Cary's door on Monday morning, right on top of the articles from her old reporters.

When Miss Cary came in, she greeted me, picked up the IN box, and closed her office door behind her.

That was the exact second the clock stopped. The closing of the door made time start playing freeze tag with me.

A hundred hours later, at noon, I tapped on her door to let her know I was going to eat my lunch and give her a chance to talk to me about the article.

"Miss Cary, I just wanted to tell let you I was going to be eating in the backyard if you want to talk to me about anything. I won't be more than fifteen minutes."

She never looked up or said a word. The only way I knew she'd heard me was the tiny nod she gave. At least I think it was a nod. After I closed her door behind me, I started wondering if it might have been a hiccup. Or a burp.

My lunch was miserable.

So were the next two hundred hours that I dragged about the print shop.

At the end of the day, I saw Miss Cary wasn't going to talk to me about the article. I went back and tapped on her door.

She grunted me in.

"I'm going home now, Miss Cary. Do you need anything more?"

"Will you be working tomorrow?"

"No, Miss Cary. Remember, I told you I'm helping my mother all day?"

"Oh. Yes. I'd forgotten. See you next week, Ben-jamin."

Instead of slamming my fists on her desk and screaming, "That's it? 'See you next week?' What about my article?" All I said was, "Yes, Miss Cary," and closed the door behind me.

I put on my traveling apron and cap and gathered all of my things.

I was almost out of the door when Miss Cary called, "Ben-jamin, please come here a moment. I'd like to discuss what you've written."

I knew it! She was waiting until the end of the day to give me the good news!

My first clue that this wasn't going to be a heaping on of praise was when she said, "You do understand you've made several major errors, do you not? Please point any one of them out to me. It should be very easy to do."

That didn't sound so good.

She slid my article across the desk to me.

I read through it, hoping the mistakes would jump out at me, but nothing; everything seemed to be perfect. I know I have a lot of trouble making commas behave, but even they looked fine.

Maybe Miss Cary was trying to trick me by pretending there was something wrong with this article when there really wasn't.

Maybe she was jealous!

With that in mind, I read through it again.

The poor souls of Buxton, Canada, many of who have already had their backs bowed by the cruel yoke of slavery, found theirself in another horrible pickle when they were exposed to a bilking cheater who took their money and sold them overpriced bottles of cheap liquor called a Magical Youth Elixir.

This con man crook goes by the name of Swami Hawley and he is shameless with his lies. He deceived everyone who came by saying he could make you feel young again. This fleecer, fraud, and mountebank put on a carnival sideshow first that was harmless to watch. But the scamming shark's true colours showed up when he bullied people into buying

*his vile elixir. This reporter, Benjamin
Alston, and everyone else there was shocked,
shocked I say, by the sharpie shyster's greed
and avarice.*

*One and all should be advised that this
smoothie and swindler is very convincing and
has a heart of stone. This is one horrible,
horrible, horrible person who should be
thrown right in jail.*

*Swami Hawley is so low that he even takes
advantage of a man with a skin condition.
Benjamin Alston and everyone else who was
there pray the man's not contagious.*

Doggone it all, it *was* perfect.

I'd even given it to Mother to read over, and it seems if there was something wrong, she'd have told me. All she'd said was, "I don't ever remember reading anything in a newspaper that seemed this . . . well . . . this *mean*, Benji."

I'd smiled and told her, "That's because most reporters are afraid to write the truth, Mother. I'm not. 'Let the chips fall where they want' is my motto."

I remembered the bottle of elixir I'd picked up. Maybe it would make a difference with Miss Cary.

I reached into one of my apron pockets and pulled the bottle out and put it on her desk.

"What's this?"

"I thought if you wanted Mr. Dickerson to draw an illustration for the article, he could use this."

She opened the bottle and sniffed.

"My word! No wonder some people love this. It's pure alcohol."

"I know, that's what my father said."

She dropped it in the trash basket next to her desk and reached her hand toward me.

I gave the article back to her.

"The easy things first, Ben-jamin. Just on a hunch, I counted the words in the last paragraph: thirty, correct?"

I nodded.

"Which means the rest of the article is exactly one hundred and seventy words long, correct?"

I smiled and did my best to look humble.

"Which means the only purpose of the third *horrible* and the final paragraph was to get you to two hundred words?"

Before I could say anything, she kept on, "And every adjective you've used to describe this Swami Hawley is a synonym of *con artist*, so we have *bilking cheater, fleecer, fraud* and *mountebank, scamming shark, sharpie shyster,* and *smoothie swindler.*

"Which leads me to ask, did the thesaurus end at the letter *S* or did you simply grow weary?

"I do note you were kind enough to keep the synonyms all in alphabetical order."

This wasn't going like I thought it would.

"Those are among the most glaring of the minor errors. For the major errors, your first is one for the ages. It's when you equate slavery with, and I quote, 'another horrible pickle.'"

She sighed and rubbed her eyes as though my article was exhausting her.

"Your next major error is just as fatal to your article, Ben-jamin."

After a pause, she said, "You don't like this Swami Hawley very much, do you?"

"No, ma'am, I think he's cheating people out of their money."

"So you don't have much respect for him, do you?"

"Well . . ."

"How can I explain this to you? This Swami Hawley may be a scoundrel and worthy of ridicule, but you must keep in mind that he and I are in the exact same business."

What? I know it wasn't what she meant, but it sure would make a great headline if I found out Miss Cary made extra money working in a snake-oil show!

"We're both in the business of words. He has chosen the spoken word, and I work with the written word. However, there is a real and important difference in the way we use our words. We both use words to influence but go about it in very different ways.

"I believe the written word is immeasurably more important."

Miss Cary waved her hand at her office.

"I recognize my bias. But that doesn't mean I'm wrong. How is your French, Ben-jamin?"

"Not so good, ma'am."

"That's something you'll have to work on. Learning a second language only enriches your grasp of English. Are you familiar with the phrase *dent-de-lion*?"

"No, ma'am."

"It means 'tooth of the lion.' It has been corrupted in English to *dandelion*.

"Now, since you have assured me ad nauseam that you are both an accomplished observer and outdoorsman, you have noticed how at the end of their season, dandelions undergo a beautiful transformation. They change from a disc of narrow, flat, bright yellow petals to a globe of ethereal, silver-gray, tiny, near-weightless seeds, each one clinging to its own parasol, each one designed to take flight at the least provocation.

"That, Ben-jamin, is a perfect representation of the spoken word.

"Like the dying dandelion, at first glance the spoken word appears to be impressive, yet something as insignificant as a gust of wind or the passage of the smallest measure of time will blow it away into something unrecognizable. The spoken word and the dandelion are available for review only through the frailest and most unreliable of human tools: memory.

"The written word is different. Once you commit something to print, you are, in effect, chained to it. It is always available to be looked at again and traced back to you.

"Therefore, written words have to be much more completely thought out; they must be crafted, arranged in such a way that they are clear, strong, and unambiguous. There is a great deal more responsibility required when using the written word.

"The spoken word allows for more room for the magician, a lot more space for flash and distraction and deception. As writers, we cannot afford to do that. We need to be bold and allow the truth to shield us.

"When writing for the press, our personal feelings should never sway the way we write. We must strive to be a clear mirror reflecting what it is we have seen and heard, not adding to or taking away anything."

"But, Miss Cary, I'm confused. First you said you use words to get across your point of view; now you say I can't let my feelings show in what I write. That doesn't make sense to me."

She smiled. "That, my dear Ben-jamin, is where the art comes in. That is also where we must respect our readers and allow them to draw their own conclusions. At most we must carefully and subtly nudge, never shove."

"This" — she waved my article like a flag — "has gone beyond shoving readers to stampeding all over them."

"So that means you're not going to use my article?"

"Yes, I'm going to use it, but in my paper? Surely you jest."

Just from her tone of voice, I knew this meant no.

"Have your parents ever had you or your siblings stand against a wall so they can use a pencil to mark both your height and the date?"

"Yes, ma'am. We do it every year on our birthdays inside the closet door frame."

"And aren't you amazed at how much you've grown from one year to the next without even noticing?"

It always does surprise me.

"That's the same thing we're going to do with this article, Ben-jamin. We'll get it framed, then I'll place it there."

She pointed at the wall behind her desk.

"We'll use it to measure your growth. Soon after you leave this apprenticeship, you will place it in an office of your own. Eventually, with your natural talents, you will hang it in the main office of a newspaper that you own. I have that much faith in you, young man. Keep applying yourself and, years from now, you shall be that good. But now? There's a greater possibility that Swami Hawley will be prime minister of Canada.

"Now, off you go."

When I left her office, I felt like she'd gut-punched me, brushed me off, slapped me back and forth, gave me a cool compress to put on my cheeks, cold-cocked me with a stiff uppercut to the jaw, picked me up, brushed me off again, then kicked me in the seat of my pants as she handed me a piece of cake and showed me the door.

Being a reporter isn't as easy as it looks.

On the train back to Buxton, my mind flitted between Miss Cary's lecture and Spencer Alexander.

Have you ever been in an argument and just knew you were right about something but couldn't find the words to convince the person you're arguing with? That happens all the time when I'm arguing with Spence.

It's sort of like telling everybody there are a bunch of fish in a barrel and no one believes you.

All you have to do to prove you're right is to dip your head under the water, get a grip on *one* fish, just one, pull it out, and you win the argument. But until you actually can get ahold of that one fish, the headlines for that day would read:

HOW LONG CAN THIS IDIOT KEEP HIS HEAD IN THE BARREL?

Up until the second you grab that fish, you're the only one who knows the headline is wrong. To everyone else, though, you *are* just an idiot with his head in a barrel.

There's no more frustrating feeling in the world.

But the very moment Miss Cary explained to me the difference between the written word and the spoken word was the very moment I was able to wrap my fingers around a fish!

When the Western Ontario Forensics Competition was over, Spencer Alexander might be the king of debaters in this part of Canada, but one of Mother's favourite sayings, "In the land of the blind, the one-eyed man is king," never rang truer. Spence might be the king of the spoken word, something not really all that important, something fragile. Or to put it as Miss Cary would, he's really just the king of a bunch of weeds.

I was going to be ruler of the written word, a much more important kingdom. Something that would last forever.

As dark green trees blurred by the train's window, I saw that when I'd gone into Miss Cary's office about an hour ago I was nothing but a boy with a dream. Now, after our talk, I was a man with a calling, and before long, just as she'd said, I was going to be the top person in the most important job on earth.

It had been a long day and I was tired from doing so much growing in such a little bit of time. I'm ten times more mature now and I can't wait to let Spence know the written word *is* more important than the spoken word. He was wrong and I was right!

The first headline I'd write as a man, not a boy, was directed right at Spence. It would read:

NYAH-NYAH-NYAH-NYAH-NYAH-NYAH!!!!

CHAPTER 20

The Letter!!!!!!

RED

Father and I sat at the dining room table, eating supper.

I finished my meal and set my knife and fork down to wait for Father to finish his.

He patted his moustache with his napkin, the sign that he was done and I could take our plates into the kitchen to wash them.

He said, "Delicious, Alvin. You've become quite the cook."

I learned to look at cooking the same scientific way I try to look at everything else. And while at first I tried to follow each recipe exactly as Mother's note cards directed, I soon learned that, just as with a scientific experiment, one achieved the best results by doing a little tinkering here and there. By not being so stuck to one idea that you can't see any other.

I reached to pick up Father's plate and was surprised to see an envelope had been underneath it while he ate.

"Father?"

"Hmm?" he said. "I wonder what that could be?"

He looked at me and smiled.

I was motionless.

He said, "Aren't you going to open it?"

I picked it up. The warmth from Father's plate had seeped into the envelope, making it seem almost alive.

It was addressed to Father and the return address was . . .

The room began to spin around me. I plopped back into my chair with the envelope in my hand.

"Oh, Father. Why are you smiling? What if I wasn't accepted? I'll die!"

Father said, "I saw Mr. Green at the courthouse today. You should know I wouldn't give you the envelope in this manner unless . . ."

The return address was Mr. Victor Green, Buxton Academy, Buxton, Ontario, Upper Canada.

My hands trembled as I began to unseal the envelope. Father's plate had warmed the glue enough that it easily came open.

My eyes refused to read beyond . . .

> *Dear Sir,*
>
> *It is with the greatest of pleasure that I am able to inform you that your son . . .*

I was in! I was in! I'd been accepted for classes from the best science teacher in all of Canada!

Father and I hugged. He kissed the top of my head and said, "Oh, Alvin. I wish your mother were here to see this. She would spontaneously combust with pride."

I said, "Oh, yes, Father, yes, she would."

Beyond that, neither one of us could talk.

If another scientist were to peek into our dining room, they would be hard-pressed to believe that I was a thirteen-year-old young man who was soon to embark upon a voyage of learning with the most respected science teacher in Upper Ontario. All that scientist would be able to observe would be a redheaded boy shamelessly sitting in his father's lap, crying his heart out with as much gusto and vigour as any three-year-old.

We hugged each other and cried until we laughed.

CHAPTER 21

The Return of the Madman of Piney Woods

BENJI

I am the only true woodsman I know. Whilst my friends enjoy the forest and feel at home there, I, on the other hand, am truly a part of it. That's why, as we sat around the fire listening to Mr. Swan on Saturday evening, a familiar chill crept down my spine. That old feeling of being watched was back.

Then I noticed him standing just inside the tree line, not forty feet away from us.

He wasn't hiding, but he wasn't doing anything to draw attention to himself either. I nudged Spence and nodded in the direction where the man stood.

Spencer looked for a second, then shrugged, unable to pick him out in the darkness. Keeping my hand low so only Spence could see it, I pointed right to where the man was standing. Spencer's eyes scanned the tree line, and a look of disbelief washed over my friend's face.

Before either one of us could say anything, Mr. Swan noticed Spencer and I weren't listening to him, stopped his story in mid-sentence, and pa-toohed a cold comet of saliva into the fire. He was preparing to give us the "And I hopes y'all's enjoyed your last time listening to the stories of Mr. Willie J. Swan" speech, the speech he gave whenever he was going to ban one of the children from his stories for life. Instead, something in our expressions made his eyes follow where we were looking.

All of the children exchanged looks of surprise when Mr. Swan stood up and walked to the tree line where the stranger stood.

Mr. Swan called out, "Well, I'll be! Seeing you's done brightened my spirits and brought gladness into my heart. This is sure a huge surprise!"

The man looked around and said, "It a surprise to me too. I been watching y'all for years and been satisfied just to sit back. For some reason lately, I been having to . . . or wanting to get closer and closer to hear better."

"I'm flattered by that, I sure am." He stuck out his right hand to the man. "You gunn come sit at the fire?"

The man stepped forward to shake Mr. Swan's hand and said, "Willie, I'm much oblige you ain't forgot me. I think I will join y'all, if don't no one mind."

Mr. Swan said, "Mind? These here young folk ain't got no idea how lucky they is that you gunn honour them by sitting in they midst. Most of 'em ain't got the sense of a turkey in a thunderstorm, but even they's got the brains to know that one day they's gunn tell they own kids 'bout this. You's a true hero to all us in Buxton!"

The man said, "Naw, Willie, ain't no one a hero. Don't say that."

As soon as *they* realized who this stranger was, Big Twin and Little Twin shrieked and bolted hand in hand into the night as if a bear were at their heels. I bet the only reason everyone else didn't follow was because fright had caused them to grow roots and plant themselves right where they sat.

The Madman of Piney Woods walked into the circle of light thrown by the fire and perched himself on the stump Little Twin had been sitting on before he and his brother ran into the darkness.

Right next to me! I could have reached out and touched him!

The twins' soul-curdling yells were fading farther and farther into the forest.

The Madman said, "Shouldn't one y'all go get them two afore they gets lost or hurt theyself?"

Mr. Swan said, "Don't worry, they's gunn run up to the door of the first house or cabin they come to and scare the bejeezus outta whoever's there. Someone'll chase 'em off or see to it they gets home. They gunn be just fine.

"They's a rare set a twins, 'cause most times with twins, you got your clever one and then you got your thick-head one; with them two, one's as big a dunce as the next, and scairt to death of they own shadows! Fra-gilest matching set of idiots you's likely to ever run up on."

The Madman smiled and said, "That ain't what's normal atall."

Mr. Swan paused a second, then asked, "You wants to say something to these young folk?"

The Madman looked uncomfortable. "Naw, Willie, I been ease-droppin' on your stories for the longest and ain't got nothin' to add. I'm just gonna rest and listen if it don't bother no one."

Mr. Swan said, "That's fine, whatever you wants."

The Madman stared into the fire with a soft smile on his face.

Mr. Swan spit into the fire again and said, "Where was we at?"

But he was talking to himself. I looked and every single boy around the bonfire had his eyes locked on the Madman.

Mr. Swan stood up and said, "I'm-a tell all you little no-goods, if y'all don't . . ."

The Madman looked up and all of the children's heads bobbed down.

The Madman said, "I do 'pologize, Willie. I suppose it a bit much for these boys to see me like this. They been hearing so much nonsense 'bout me that this gotta be a shock. You caint hold it 'gainst 'em."

Mr. Swan said, "Uh-uh, ain't no reason for them to be rude like this. Every last one of 'em, wit' one or two 'ceptions, come from good people and know better.

"I'm 'bout ready to quit telling these ungrateful brats my stories. I think they've heard 'em all."

The Madman said, "What was you telling 'em 'bout, Willie?"

"We was discussing all the places the demons and haints and monsters is hiding out in the woods."

The Madman smiled.

"In that case," he said, "maybe I got something to tell 'em after all."

"The pulpit's yourn, my brother."

The Madman said, "What you think, Willie? You think they's old enough that they ready to get scairt for real?"

The Madman seemed to become lit up with such a light that Mr. Swan stopped chewing and gave him a cautious look.

The Madman looked into the fire and began rocking back and forth, his arms wrapped tightly around his buckskin-covered shins.

"Willie, you 'members when we was young how we looked to hear stories what would prevent us from sleepin' for a while? You think that what these young'uns wants?"

It's not possible, but it seemed like even the crickets

stopped chirping and the toady-frogs in the pond quit making sounds when the Madman spoke.

He pointed at the six youngest children and said, "Y'all run on home now. None of y'all's ready for this. Y'all's too young to even have places in your heads where you can rest what I'm 'bout to say."

Some of the youngsters, already rising, looked at Mr. Swan. He said, "Get on home. Stick together."

None of them said a word about wanting to stay.

I didn't know if he could keep this up, but, judging by who was saying it and by the tone of his voice and by the look in his eyes, this had to be the best introduction of a scary story ever told on earth!

He said, "Now, if any the rest of y'all's been blessed with a sensitive nature, listen here: That ain't nothin' to be 'shamed 'bout, but if I was you, I'd use this time to follow them li'l babies back on out these woods."

Even if any of us wanted to leave, and it wouldn't take too much encouraging to get even me out of here, what he said meant whoever got up might just as well hang a sign from their neck saying SENSITIVE-NATURE CHILD, and that's one thing none of us wanted to be accused of!

He took his eyes off the fire and, with his body becoming as still as death, he started looking like an owl! A great horned owl! He rotated his head and its tangle of hair to look around the circle, catching hold of the eyes of each of the seven of us left.

Some cast their glances down, a couple bawled quietly. Spencer stared back, his face twisted in pain. By the time the Madman's head rotated in my direction, I thought I would be ready. I thought I could be like a reporter observing a scene. Plus, we were almost like old chums. No one knew it, but I'd already talked to him.

But when those black eyes snatched hold of mine, I knew I wouldn't have been able to prepare for this if I'd had millennia. There was something different about him now. I wasn't sure if it was the light of the campfire or the darkness that was all around us, but he was much more frightening now than he was during our talk.

I was glad I hadn't told anyone. As terrifying as he was now, even I wouldn't have believed my tale.

As the Madman of Piney Woods's eyes captured mine, I remembered this feeling. Once the fear in me quieted down, I remembered a trip when I was eight years old and the mayor had loaded most of Buxton's young folk in wagons and taken us to visit the falls at Niagara. We don't really have a mayor in Buxton, but everyone knows if we did have one it would be him.

They'd stopped the wagons two miles away so we could more clearly hear the low rumbling growl that had been creeping up on us. The closer we got, the louder it became.

Something in the air made the younger horses pulling the wagons skittish and prone to rear up. At the same time, the air made me and the other children giddy and silly. We seemed to lose control of our arms as they flapped ridiculously about.

We were still a half mile away when they stopped again. The vibration of the falls rumbled up through the floor of the wagon. Small bits of straw, dirt, and dried leaves trembled and leapt on the boards there.

We came upon the falls and my first surprise, other than how loud they were, was that every description of them I'd read or been told had been wrong.

Yes, they were unbelievable.

Yes, they interfered with you breathing natural because it seemed the air was charged like lightning.

And, yes, it was a memory you knew was yours forever.

But the one thing they were *not* that every description said they were was beautiful.

The falls at Niagara were anything but beautiful.

They were harsh and terrifying. They were ugly and confusing. They looked to me like a festering wound in the earth.

I got even scareder when the mayor had made all of us under ten years of age get tied to one another with one adult at the front of the rope, one in the middle, and one at the rear.

Then we were led to the wooden railing at the edge of the falls and I understood why we needed the rope.

The strongest feeling surged over me when I looked down where the roaring water crashed below. If it weren't for the rope and Patience and Stubby clinging desperately to each side of me, I'm sure I would have calmly climbed up on the railing, stepped over the edge, and allowed myself to be swallowed by the water.

There was such a magnetic pull to go over that my knees buckled and I strained against the rope.

That was the same electrical feeling I had as the Madman of Piney Woods, sitting mere feet from me, locked his eyes upon mine. For some reason, I knew I could jump into the swirling madness I saw there. I didn't fear the rush of movement and noise and currents that lay behind his eyes. I wanted to look deeper.

Either that or run as quickly as I could after those lucky little brats who had been excused earlier.

Good sense prevailed and I was just about to tell Mr. Swan, *I'm not comfortable with those children walking alone in the woods, sir. I'll escort them home and come right back.*

Before that lie could pass my lips, the Madman freed my eyes and, peering back into the fire, said, "If what you looking to hear is something that's truly frightening, you done come to the right place, your call been answered by the co-rrect man."

Mr. Swan seemed worried. "Uh, look, I ain't so sure now's a good —"

The Madman said, "Naw, Willie, let me tell 'em. I'm-a tell 'em something true and frightening. I'm-a let 'em know the truth 'bout demons and monsters. I'm-a show 'em 'xactly where they's laying in the cut waiting for 'em. I'm-a show 'em like no one took the time to show us. I'm-a give 'em the news 'bout who them demons truly is and where they be waiting."

The Madman never took his eyes off the fire. Time froze during those few moments of waiting for him to speak. They were the longest, most fearful moments I'd ever had.

The Madman hadn't lied. Once he began talking, I didn't see where in *my* head his words could rest without causing huge distress to my every hour, waking or sleeping. I wished I had shown the same wisdom and bravery that the twins had shown and bolted screaming into the woods, never to be exposed to his horrible insanity.

The Madman of Piney Woods began the process of absolutely destroying the sleep of seven children from Buxton by whispering one word: "*Monsters . . .*"

There was no way to tell what made that word so terrifying, if it was because of what he said or because of the way he said it.

He didn't use any of the tricks Mr. Swan did to make his stories scary: He wasn't lowering his voice to make you lean in closer; there weren't any long pauses followed by

179

sudden shouts that blasted coldness and shivers into your bones; he wasn't waving his arms and pointing, suddenlike, off into the dark forest.

He just started talking.

"Let me open your eyes 'bout demons and monsters. I'm here to speak the truth, so get ready. Sometime that be the hardest thing to hear.

"I know all them tales 'bout haints and dead chiefs and such wandering 'bout these woods once the sun's gone down. And, no disrespect to you, Willie . . ."

The Madman looked right at Mr. Swan, who said, "None taken."

"I was tolt them same lies when I was little. All us young folk was. Them tales was entertaining, but they was lies and that's where we starts going wrong, filling young folks' heads with folderol that don't make no sense just like it the stone-cold truth."

He stared back into the fire.

"Young folks is lots smarter than they gets credit for and all them stories and lies end up doing is planting seeds of doubt 'bout *everything* they's tolt. Things what they should re-ject the second they hears 'em lingers in they head. The only thing them stories and lies do is crack the door open for every other pretty lie they hears, don't matter how foolish it be, to blow in, lay down roots, and start growing in they 'maginations.

"These young'uns starts up having pause at anything they ma and pa say, and caint no one blame 'em neither, 'cause they ma and pa be tellin' 'em stories 'bout ghosts and Easter bunnies and the most ridiculous set of nonsense. And they tells 'em with the same straight face they tells 'bout not hurting no one else or treating folks the way you wants to get treated."

He stopped.

Every eye around the circle was locked on him, every one of us waited.

"Yessir, I got tolt 'bout the ghosts in the woods what come out at night too. But if y'all youngsters is smart, that there is your first clue that these is lies. Anytime someone start they story by saying it happened in darkness or fog or smoke, anything what cloak they words, you needs be suspicious 'bout what follows. Darkness hide a whole lot of things, but in talkin', it's used most of all to hide the holes in the words of whoever be talkin'.

"Darkness? Real demons and monsters and devils ain't gotta wait on no darkness.

"Darkness?

"*Darkness?*

"They work get done as much at high noon as at the blackest midnight. They ain't no respecter of the 'mount of light washing over the earth. They gunn get done what they need get done."

The Madman's voice changed. It became steady and near monotonous, in the exact way Mrs. Brown warned us against during forensics lessons.

I had no idea if the other boys were feeling what I was. All I could see, all I could hear, was this man with the huge head of wild hair.

"I seent devils and demons and beasts and mostly I seent monsters. I seent how they walks upright, on two legs. I heard 'em talk and they sounds a whole lot like you and me."

He stopped and I realized I'd been holding my breath.

Mr. Swan said, "Uhh . . . thank you, that . . ."

"Uh-uh, Willie, lemme finish. These here boys wants to hear 'bout monsters and they ain't got no idea they's inviting them monsters right into they hearts. I seent how they likes playing war and soldiers in the fo-rest; I seent how they crashes 'round hollering and frightening every living thing in the woods. Let me tell 'em, let me tell what no one ain't had the sense to tell us when we was young and excited by that foolishness. They needs to know what they's playing at."

There was no stopping this. In the same manner that water in the Niagara River gets to a certain point and its fate is sealed, the Madman was unstoppable in pulling us into his nightmare.

He moaned, "Lemme tell y'all 'bout who the monsters is and where they be hiding. It gonna be a big surprise, I promise y'all.

"I always looked younger than I was. I'd just turnt seventeen, which was old enough to join up as a soldier, but they thought I was thirteen at the most and would only let me be a drummer boy. I knew at the first chance what come, I'd throw that drum down and pick up a rifle and kill me some of them Johnny Rebs. I knew it was gonna happen. But I sure didn't think it would happen so soon and in the way it did.

"I got attached to the Sixth Regiment Colored Artillery outta Mississippi, and the day I did, we was in a skirmish at Vidalia. It near cost me my life. But it open my eyes good.

"We got charged by the Confederates, right after they'd shot us to tatters. I dropped my drum and grabbed the first dead man's rifle I seen. The sergeant told us to prepare bayonets, but them rebs was atop us afore I got the chance to get the bayonet fixed on my rifle. The man next to me got a hole blowed in him, and the sight made me drop my rifle. I run. I ain't ashamed to say it, I run.

"I run down a little swale and could hear a reb right behind me. I didn't get thirty yards afore a root reach up and grab me and drop me on my face. I felt the reb's bayonet poke in my back.

"He shouts, 'Turn around, darky. I ain't never shot no one in they back and I ain't 'bout to start with you. I wanna see your eyes when you die.'

"I turnt over and the rifle was pointed 'tween my eyes. I stayed still to give him a clean shot, but he lowered his gun. He looks at me and says, 'Why, you ain't nothin' but a baby. I got kids at home older than —'"

The Madman of Piney Woods stopped talking.

When he started again, his voice was dead.

He said, "That's when I fount out where the real monsters was hiding. That's when I seent who was truly a devil. The man reached his hand down to pull me up. I didn't even know I hadn't dropped the bayonet. I swung at him and it seemed like his chest welcomed it in. It went in that easy. And that deep. Must've pierced his heart. He fell atop me. And bled out right there.

"I knowed right then I had good cause to be afeared of all the monsters I got told 'bout. I knowed right there that devils was real. I knowed I *should* be afeared 'cause I was carrying the devil 'round inside me. He waren't hiding in no darkness; he was me. All he was doing was biding his time. Waiting for a sign. Waiting to come out."

I was dumbstruck. I waited for Mr. Swan to make him stop, but he was as stunned as the rest of us.

The Madman wasn't through.

"I caint remember nothing what happened for two days. I only know we run them rebs off. But I soon got to see more 'bout them devils.

"A couple weeks later at Fort Pillow, I seent more monsters treading the earth, watched 'em doing they evil work.

"We was outnumbered bad. Four or five to one. Y'all know how in one n'em big storms what blows so hard, the rain be coming at you sideways? That just how them bullets was coming at us from the rebs.

"I was hunkered down praying that one n'em rifle balls would plant itself in my forehead and make this go away quick. If I coulda got my hands on a gun, I'd-a done it myself.

"Must've got grazed and knocked cold. In the time I was out, the monsters come upon the earth to practice doing they filth.

"I 'members opening my eyes and thinking it was over 'cause I couldn't hear no shooting nor cannons. But then my ears sharpens and I'm blast by wails and caterwauls like I ain't never heard afore. I'd heard wounded men on the battlefield afore, but this was something worst. I raises up and —"

He stopped; I breathed.

When he started talking again, his voice sounded like one of the youngsters at school tiredly reciting something they had to memorize.

"You's half-unconscious and dazed and laying on your side and not understanding how come so many of your friends is laying 'round you with red caps pult tight over they heads. You might even laugh, 'cause you know that red caps ain't no part of no uniform.

"Then you sees. You sees they's all been worked over by them monsters using bowie knifes to cut the scalp clean offen 'em. Seent laying not five feet from me the bleeding head of the man what I was talking to half a hour afore the rebs attacked. Same man I et breakfast with that morning. Same man what talked 'bout his family and listened whilst I talked 'bout mine.

"Then something's got a claw in my hair, snatching at my head so rough I feared my neck's broke. There waren't no real pain. All I feels was something score a line 'cross the back my neck at the hairline and I feel metal hitting bone, making a sound I recognize is the same sound I heard a thousand times afore when a goat or a pig's getting slaughtered.

"I looks back and up into the eyes of the demon what was scalping me and he waren't mad nor fult up with hate. He waren't in no rage with teeth bared and foam on his lips. He waren't feeling nothing what a human would feel doing this. He was calm as if he was washing his socks at a crick or shaving stubble offen his chin in a camp mirror.

"Then I feels this terrible sawing at the back of my neck. But the main thing is the sound as the monster commence ripping at my scalp. It sound just like a thunderstorm got trap in my skull. It sound like cannons booming in my head."

The Madman raised his voice as if he had to shout over the sounds.

"Then it stop. My head got dropped back down to the dirt, and once the thunder quit booming in my ears, I hears a voice. I looks over and seent a different white man pointing a pistol dead at the demon with the bloody knife what was standing astride me.

"They argues back and forth afore the one what been ripping at my scalp bend back over and snatch my head up again. The person with the gun holler at him louder and the monster growl something terrible back to the gunman and I feels that knife hit bone again, then hears a shot, and the monster what was stealing my hair fall atop me with a gaping hole where his heart use to be. I seent a swarm of them other gray demons with knives overtake the one with the pistol. Then I passes out."

When the Madman of Piney Woods stopped talking, his voice echoed in my ears like the fading ring of a church bell. I don't know when it happened, but sometime during his story, he'd quit looking at the fire and locked onto my eyes again.

He misread my look and said, "What? Y'all think I's lying? Y'all thinking I ain't had no truck with monsters?"

I looked around the circle and the only people still there were me, Spencer, and Mr. Swan, who had stood up and was reaching a hand toward the Madman.

"I ain't afeared of the truth, and neither should y'all be. This is the truth. Look and tell me if I's lying."

He stood and turned his back to me and dropped his chin to his chest. Then he used both hands to grab the thick hunk of hair that hung down his back. He lifted his hair as if he were raising up a trapdoor, showing me and Spencer and Mr. Swan the back of his skull.

And that's all that was there, his skull. Where you'd have thought would be more of the thick hair, there was a slice-of-bread-sized grayish-white patch of bone bordered by a band of thickened, shiny black skin.

I couldn't pull my eyes away as the Madman, with his back still to me and Spence, said, "I ain't got no clue how long I slept after. When I finally gets up, it was long enough for clouds of flies to be rolling over Fort Pillow like waves. It was long enough for maggots to set up in my wound. I picks as many of 'em out as I can, then crawls to the river and packs mud on my head to try to cool it down."

He laughed and the bitterness of that laugh grated on every nerve in my body.

"They tell me them maggots and that mud what saved my life."

I can't say for sure if it was me or Spence who made the first move toward bolting. Being a much faster runner than he is, I was already in the house with my chest heaving and my back leaning against the front door when I heard Spencer's wails as he ran past.

Spencer's howls, my gasps, and the slamming door disturbed Mother and Father from their bedroom.

They appeared at the top of the stairs, Father holding a fireplace poker, and Mother the small coal shovel. Stubby and Patience joined them; she had her carving knife in hand.

"Benjamin Alston," Mother said, "what is the cause for this commotion?"

"Mother, Father, I met him face-to-face! He sat right next to me!"

Father said, "Who? *What?*"

"The Madman of Piney Woods! He's been scalped! His skull is showing, white as snow!"

Mother said, "This was at Mr. Swan's storytelling?"

"Oh, yes, Mother."

"Is he still there?"

"I don't know, but there's more I haven't told you." Even though I knew they might ban me from going in the forest if they knew, I had to admit I'd talked to him earlier.

She said, "It can wait, all of you go to bed."

All three of us said, "But, Mother . . ."

She raised her voice in a way I'd never heard before. *"Now!"*

There was no thought but to listen.

Mother and Father didn't even change out of their night clothes. They hopped at the front door, pulling on their shoes, not even bothering to lace them.

Mother said to Father, "Hurry, hurry, Tim. What Miss Ennis said must be true. He's starting to talk to people again. That poor man has to be so lonely, maybe this time we can . . ."

They left in such a rush, they didn't notice that me and Pay and Stubby had ignored Mother's order and were still standing on the stairs.

The front door closed, the screen door banged, and they were gone.

Patience said, "Benji? What should we do?"

"I don't know. Maybe we should just go to bed like Mother said."

Stubby and Pay had their arms wrapped around each other.

He said, "You really saw him, Benji? Honestly? Was he horrible?"

I didn't even have to think. "No, he was very scary, but most of all he seemed . . . I don't know, I can't describe it.

Maybe Mother was right; maybe the only word to describe him is *lonely*."

Patience said, "Benji, did he really get scalped?"

I could see that even Pay was frightened. I suppose it would be really terrible to hear about this the way they just had. I mean, even Mother and Father had looked horrified, and Mother had roared at us like a lion. It's easy to see how this could shake a young person up.

"Patience, it was dark. Now that I think about it, he probably wasn't really scalped; it must have been some kind of trick."

I felt rotten about how shook up I'd got my brother and sister.

I really wasn't doing it only for me when I said, "Stubby, if you go get a blanket, we can wait on the couch for them to come home."

He ran upstairs.

Pay stood close to me and I wrapped my arm around her.

She whispered, "Don't tell Timmy, but Mother used to know him very well."

"*What?*"

"Shh! It's true. That's why she gets so upset when people call him Madman. He was —"

Stubby charged down the steps, dragging the blanket from his bed.

I sat on the couch, and Pay and Stubby sat on each side

of me. I flapped the blanket a couple of times until it set-tled over all of us. I felt like a mother hen when he snuggled under one of my arms and she the other.

Stubby said, "Do you remember when we all slept in the same bed and you used to tell us stories to help us sleep, Benji?"

I sort of did. I used to try to get them to sleep so I could sneak out of the bedroom window to run the woods at night with Spencer.

Patience laughed. "I do! They were so funny and it seemed like I always had good dreams afterward."

I began to remember, but my memories went further back than theirs, and they came because I used to feel that same way when Mother would comfort me after a night-mare or when sleep just wouldn't come.

After Mother sang me a lullaby or told a silly story or just let her warm hand rest on my forehead, I felt com-forted. I knew there'd be no more nightmares. I knew it was safe to sleep.

They waited.

I said, "All right. I'm rusty at this, but I can try."

I remembered they always wanted the stories to start the exact same way.

I said, "A long, long time ago, even before there were clocks, in a forest so far from here that only eagles know the way there, lived two little trolls named Patience and Timothy. One wintry summer day, they decided . . ."

I couldn't believe how easy the stories started coming back.

Pay and Stubby fell back to sleep much too quick. I wished they'd stayed awake longer.

I was left alone with my thoughts.

I wonder if he'd been right when he said the forest had judged me and him to be just alike. I think that's what scared me most about seeing the Madman at the storytelling — not his wild eyes, not his scalped head, but the thought that he was right.

Could that be me someday?

Had he started out as someone like me who loved the woods too much and that made his mind slip off the tracks?

My right arm started tingling and going numb from Stubby's head.

I slid my arm from underneath him.

No, there isn't any way that loving the woods could make you lose your mind. There had to be something more.

Mother said he was lonely, but could that make you go mad?

My left arm started feeling like it was going to sleep.

I lifted Pay's head. I took the knife she was still holding and set it on the back of the couch.

Then I understood. If it was loneliness that had caused the Madm . . . had caused Mother's friend to be so disturbed, then I didn't have to worry. I had Mother and Father and Pay and Stubby to protect me from that.

It's funny. While they slept cuddled next to me under the blanket, I thought about the monarch butterfly cocoons that pop up every fall in the woods.

This blanket was like a cocoon, and me and Stubby and Pay were three caterpillars safe inside.

I stopped worrying about Mother's friend; he wasn't interested in hurting us or anybody else. He was wrong. Maybe the woods told him we were the same, but the woods didn't know me when I was at home. But he was right when he said I was to be envied. I could do one thing he couldn't. I could leave the woods and come home to my cocoon, my family.

PART TWO

BENJI
⟩ AND ⟨
RED

CHAPTER 22

A Boy Named Red

BENJI

Being a reporter puts you in some real uncomfortable, dangerous spots. I'd followed Father's advice and was taking the initiative with my work.

Without Miss Cary assigning it to me, I was going to report on the Upper Canada Forensics Competition. I'd be at the contest to support Spencer anyway, so I could kill two birds with one stone.

This time I was sure she was going to publish my article. How couldn't she? It was going to be a touching story about how Spencer Alexander overcame so many things to be Buxton's finest public speaker. I'd already written two endings for it, just in case. In the first ending, he was a gracious winner and thanked everybody he could think of. In the second ending, he was a gracious loser and thanked everybody he could think of.

I was this close to passing out in the Buxton church where the contest was going on. Even though it was late September, it was hotter than July inside. All of the windows were open, but every breeze in Canada ignored the church.

Right after the first speaker, I opened the rear door of the church to escape for a minute. After the heat from inside washed around me, and my eyes became accustomed to the bright light and the way everything seemed to shimmer, there he was, sitting on the back steps.

One of the white Chatham boys had the same idea as me.

He was wearing a wool jacket, a necktie, and knickers with thick wool stockings. A heavy wool cap sat next to him on the porch; he'd had sense enough to pull it off.

It was hard to tell what this boy would look like on a day that wasn't so hot, but with his bright red hair and freckles, it made me think someone had lit a match, then as a joke dressed it in knickers, a suit jacket, and a necktie.

He gave me a little smile.

"Hot enough for you?"

For a second I wondered if he said this because he was being racialist. So many white Chatham people think, since most Buxton people come from the southern United States, we all love the heat. But it was just too hot to get worked up over words, no matter what they meant.

He was friendly when he spoke and looked right in my eye. That said something.

I answered, "As hot as it is for me, I know it's ten times hotter for you. Are you wearing those winter clothes because you've heard there's going to be a sudden blizzard?"

He laughed. "I suppose I could take the jacket off. My grandmother's nowhere around, after all. I only have one suit and it's for winter; she insisted I wear it."

His jacket had been carefully patched at the elbows, his shirt was soaked, its collar and cuffs frayed. His clothes were far from new, but everything he wore had been pressed and washed and starched to within an inch of its life.

He carefully folded the limp, damp jacket over his knee. "Whew!"

I said, "Are you in the forensics competition?"

"Oh, no, I'm here supporting my friend. When he wins the competition today, it will be his third time."

That meant he was here with that Holmely boy from Chatham. The one who was cheated out of first place two years ago.

I snorted, "Well, we'll see."

He said, "Oh. You're supporting someone else?"

"My friend Spencer Alexander. You and that Holmely boy shouldn't start counting your chickens yet. Spence has got a pretty good chance to win, you know."

The boy said exactly what I was fearing. "I hope your friend hasn't gotten his hopes up too high; you know his only *real* chance is second place."

What could I say? The reddish white boy was right, and I could tell he was joshing me. Plus, he did give a huge beaming smile when he said it.

His gums seemed to follow suit with his hair. I was surprised that his teeth weren't red too.

He said, "Don't fret. Second place isn't bad . . . it's just not quite as good as first."

We laughed.

"My name is Benji Alston."

I stuck my hand out. His hand was as hot and sweaty as you'd expect it to be, but he gave me a very firm shake.

"I'm Alvin Stockard. But I'll bet you a wooden nickel that you can't guess what everyone calls me."

I couldn't help smiling. It would be hard for even as good a debater as Spencer or the Holmely boy to disprove that a cardinal and a beet hadn't been married and given birth to this boy. Then baptized him in a tub of red ink.

I said, "Uh, let me guess. Do they call you Tex?"

He looked surprised. "Why, no, they call me Re — Oh, you're being facetious."

"Does it bother you when people call you Red?"

"It did when I was younger, but if you get called the same thing enough different times by enough different people, you catch on that the writing's on the wall. You can either fight every day of your life or learn to live with it."

"OK, if you don't mind, I'll call you Red."

"And I shall call you Benji."

We shook hands again.

"So why aren't you in the forensics competition, Benji?"

I was proud to answer, "I'm a newspaperman. I like telling about things that are happening, not arguing about them. Why aren't you?"

"I'm not an arguer either. I'm a scientist. I can't think of any occupation that's more important than understanding what makes things tick, and science is the best way to do that."

He stopped and then said, "But of course being a newspaperman is probably important too." His eyes rolled.

I said, "So I guess when it comes to having an important job, I'm just like Spencer in some ways; I have to get used to second place."

He sounded surprised. "Benji! As a scientist, I must say I've observed that you have a great and winning attitude when dealing with your circumstances!"

"Well, as a newspaperman, I have to say I've only known you for a minute and I can report that you are a huge pain in the buttocks. I've also observed that if you keep sitting around in those winter clothes, you'll soon be coming back to this church for your own funeral."

I sat on the step next to him and started pulling off my shoes and stockings.

"But, Red, you've helped me make up my mind. Since everybody already knows who's going to win this competition, and I've already got most of my article written, I'm not going to sit in there and come to a slow boil just to watch Spencer get second place. There's a great swimming hole not far from here. Want to go cool off?"

My words really distressed the boy. His eyes darted from the door of the church to his jacket to me, then to the woods, then back to his jacket. You would've thought I asked him to tag along while we robbed a bank and murdered a teller or two.

"Uh, I . . . well, my grandmother told me not to wander from the church."

"Suit yourself, but if you go back in there, it would be thinking scientifically to leave that coat off."

I tied my shoes together, stuffed my stockings inside, and stepped off the front steps.

I shouted over my shoulder, "Tell Spence congratulations on coming in second."

I hadn't gone fifty yards when I heard, "Ow! Ow! Benji! Wait! Ow! Ow!"

I turned back. Red had pulled his stockings off and stuffed them in the shoes that dangled over his shoulder with his jacket.

He was very much a tenderfoot. Every step he took started with a scowl and ended with an "Ow!"

I said, "My feet are like that in the early spring when I haven't gone barefoot for months; you might want to put your shoes on until they toughen up a bit."

"Good idea. I'd hate for my career as a pioneer to be ended so quickly by a thorn."

He sat on the trail and slipped his feet into his shoes.

"Oh, that's so much better."

We weren't even into the forest when Red started losing his courage.

"So how far off is this swimming hole, Benji?"

"Not far."

"How long do you suppose we'll stay there?"

"Not long."

I knew once he got into the water, he'd see what a good idea this was.

"Are you sure we're going the right way? Everything looks the same to me. We aren't lost, are we?"

"Look, Red. You've got to trust me. I told you I was going to be a newspaperman, but the second career I have in mind means I know the forest."

"Really?"

"Really. If I can't be a reporter, my plan is to learn how to be a hermit."

He laughed. "Where does one go to learn how to be a hermit?"

I waved my arms. "This is my classroom right here. And these are my teachers. The trees and the sky and the animals and most especially the floor of the forest. If I need to get information on anything that's happened, I look at the ground and it's like I've opened a book."

Red said, "How's that?"

Maybe I wasn't being fair, but this little Chatham boy was the most naïve human being I'd ever met.

He was smart, but he believed everything I said about the woods. I told him that I could tell by the piece of deer scat on one of the trails that it was a sign that the Madman of Piney Woods had taken his pet bear out for a walk with a raccoon riding on its back when a giant eagle grabbed the raccoon and flew off to the mountains.

My conscience started bothering me right after I told it. This was too easy. This was shooting fish in a barrel. It reminded me of the way Patience used to believe everything I said when she was really young. There had been no sport in teasing her then, and there was none in teasing Red now. He seemed like a decent enough boy, so I held off.

My way of apologizing without actually saying sorry would be to show him the secret swimming hole. That would make up for far more than a little teasing. Besides, it seemed like this little redheaded boy from Chatham could dish it out just as well as he could take it.

CHAPTER 23

A Lad Named Benji

RED

This Buxton lad named Benji proved to be a fine favourable fellow. Not only was he exceedingly clever, he also knew the woods as well as he knew the palm of his hand. And what most amazed me was, even though I'm sure he wasn't aware of doing it, he was applying his knowledge in a manner that was purely scientific!

He wasn't making his judgments based on being familiar with a particular section of the woods; he had what we scientists call a paradigm and applied it to each situation. As we walked deeper and deeper into the forest toward the promised swimming hole, he never let the conversation lag. He pointed out many things that my eyes had simply brushed over and thought nothing of.

Where I barely noticed a mishmash of tiny, bleached bones at the base of a huge oak, he looked up and pointed out the massive, hidden nest of a great horned owl. One, he said, judging by the bones, that had been living there for six years.

Where I saw grass, he saw a place where a doe had hidden its fawn a few hours before.

Where I saw stones and moss and lichen and twigs, he saw stories. Stories available only to those who knew the language, only decipherable by those who paid careful attention. If this little Buxton boy hadn't been so confused and misled by his desire to be a reporter, he might even have made a halfway decent scientist. I was very impressed!

I was less impressed by his attempts to explain why being a reporter was so important. Besides leaning a tad too much toward braggadocio, he talked to me as if I was something of an idiot. Maybe in his eyes I was, maybe since a leaf was nothing but a leaf to me, he assumed I was dense in all areas.

"So," he said, "there are two reasons that I'm more of a noticer than most people, most people our age especially. The first reason is —"

He stopped walking and pointed at a small group of saplings.

"Red, do you remember the fawn I told you about before?"

Of course I did; it had only been a minute or two earlier.

"The poor thing is dead."

"Really?" I peered at the young trees he was pointing out. "How can you tell?"

"By the way that one sapling is leaned to the side. The doe put up a brave fight to save her fawn's life, but in the end, she was no match for the coyote. Though all didn't turn out well for the coyote either."

He pointed at an area that to me simply looked like a growth of weeds where a few had been blown down.

"Just as the coyote settled in to eating the poor fawn, a rare North Woods alligator ambushed the coyote and ate both of them."

This was too much! "An alligator in the forest?"

"I told you it was a rare alligator; not many people know about them."

It was incredible! All I could see were some weeds and a small tree leaning as if it were trying to get the sun's rays. Perhaps Benji's eyes were keen far beyond mine, but while my heart wanted to believe him, my head wasn't buying this story. I began to suspect he was as good a storyteller as he was a woodsman.

He continued, "The first reason I'm more of a noticer is exactly because I'm studying to be a newspaperman. I can't think of anything, *anything* that's more important than that. A reporter lets people know what is happening in the world, and what caused them to happen."

Benji misinterpreted my look; he thought I didn't believe him. It wasn't that at all. I was still in thrall at his ability to read the woods, and I remembered what

Father had told me, that many times a flaw in an argument is so obvious that we tend to look right past it, that it was so hard to see because it had been hidden in plain sight. And this alligator story had big flaws from first word to last.

"I've even got books that prove nothing's more important than a newspaper," Benji said. "One book says, 'The press is at once the eye, the ear, the tongue of the people. It is the visible speech if not the voice of the democracy. It is the phonograph of the world.'"

He gave me a look.

"You do know what a phonograph is, don't you?"

"Of course I do! Our Father Ted has two of them."

He stopped walking.

I looked around to try to see if I could figure out what the next woods lesson was going to be.

I was certain I picked it out. There was a spot where a stone rested at an odd angle against the side of a tree. Several pinecones were arranged around the rock in a way that, once I studied them, didn't appear random or haphazard.

I pointed at the spot with the strangely placed stone and pinecones.

"What do you suppose happened there?"

He glanced at the spot I pointed out and started walking again.

"Looks to me like a rock is leaning against a tree."

The only time I was absolutely sure he wasn't pulling my leg was when he talked about being a newspaperman. Unlike the forest tales, his eyes burned when he spoke of the press.

"Do you read the newspapers, Red?"

"Every morning, Father and I read the *Chatham Times* and the *Toronto Globe*."

Benji scoffed. "Sorry to tell you, they're not good papers."

"Oh, really?"

"Really. I find them to be very dry. When I'm editor of my own paper, I won't make the same mistakes they do. Those big-city papers don't do anything to snatch the reader's attention, to force you to read more."

"I never noticed."

"If you saw the way it's supposed to be done, even someone like you would notice the difference."

"What is the difference?"

"Another one of my books says, 'Always remember, if you don't sock a newspaper reader right between the eyes with your first sentence, don't waste your time writing a second one.'"

"I don't understand."

Benji very patiently explained to me, as if he were talking to a four-year-old. A very dense four-year-old.

"Let me give you an example, and it's not really fair because this is something I practice a lot every day."

The air changed. It became heavier, and it wasn't only the increasing darkness caused by the thickness of the woods. We were getting near water.

"I'm listening."

"OK. What I practice is writing headlines, or what we newspapermen call leads, for everything that I see around me."

"I still don't understand."

"For example, to show you how using the right words can make all the difference in the world, why don't you pretend you're writing a headline about you and me meeting this afternoon, then I'll do the same, and we'll see which is better."

"But who shall be the impartial judge? What's to stop you from saying yours is better and me from saying mine is?"

"Oh, don't worry. Mine will be so much better that even you will have to admit it."

I laughed and took the challenge.

"All right, let me see."

Through the thick trees, I could see a pond maybe twenty yards away.

I thought for a moment, then said, "Here we go; my headline for today's events would be 'Two Lads

Meet at Forensics Competition, Go for Cooling Swim.' How's that?"

Benji said, "Not bad. But don't forget this competition isn't fair, so I don't want you to be crushed when I give my headline."

The only thing that stopped him from being completely insufferable was that he always smiled when he made his questionable comments.

I said, "I promise not to be crushed."

"Good. Here's the *real* headline, and you tell me which story you'd rather read."

Benji cleared his throat and punctuated each word by jabbing his finger in the air as if he were reading something there.

He said, " 'Overheated Chatham Boy Not Heard From in Weeks. Last Seen in Company of Stranger from Buxton. Has the Young Hatchet Cannibal Struck Again?' "

He tilted his head to the side, widened his eyes, and made chomping sounds with his teeth. His right hand was hidden behind his back as though he were carrying a . . .

For a moment, probably not even that long, I admit the same jolt of electricity that I'd experienced when I met the South Woods Lion Man ran through my veins. Grandmother O'Toole had told me if I wandered away from the church, I might be murdered and carved up by one of the people from Buxton, and now I realized I was totally lost in the woods and at the complete mercy of this terrifying growling and snarling Buxton boy.

It all stopped when Benji shouted, "Last one in has to marry his own grandmother," and, pulling off his shirt, jumped from a rock and disturbed the calm waters of the beautiful swimming hole.

I was embarrassed that I'd had even a moment of fright, but I was almost nauseated from the thought of being trapped in wedlock with Grandmother O'Toole. I kicked off my shoes, folded my clothes, and threw myself in the water after Benji.

The coolness was shocking. All of the clamminess and closeness and heat of the day that clung to me so stubbornly was stripped away the moment I hit the water.

This is how a moulting snake must feel after it has shed its skin. I was so reinvigourated that it wouldn't have surprised me if I saw my old, hot sticky skin walk out of the lake and disappear into the forest.

I knew Benji would be able to track it to the end of the earth.

CHAPTER 24

Strange Friends

BENJI

We swam and splashed about for maybe an hour, then sat on a rock with our legs dangling in the water.

Some of the time, it's as easy to read white people as it is to read the forest floor.

Red wanted to ask me something but didn't know how. That meant it had something to do with my skin colour or my hair or some other difference between us. I was surprised since he was friends with the Holmely boy. Most often, white people act like this only if you're the first black person they've met.

I let him wiggle uncomfortably for a bit, then said, "So what is it you want to ask me?"

He stopped swishing his legs in the water.

"What? I didn't want to ask anything."

I waited a second and said, "Except . . ."

He looked at me, hesitated, and finally said, "Well, I *was* sort of wondering if you'd been injured in some type of explosion?"

"*What?*"

"I hope you don't take offense, but when you pulled off your shirt, I noticed how your arms and face are so much darker than the rest of you. The only time I've seen anything like that was when Miles Dennis was blasted by a fireball at the smithy and his arms and face, anything that wasn't covered by his clothes, remained much darker than the rest of him ever since. I thought maybe you'd had the same misfortune."

Some of the time, you don't know whether to laugh or cry. I was going to come up with a tall tale but then stopped. I supposed it was an honest question.

"No, Red. I haven't been in an explosion. I spend a lot of time working and playing outdoors. Just like white people, our skin gets darker the more it's in the sun."

He looked surprised. "*Really?*"

I rolled my eyes and said, "OK, since we're asking stupid questions, it's my turn."

"Go ahead, but Father says there's no such thing as a stupid question."

"He was being kind to you, probably because you ask a lot of them. What I want to know is are your mother and father such . . . well, such big redheads like you?"

"No. Father says his hair used to be dark brown and Mother was quite blond."

The word *was* really stuck out. But now wasn't the time to ask.

Red sounded sad. "I guess it's just genetics that I turned out this way."

There was a long silence before I tried to move the conversation on to something else.

"So what on earth made you want to be a scientist?"

It worked. He got some starch back in his sails. He gave me a pitying look and said, "Perhaps you're right. Perhaps Father *was* just being kind. That really is a stupid question. Who in their right mind wouldn't want to be a scientist?"

"Well, I'd say half of the people at this swimming hole, for a start."

My words caused a flood to pour out of the redhead boy. He started talking about science the same way Stubby and Patience talk about carpentry, probably the same way I sound when I talk about newspapers. Or the woods.

He said, "Can you honestly tell me any other vocation or even avocation that gives one an infinite number of mysteries to wonder about? You say the forest is your classroom and you can read it; have you thought about why it's so predictable that you can make an accurate guess as to what each thing means? You're studying and reading patterns. That's what scientists do. If I were given time and a bit of forest in which to conduct experiments, I would eventually be able to read the forest as well as you do. It may take many years, but I could do it. Science gives one that power."

I didn't say anything because he sounded like he was talking about religion or something, but truth told, there's a lot more to knowing and loving the woods than that.

"So what's the headline going to be for today?" Red asked.

"I don't know yet. I'm debating between two."

"Really?"

"Yes. The first one says 'Sympathetic Ace Newspaperman Pities Doltish Chatham Boy and Befriends Him.'"

He said, "How kind of you. What does the second one say?"

"'Best Swimming Hole in the North Woods Mysteriously Evaporates When Red-Hot Chatham Boy Dives into It! Many Fish Left in Great Distress.'"

Red said, "How about this for a third choice? 'Lonely Buxton Boy Found Drowned in Pond Filled with His Own Sarcasm and Hubris.'"

We laughed. He talked too much like a grown-up. I had no idea what *hubris* meant, but I knew it wasn't a compliment.

I didn't say anything, but the more we talked, the more I knew what the day's headline would *really* be:

UNUSUAL FRIENDSHIP BLOSSOMS BETWEEN
STRAPPING BUXTON NEWSPAPERMAN AND
CARDINAL/BEET ABOMINATION.

CHAPTER 25

The Invitation

RED

That old adage that time flies when you're having fun has never proven truer than it did on the day of the forensics competition.

It felt as though Benji and I had been talking for only a few minutes, but I realized how much time had actually passed when Benji said, "Well, Red, it's got to be around four o'clock. I don't know about your folks, but if I don't show up for supper, mine don't have any problem in sentencing me to time in the Amen Corner, and that's not something I'm looking forward to after I did my last stretch."

"The what corner?"

Benji explained a punishment his parents had designed where he or his siblings had to sit in a corner for days on end and read the Bible.

I said, "That seems odd that they'd make it a punishment to read the Bible."

He said, "See! That's just what I thought. I tried explaining it to them too, but it didn't work. Father told me, 'You can lead a horse to water but you can't make it drink, but you *can* sure make him stand there looking at the water for a long time.' Mother said she knows we probably wouldn't be doing much reading while we were in the Amen Corner, but she hoped being in the same general area as the Bible might cause something good to rub off."

As we gathered our clothes, Benji said, "What can a person do? The competition should be over soon. I hope we're back in time for the awards ceremony."

I became a bit nervous.

"Let's move quickly, Benji. If we don't get there in time, I'll have to walk back to Chatham. If that happens, I'll invite your parents over so Grandmother O'Toole can demonstrate the proper way a punishment is supposed to be given. Believe me, there's no reading involved, but it *is* very Biblical. It's full of smiting, striking down, and pestilence raining onto the head of a certain worse-than-a-serpent, ungrateful child with red hair."

Benji said, "Don't kid yourself, Red. The Amen Corner is the gentle end of Mother and Father's punishments; they can get a whole lot more Old Testament."

We started back and I must admit I felt some sadness that I'd probably never see this Buxton lad again. Maybe we'd bump into each other when he came to Chatham to work at the newspaper or when I went to Buxton for Mr. Green's classes.

When we reached the church, people were just coming out.

One of the Buxton lads saw Benji and shouted, "Benji! There you are! Can you believe it?"

He ran up to Benji, holding a silver bowl attached to a wooden base. He was positively beaming.

My heart sank. Had Hickman been robbed once again?

The lad held the bowl over his head and said, "What? You think fat meat ain't greasy? I did it! I did it!"

I had no idea what that meant.

Benji said, "You won, Spencer? I can't believe it!"

"I know! I'm shocked!"

Benji said, "Spence, I want you to meet someone. His name . . ."

I interrupted. I've found it's always better to beat the other person to the punch. I said, "I bet you a wooden nickel you can't guess what my nickname is."

Spencer said, "You can keep the wooden nickel, *Red*."

He handed the beautiful silver trophy to Benji. Benji read the inscription.

I looked to the door of the church just as Hickman Holmely was coming out. He was surrounded by people patting him on the back and saying those horrible words people say to someone who's been cheated. "Great job, Hicks!" and "You should be very proud!"

Under Hickman's arm was another silver bowl, this one twice the size of the one Spencer had handed to Benji.

I didn't understand, and as he read his friend's bowl, Benji appeared to be just as perplexed.

He said, "Wait a minute, Spencer, I think you got so excited you picked up the wrong bowl. This one reads 'Upper Canada Forensics Competition 1901. First Runner-Up.' Does that mean first runner-up as in second place?"

Spencer looked up to the porch where Hickman was accepting more congratulations and back slaps. True admiration filled his eyes as he said, "Are you kidding me? That's *Hickman Holmely*. The only real competition was who'd come in second."

Benji and I looked at each other and laughed.

Hickman ran over to some new friends to great cheers and huzzahs.

Benji reached his hand out and said, "Red. It was a lot of fun meeting you. Maybe I'll see you in Chatham or when you're coming to school in Buxton."

"I'd like that, Benji. I was thinking the same thing."

I walked to the wagons that would return to Chatham.

I was pleased and surprised when I heard, "Hey, Red! Wait a minute."

Benji ran toward me.

"I was thinking. You know how you feel so jealous because you don't have brothers or sisters?"

It was true, but I'd never said that to Benji.

"I don't recall saying —"

"You don't have to recall. You get that same look that Spencer gets when I talk about those brats. An expression of *Ooh, it would be so nice to have siblings. Ooh, I'm so lonely being all alone* comes over your faces.

"I've done my best to correct Spence, and I think it's only fair I do the same with you. Do you think your evil grandmother would let you come over for supper with us one day?"

She never would if she were to find out I was going to Buxton, but I know Father would consider it fine. He's always suggesting to me I need to be more open to making new friends.

I said, "That would be great!"

Benji said, "OK, I'm in Chatham on Tuesday at Miss Cary's shop. If you come by then, we can make all the arrangements. We don't live far from the station."

"That would be wonderful. I'm really looking forward to meeting your brother and sister."

He said, "You say that only because you don't know Stubby and Patience."

I said, "We'll see." I'd heard that some of the Buxton people had unusual names, but "Stubby"?

Benji said, "One more thing, Red. Did you know the word *gullible* is not in the dictionary?"

"What?"

"Seriously, it's a real mystery. *Gullible* is nowhere in the dictionary."

"Why, I'm quite sure you're wrong, Benji."

"I'm not. Take my word and don't waste your time looking it up."

I didn't say anything more, but as Benji walked toward Buxton, I couldn't wait to get home and prove him wrong.

What a grand day this had turned out to be. Hickman hadn't been cheated this time, and I'd soon be going to Buxton to have supper with my new friend!

We sang and laughed all the way back to Chatham.

We were so proud of Hickman that we could have collectively burst.

CHAPTER 26

Supper with Red

BENJI

"... and finally, Lord, make certain that Benji's friend Alvin is comforted and at ease whilst he is under our roof. We ask that You let Your love fill his heart as abundantly as it has filled ours."

Mother finished with "Amen."

All the Alstons and Red echoed, "Amen."

He kept his head bowed for a second as his right hand danced across his chest and his face.

Stubby and Patience exchanged a confused look.

I wish Mother had said a word or two to Jesus for *me*. I could use a little help to feel comforted and at ease too. Bad things had started today at the newspaper when Miss Cary hadn't mentioned my article about Spencer's second-place victory.

I'd said, "Miss Cary, do you think my article will come out in the paper?"

She'd said, "We'll get to that in a moment, Ben-jamin, but first, do me a quick favour."

"Yes, ma'am?"

"Go out onto the front porch and check the skies for me."

I already knew there wasn't a cloud in the sky but went anyway.

When I came back into her office, she'd said, "Were any hogs or sows zooming about up there?"

Hogs or sows? Had Miss Cary lost her mind?

"In the sky?"

"Um-hmm."

"Why, of course not, ma'am."

"That's what I thought. Now, to answer the question about your article, let me know when you look to the sky and *do* see pigs flying about, because the way you're writing, that will be the day one of your articles appears in my paper. Now, off you go!"

I'd left her office beat up again, but this time there wasn't any cake.

I also needed Mother's prayers because I couldn't shake the feeling that this dinner Red was sharing with us was bound to end in catastrophe.

I'd spent the night imagining everything that could go wrong.

I was afraid everyone would be too stiff, that Mother and Father would behave like they were questioning Red as though they were hiring him for something. I could see he might be so frightened, he'd answer everything with a yes or no and wouldn't talk beyond that. I thought maybe Patience would sit and glare at him evilly and that I'd be so nervous that my old habit of laughing at everything, even if it wasn't funny, would come back.

Father said, "My friend Victor Green tells me you're quite the student, Alvin."

For some reason, this was hilarious. I guffawed. Strange looks were directed at me from every side of the table.

Red said, "Thank you, sir. I'm really fortunate to have such a good instructor. Mr. Green is known to be the best science teacher in all of Upper Ontario. It's very difficult to get into his classes."

There wasn't any possible way that was funny, but out exploded another laugh.

Mother looked at me and furrowed her brow.

I was certain I didn't have to worry about Red or Pay saying anything unfortunate; it was Stubby who had me on pins and needles.

If he had a question or comment, he was going to let everyone know. He hadn't learned yet that many things are best left unsaid. He was the loose cannon on deck.

And he didn't disappoint.

Not two minutes after Mother had prayed for Red's comfort, Stubby made all of us uncomfortable by looking at Red and saying, "So. Does it hurt?"

I held my breath.

Red said, "Does what hurt?"

Stubby said, "Being that colour."

Mother slammed her fork on the table.

"*Timothy Eric Alston!* Plan on spending some time in the Amen Corner, young man!"

"Why, Mother? That's not a rude question. A white girl at school touched the top of my head and said my hair was so stiff that she felt sorry for me because I must go through every day with a headache. I didn't get mad."

Mother almost smiled before saying, "Just because someone has asked you an ignorant question or made a rude remark doesn't mean you have license to do the same. Now, Timothy, you know what you must do."

Stubby said, "Yes, Mother. I apologize, Red. I really wasn't trying to hurt your feelings."

Red smiled and said, "I get asked questions like that all of the time. You didn't hurt my feelings."

Stubby couldn't help himself. He said it again. "So, then. Does it hurt?"

Before Mother or Father could react, Red answered, "To be truthful, Stubby, I have the same problem as your big brother.

"These" — he pointed first at my face, then at his — "are completely painless . . . unless there's a mirror in the room."

Red had done the impossible. He made it so not one Alston knew what to say. Silence and expressions of surprise hung over the table.

Father and Mother howled first, followed by Stubby and Patience and Red. Finally, I laughed too. Mine wasn't a laugh of humour; it was a laugh of relief.

Pay pointed at me and said, "Ahh! He got you good, Benji! I don't know how many times I've seen you staring in the mirror with tears in your eyes!"

"You're right, Patience. I cry because I have you for a sister."

Those words and those laughs were like an abandoned fishing shanty crashing through a frozen Lake Erie at the end of winter. Just like that, the ice broke and all my worries disappeared. Stubby had taken his best shot and I didn't have anything to worry about. My new friend, this Irish boy from Chatham, could take care of himself.

I relaxed, the other Alstons relaxed, Red relaxed. Mother's food seemed even more delicious than usual and our everyday chatter filled the room.

Other than when Stubby asked Red why he talked like a schoolteacher instead of a normal child, the dinner was wonderful.

I was glad I'd invited him.

*   *   *

228

When it was close to time for the train to leave, Red and I stood at the door as he thanked Mother and Father for supper.

"You're welcome here any time, Alvin."

Red said, "Thank you, Mrs. Alston. You can call me Red, ma'am."

Mother laughed. "I'd rather not."

Father said, "Tell the judge Timothy Senior sends his best."

"Yes, sir, I will."

Mother and Father walked into the kitchen.

Patience and Stubby started pulling on their shoes and stockings.

"Hold your horses," I said. "Where do you two think you're going?"

Stubby said, "We're going with you to walk Red to the station."

This was surprising. They never wanted to do anything if I was involved in it.

I said, "That's very sweet, but it won't be happening this time. Take those shoes and stockings back off."

Patience never stopped lacing her shoes and shouted, "Mother!"

Mother called from the kitchen, "They're going with you, Benjamin."

I thought I was whispering when I said, "Fine, but I'll

pound either one of you if you open your mouth to say one word."

Patience yelled, "Mother!"

"They're allowed to talk, Benjamin."

I made the sign of cutting my throat, then pointed at Pay and showed my teeth.

"*Mother!*"

"Benjamin, do I have to come out there?"

"No, Mother."

I said to Red, "Do you see now?"

He smiled.

At least Pay and Stubby had the sense to follow a little behind us as we walked.

I could tell something was on Red's mind. I said, "So what do you want to ask me now?"

A devilish smile crossed his face. He said, "I didn't want to ask you anything, but there is something I want to tell you."

He reached in his pocket and removed a small piece of paper. He unfolded it and said, "Do you remember the other day when you told me the word *gullible* isn't in the dictionary?"

"Of course I do. It isn't."

Red made a show of clearing his throat and read from the paper, " '*Gullible. Adjective. Meaning easily misled and prone to being tricked and taken advantage of.*' "

He smiled and waved the paper under my nose.

He said, "It seems as though Mr. Webster disagrees with —"

It dawned on him. He stopped walking and turned the most amazing shade of crimson.

"Oh, dear," he said.

Me, Pay, and Stubby almost collapsed from laughter.

Pay said, "Don't feel bad, Red. Everyone falls for that stupid joke."

Red's smart; he changed the subject. "I hope you don't mind me asking, Timothy, but I noticed you have all of your limbs and fingers and toes, and you are by no means short for someone your age. Why on earth are you known as Stubby?"

Stubby said, "That's Benji's fault. Last year when he found out Mother and Father were going to let Pay and me apprentice with the carpenter, he got so jealous that he tried his best to make us feel bad."

Pay said, "But since Benji's not very bright, the worst he could come up with was to give us stupid nicknames. He called Timmy Stubby and me Ninah."

Red said, "Where on earth did those names come from?"

Stubby said, "He asked me to look at all of the carpenters we worked with and notice if they had anything in common."

Patience said, "And they did. Nearly every one of them was missing a finger or a thumb or at the least a hunk or tip of a finger."

"Benji told me it wouldn't be long before I chopped something off of me too, so to toughen me up and help me get used to being teased, he started calling me Stubby. Now everybody but Mother and Father and Patience do."

I said, "That's right. When someone gets hit with a perfect nickname, it always sticks. And I've got to tell you, Red, I'm shocked . . . shocked, I say, that to this day, the boy has never uttered one word of thanks for me helping him prepare for his future life."

Red asked Patience, "Why did he give you the nickname Ninah?"

I *really* didn't want this sad story to be told.

I said, "Truth told, Red, the only nickname that ever stuck with Patience is Li'l Toot."

He said, "Why is that?"

Pay said, "When I was young, I was very hard-headed and strong-willed, just like our mother. Some people call her TooToo and they called me Li'l Toot."

Red said, "That's an unfortunate nickname. But why did Benji call you Ninah?"

Pay said, "According to Benji, when I cut off one of *my* fingers, I wouldn't have ten left, I'd just have nine, which means I'd be a Niner, a Ninah. But no one calls me that, and they never will."

"Why not?"

Pay smiled. "Ask him."

I lied. "Oh, I don't know. Some names stick, some don't, that's all."

Pay said, "It didn't stick because the night after he said it, I made sure he was sound asleep, then sneaked into his and Timmy's room. I tied a string around two of his fingers on his right hand as tight as I could and waited."

Stories like this were the exact reason I didn't want these two to come along.

Pay continued. "Before long, he twitched around a bit and whined and shook his hand in his sleep. When his eyes came open, the first thing he saw was me looking down at him. I was holding a lit candle and had my knife between my teeth like pirates do.

"I took it out so I could talk, put it under his nose, and told him, 'Guess what. Your new nickname is Eight-uh. If anybody ever, *ever* calls me Ninah, your next nickname will be Lefty.'

"He felt the pain from the string cutting off the blood to his fingers and thought I'd chopped them off. He grabbed his hand, screamed, crawled under the bed, and cried for his mommy like the baby he is!"

Stubby said, "I'll say! His screams woke all of us up. Father rushed into the room holding a fire iron over his head. Him and Mother thought Benji was getting murdered!"

Patience said, "That was worth the week I spent in the Amen Corner. I would have gladly done two!"

Red and Stubby and good old Ninah enjoyed a long laugh at my expense.

When we reached the station, the train was already boarding. I shook Red's hand, so of course Stubby and Pay had to do the same thing.

Red opened his mouth in surprise.

"My word, you two have the roughest hands I've ever touched."

Patience said, "Thank you!"

He climbed the stairs to the train and, once he reached the top, turned back around.

"Don't take this the wrong way, Patience, but there's something I simply must tell you, particularly since your older brother is so full of himself."

Pay said, "What's that?"

Red said, "It was a pleasure making your acquaintance. I can't wait to see some of the furniture you and Stubby have worked on. I hope your family will invite me back . . ."

He paused, laughed, then added, ". . . Miss *Ninah*! I shall see *you* in Chatham for supper at my home next week, Lefty!"

I'm certain he meant that as a good-natured joke, but he has absolutely no idea how bleak and cold Pay can be. There are still nights when I awake startled from my sleep and check to make sure all ten fingers are still connected to my hand.

Maybe Red would feel some sort of remorse and understand how painful words can be if he read that day's headline:

WORLD-FAMOUS NEWSPAPERMAN HORRIBLY MAIMED IN HIS SLEEP! VICIOUS SISTER PROVIDED WITH AIRTIGHT ALIBI BY SIMPLEMINDED YOUNGER BROTHER!

→ CHAPTER 27 ←

Dining with Benji

RED

Three weeks after my delightful supper with the Alstons, on the evening Benji was supposed to join Father and me for supper, I was in a complete dither.

I checked, double-checked, then checked a third time that Grandmother O'Toole had indeed gone to Windsor for her end-of-each-month, weeklong visit with Great-Aunt Margaret. I lived in dread that just as Benji, Father, and I settled down to eat, she'd come bustling in from a missed train with her "Faith and begorra this . . ." or "Faith and begorra that . . ."

I shivered in horror through the night fearing what she would have to say to and about Benji if she saw him. Grandmother O'Toole had a ranking of the different kinds of people she hated most. On top of her list were Canadians, followed closely by English people, followed closely by anyone with brown skin, especially the brown-skinned people from Buxton. The list went on and on, but the top three were all I had to deal with now.

Unfortunately, Benji would be at the top of the list even above Canadians because he was both brown-skinned and Canadian. She always had the most incredibly cruel and ridiculous things to say about Canadians and especially the Canadians who came from Buxton.

I'd resigned myself that if Grandmother O'Toole did show up during supper, before she had the chance to utter one vicious word, I'd immediately grab my innocent friend and the two of us would hurl ourselves through the glass of the picture window to make a grand escape.

Taking a chance on being shredded by sharp shards of glass would be far better than the guaranteed pain and anguish Grandmother O'Toole's angry, mean-spirited tongue would doubtless mete out.

The fourth time I asked Father if he was absolutely, one hundred percent, beyond-any-doubt positive she wouldn't be back and that the train had come through on schedule, he said, "Alvin, believe me, I understand your trepidations, but we're fine.

"She didn't take the train this time. Her sister was in Toronto for an appointment, hired a carriage to take her back to Windsor, and they've already picked up Mother O'Toole.

"As we speak, the dear is wreaking havoc at the home of your great-aunt Margaret in the beautiful City of Roses. We have nothing to worry about. Our dinner tonight with your new friend will be a time of relaxation and peace."

I trusted my father.

But that didn't mean I didn't still have my doubts.

At the very moment Grandfather Stockard's clock chimed for the seventh time, a soft knock came from the front door.

I almost didn't recognize the boy who stood on the porch with a pie in his hand.

He was dressed in a starched white shirt with a blue bow tie and full-length trousers that were held up by a pair of braces made of the same blue material as the bow tie.

Benji looked so different. I am accustomed to him being either in the heavy denim apron and folded-newspaper cap he wore whenever he was on his way to or from work, or barefoot in cutoff pants with a short-sleeved shirt and ragged straw hat. I'm fairly certain that he wore the apron and cap so people on the train or in Chatham would notice that he was a newspaperman and might want to engage him in conversation.

Tonight, however, Benji appeared to be as stiff as one of the manikins in Curly's mother's shop. Or maybe even a corpse.

"I'm sorry, sir," I said, "you've come to the wrong home. The mortuary is three blocks down."

Benji laughed without humour. He put his finger in

the shirt's collar and pulled at it. "Heh-heh. My mother made me wear this."

He looked over his shoulder.

"I thought about changing out of it, but you can never be sure that Patience and Stubby aren't out spying."

I took the pie from him. "Thank you, Benji. Come on in and meet my father."

Father stood when we walked into the parlour.

"Father? I'd like to introduce you to my friend, Benjamin."

His name sounded odd to me. I don't think I'd ever called him anything but Benji before.

Benji stepped over to Father and they shook hands.

Benji unblinkingly looked Father in the eye. He spoke as if Father were partially deaf.

"It is a pleasure meeting you, sir. Heh-heh."

Father said, "The pleasure is all mine. My goodness, Benjamin, you have a very firm handshake."

"Thank you, sir."

"We're pleased that you could join us for dinner tonight."

"Thank you, sir. You have a lovely home. Heh-heh."

"Thank you, Benjamin."

Benji near shouted, "My father told me to make sure I passed along his greetings. He filed a deed with you a while ago, sir."

"Yes, I remember. Tell him and your mother I say hello as well."

"Yes, sir, I will. Heh-heh."

I had to do a double take. Who was this lad speaking in this manner? Surely not my talkative, boisterous friend from the swimming hole.

It was simple to deduce what was occurring. I was certain I'd be able to predict how this evening was going to unfold since I knew the checklist that Benji's parents must have insisted he run through. It had to have been similar to the list Father had made me swear to follow when he gave me permission to go to Benji's house for supper.

1. Shake hands firmly.
2. Make and maintain eye contact.
3. Speak clearly; no mumbling; make certain you're speaking loudly enough to be heard.
4. Compliment your hosts' home.
5. Don't sit until your hosts do.
6. Make certain you put your napkin in your lap.
7. Don't talk with your mouth full.
8. Compliment your hosts on the meal.
9. Thank your hosts for a lovely evening.
10. Firmly shake your hosts' hands as you leave.

Father said, "Please be seated, Benjamin. We'll be eating shortly."

"Oh, no, sir" — Benji waved his hand at Father's chair — "after you. Heh-heh."

He waited until Father sat, then looked at me.

Benji prided himself on being such a joker that I decided this was as good a time as any to throw a hammer or two at Thor.

I started to sit, but before my bottom hit the cushion of the chair, I stood back up.

Benji did the same.

Twice more I became partially seated but sprang back up. Benji followed like a jack-in-the-box.

He looked in my direction as though he wanted to strangle me.

There's an old Irish saying for when a prankster gets his comeuppance and the joke ends up being on him. I have no idea what that saying is, but I know, just as with everything else that happens, there's an old Irish saying for it.

My comeuppance came when the fourth time I almost sat, an Irish woman's voice boomed from the just-opened front door, "Chester Stockard, you're supposed to be the wisest old judge in Chatham, yet ye leave the front door wide open so that any jacksnipe can come in and get his foul revenge on ye and your poor innocent family?"

As a cold shiver ran through my body and heat flushed through my face, I quickly lost my courage and forgot all about leaping through the picture window. Even more shamefully, I also forgot about my heroic plan to grab Benji and escape with him.

Knocking over the chair I had been pretending I was going to sit in, I ran toward the kitchen and shouted, "Oh, Benji! Please! For the love of God, *run!*"

I'm not certain if I could have reacted as quickly as Benji did were it me being yelled at in such a manner, but my friend never hesitated.

I can only imagine the confused look that must have come to Father's face when Benji hollered over his shoulder, "Thank you very much for having me over for supper, sir, the conversation was stimulating, your company was exhilarating, and that was one of the finest meals I've ever had!"

Benji jostled past me as we ran through the kitchen and spilled out onto the back porch.

"Keep running!" I yelled. "Don't listen to anything she says; she's very confused!"

Three blocks from home, just outside of the funeral parlour, I grabbed the back of Benji's jacket and pulled him to a stop. I leaned over, put my hands on my knees, and gasped to him, "She has rheumatism. I'm fairly certain we're safe. I don't think she can run this far."

"You don't think who can run this far? Who are we running from?"

"Grandmother O'Toole!"

"*Who?*"

"My mother's mother."

"Your grandmother? We're running like this from your *grandmother?*"

He did make it seem fairly ridiculous.

"Take my word for it, Benji. She's not like anyone you've ever met."

This made no impression whatsoever on him, so I added, "You don't understand. She's directly from *Ireland!*"

Benji still failed to grasp the seriousness of my fears. He looked around and said, "I sure hope Stubby and Pay aren't out here spying on me. I'll bet you anything Mother would say that running out of your house like that is the height of disrespect and rudeness. If they did see what happened, I'm going to be spending a lot of time in the Amen Corner."

We must have presented quite the cowardly sight. I was looking fearfully down the street, half expecting to see a thousand-year-old Irishwoman toddling after us with her cane cutting through the air much like the grim reaper's scythe, and Benji was nervously sweeping his eyes from pillar to post to be certain he hadn't been seen by his sweet young siblings.

"Well, if your parents do try to give you time in the Amen Corner, I'll be happy to testify on your behalf. I'll let them know you were the most polite and well-behaved guest we've ever had. I don't believe anyone else has ever complimented Father on how stimulating his conversation was before he'd said even three words!"

Benji said, "Ha-ha."

"And I must say I've never seen anyone go from a complete standstill to full speed in such a short period of time."

Benji said, "If you could've seen the shade of red you turned when you heard your grandmother's voice, believe me, you would have gotten out of there just as fast as I did!"

I said, "Regardless, I'm so pleased that you enjoyed the food as much as you did; it has to have been special if you loved it without even tasting it!"

He laughed. "It was a mystery at first, Red, but I'm beginning to understand why you have no friends. Do you think if we apologized to your father, he'd still serve us supper?"

Oh, no! How could I explain?

"Benji, I don't think that's a good idea. Maybe you should come back at the end of next month or . . ."

"Alvin Stockard! There ye are, lad!"

The woman's heavy Irish brogue made panic course through my veins for a second time.

"And what on earth caused such a rude display? Your poor mother must be spinning in her grave!"

I began to run but heard "Ye must be Alvin's friend, Benjamin. 'Tis a pleasure to meet ye. My name's Lily Collins. I'm a friend of Alvin's dear grandmother."

I turned back and saw Grandmother O'Toole's best friend, Miss Lily the baker, shaking hands with Benji.

"Pleased to meet you, ma'am."

"We'd've met a bit earlier, but the way the two of you bolted from the house like it was afire prevented that. Alvin's father had asked me to bring a pie over for your dessert tonight."

She looked hard at me and said to Benji, "Do accept our apologies for the doltish lad here. Some of the time, we think he's too bright for his own good."

"No need to apologize, ma'am. I look at my friendship with him as a huge act of charity."

Miss Lily laughed. "Ye've a fine sense of humour, Benjamin. We have a saying in Ireland that a light heart lives long. I suspect ye'll be around for quite a while."

"Thank you."

I said, "It's good to see you, Miss Lily."

She said, "You!" She slapped the back of my head as she walked away.

Benji said, "Now, let me understand this. We're

supposed to be afraid of only certain Irish grandmothers, not all of them?"

"You'll never understand, Benji."

"All I want to understand now is if that food is really as good as I told your father it was. I'm starving. Do you suppose if we keep a sharp eye for Irish grandmothers, we might go back and I can get seconds of the best meal I've never had?"

I was so relieved that I said, "For sure, Benjamin."

I couldn't resist adding, "But you know, my father is a bit hard of hearing. You should probably speak a bit louder to make certain he's understanding everything you say."

Benji said, "Thanks, Red."

I couldn't wait to get home and hear this!

Chumming around with Benji was turning me into a real trickster.

→ CHAPTER 28 ←

The Lung-Shot Doe

BENJI

Miss Cary enjoys rejecting articles. Not only mine.

More than once, I was working about in the shop when one of the real reporters would come out of her office with a very upset expression and the cheerful words "Now, off you go" following behind them.

The only good thing was I could see it wasn't personal.

Right after Mr. Thames came scowling out of her office, Miss Cary called, "Ben-jamin!"

I went in.

There was another flyer on her desk.

"How about three hundred words due on Monday at nine sharp?"

The flyer told about a farmer charging people to see the mounted head of a huge deer. It was supposed to have a record rack and weigh more than three hundred pounds. He'd shot it near one of his fields.

I could never shoot a deer. Maybe it has something to

do with the animal's size. Maybe the bigger something is, the closer it is to God.

Or maybe it's their eyes; a deer's eyes are so . . . so . . . *Gentle* is the only word I can use to describe them. Whatever the reason, even if I was carrying a rifle large enough and sighted in on a deer, I know my finger would be a frozen lump on the trigger.

I told Miss Cary, "Yes, ma'am," but my heart wasn't going to be in this article.

When I reached home, Mother and Father were sitting on the front porch.

"Good evening, Benjamin," Mother said. "How is Miss Cary doing?"

"Good evening, Mother, Father. Miss Cary is fine."

Father said, "Any good word on getting something published?"

"No, Father, nothing. She's given me the assignment to write an article about a huge deer getting shot."

Father said, "I heard 'bout that. Up near Chatham, on Lennox Burroughs's farm, I think."

"I don't want to write it. I don't see how anyone can shoot a deer."

"Benji," Father said, "it just ain't in some folk's nature to kill, not no large game anyway. Some folks is just too fra-gile to do it."

I scowled. Nobody wanted to be called fragile.

Mother quickly added, "Now, son, there's not a thing wrong with that. This world would be a whole lot better place if we had more gentle-souled folks rather than those who are happy to shoot anything they see."

Father smiled that little lopsided smile of his and said, "TooToo, you should say they's happy to shoot anything they sees . . . long as it ain't shooting back."

He added, "It brings to mind what happened a ways back in the North Woods, Benji. You wasn't but six or seven and we was headed back from fishing."

Mother sighed. She'd heard this story more times than she wanted to.

I don't remember the things Father described and have always wondered if it was true, because if it happened the way he says it did, it would be something hard to forget, even for a six-year-old. I don't know if Father always brings it up to teach me a lesson or to poke fun at me or maybe he's just misremembering what really happened.

"You and me was out in the North Woods coming back from fishing. Even back then, I knew you was gonna be a great outdoorsman one day 'cause we're walking along and you all the sudden stops and shushes me.

"I stopped and I'll be blanged if there wasn't a strange sound.

"I remember you said it was off to the right and I said it was off to the left, and you was right.

"The sound was coming out of some thick underbrush. I told you to wait while I checked what it was.

"I pulled some of the growth aside and my heart broke. I told you, 'Some fool's done lung-shot a doe. Give me your knife, Benjamin.'

"You give it to me, then when you saw the doe, Benji, you done something I never expected. You looked like you was dumbstruck; you put your hands atop your head and started walking back home without saying a word.

"That's probably why you's a little sensitive about deer, son, but like your momma say, ain't nothing wrong with that."

I don't know why Father tells that tale. Usually, Mother's the one you can expect that sort of thing from, what the old folks call prettying-up a story. Father's stories are usually close to the truth.

Whenever he'd recount the story of the deer in the forest, it always left me scratching my head in wonder.

I should have started over to the Burroughs' farm to write my article. Instead, I went into the woods to think about how I was going to do it. I know a good reporter wouldn't let his personal feelings get in the way of what he was writing unless he could do it in a very sneaky way.

I was sitting near the river when the woods whispered, "He's near."

He was coming from the back, but I didn't let on I knew.

He said, "I hear tell you's a reporter."

I never turned around.

"Yes, sir, I'm trying to be one."

"You report on you and me talking?"

"Why, no, sir, that's no one's business but ours."

"Good, good."

He threw a stone into the water.

"So what kinda things you reporting on?"

"Not that anyone will ever know, but I'm supposed to do an article on a deer."

"Deer?"

"Yes, sir."

"Folks so desperate for news now that they looking to read about deer?"

"This was a special one. He's supposed to have had the largest rack on any deer in Canada and weighs three hundred and sixty-five pounds. It's supposed to be a record."

"He's dead?"

"Yes, sir. Mr. Burroughs shot it on his farm. He's charging people to come look at it and I'm supposed to —"

"He shot him?"

"He shot the buck, sir."

"Huge rack? Three hundred sixty pounds?"

"They say."

"A shame, a rotten shame. That the Old Grandfather. That deer older than you by a lot. A shame, a rotten shame. And they showing off his head?"

"Yes, sir, he's charging . . ."

I turned around and he was gone.

They didn't say it exactly, but I took that to mean the woods were telling me, "Go fishing. Your deadline for the article isn't up for four days. You can do it later."

I went to the tree where I hide my pole and took the woods' advice.

I'm going to have to listen to the trees more carefully! Their advice to wait to write the article was perfect.

I went to the Burroughs' farm on Sunday and as soon as I knocked on the front door of the farmhouse, I was greeted by a double-barrel shotgun behind the screen!

I put my hands in the air and said, "Sir, I'm a reporter for the *Chatham Freedman* come to do a story on your deer head."

My heart was doing somersaults in my chest.

The farmer pushed open the screen door and pointed the gun at the ground. He was a large white man with a wad of tobacco in his cheek.

"Well, you're too late, boy. Someone done run off with the head."

"It was stolen?"

"That's right. Had it in the loft of the locked barn with dogs all 'round it, and some thief got it anyway."

He swore and spit to the side.

"Maybe I can write about that and someone will give it back."

He said, "Write what you want; it's probably in Toronto by now. That buck was worth a lotta money. I'd-a had the record."

He showed me where he had kept the deer's head and he was right. It was high in the loft of his barn. He'd first had to shoo away three huge dogs.

I wrote my article when I got home. It was pretty good. It turned out to be interesting because it had a mystery in it.

One thing that wasn't mysterious was what happened when I turned my article in.

It was no surprise on Monday morning when the words "Now, off you go" chased me out of Miss Cary's office.

→ CHAPTER 29 ←

A Murder in the Woods?

RED

Curly said, "Pa come home drunk and real upset early the other morning."

This caught my attention. Not that Curly's father had stumbled into their house drunk and raised Cain, but the fact that Curly was talking to me about it. His father's drunkenness was Curly's most tender spot. It was the place where we dared not tread, the same as Petey's mixed blood or the Baylis boys' older brother who had been hanged in the United States. Besides, it would be a stretch to say Curly and I are friends, especially not friends who would confide in each other.

His words hung in the air. I didn't know what to say.

He went on, "I ain't never told no one this, Red, but every once in a while when Pa's on a bender, he whups us. He's been hitting us like we was full-grown men for years. He didn't this time, not to start, but he roused us all out of our sleep and made me and Quincy and Ma sit 'round the table at about three in the morning. When I saw that he had the Bible on the table in front of him, I wished we'd-a just got whupped."

I nodded.

"He said we was all gonna stand up and, one by one, with our hand on the Bible, swear we wouldn't tell a soul what he was gonna say."

He paused.

"Ma swore first and slid the Bible to Quincy. He told Pa the same thing I was feeling. He said he waren't doing it, that he didn't trust his own mouth and didn't want to go to hell for breaking his word on the Bible. Said Pa shouldn't tell him no secrets, that he should just let him go back to bed in peace."

"So what happened?"

"Ma starts bawling and begs Quince to swear for Pa, that it won't hurt him to do it, that God will forgive him if he makes a mistake.

"Quince still won't do it. Him and Pa are standing face-to-face. I was across the room and could smell the rotgut on Pa's stinking mouth from that far."

Curly went quiet.

"So Quincy didn't swear not to tell? You didn't either?"

Curly said, "I saw what Pa done to Quince. He ended up swearing on the Bible anyway, so I swore too."

He laughed. "Only difference was I didn't come out of it knocked loopy with a busted lip."

I still didn't know what to say.

"That ain't right, is it? You can't get forced to swear to do something wrong on the Bible. Right, Red?"

I felt as though I'd been slapped.

I said, "It doesn't seem right to me, especially if you were forced to do it. But . . ."

Curly said, "But nothing. Pa was wrong and what he done out in the woods was wrong."

I was dying to hear what Curly's father had done, but Curly was having second thoughts. He started doing what Father says people do in court if they're uncomfortable with telling the whole truth right off the bat. Father says they gift wrap the story. I was going to have to listen to a bunch of ribbons and bows and wrapping paper and excelsior and wadded newspapers before I finally got to Curly's gift, the thing he really wanted to say.

"Pa starts this demon laugh he's got and says, 'They needs to give me a medal. I should be in the papers for what I done! But you think that'll happen? Of course not; one of 'em will have something smart to say about it, and sooner or later, it's all going to boil down to 'Let's throw Phineas in the hoosegow.'

"Pa says, 'Folks been talking 'bout that scoundrel for years, but these fools in Chatham ain't done a thing. They ain't real men; they all talk.'

"Pa threw a plate into the wall and said, 'Well, Phineas R. Bennett will be respected from now on! They won't want to, but now they ain't gonna have no choice. They'll all have to say I'm a man what gets things done! I'm a real man.'"

Curly stared out at the river.

I said, "Curly! What did he do?"

Curly said, "Me and Quincy looks at each other. Pa ain't talking to no one in particular, and if it waren't for Ma being trapped there, we'd-a left. Or jumped him.

"Pa drops his head down on the table and starts sobbing, and that ain't never good.

"The carving knife wasn't but a couple of inches from Pa's hand."

Those words caused a cold blast to run across my scalp!

Curly said, "I seen the knife and seen how his back looked a mile wide while he had his head down. I figured this would be the perfect time and place to bury that knife."

"Oh, Curly, say you didn't, say you didn't pick up the knife!"

"I was going to. I swear it, Red, but before I could, Pa raises up his head and says in this whining voice, 'He startled me; he ain't got no business being in our woods no way. He know he suppose to stay farther south.'"

I said, "Who? Who was he talking about, Curly?"

Curly said, "Pa gets up and walks over to where Ma's sitting and falls to his knees. Ma's stiff as a board when Pa puts his head in her lap and . . ."

Curly starts crying. I wanted to reach out to him, but my hands hung like weights at my side.

He said, "This is what happens all the time. First he's sorry and weepy to Ma, then he's tanning her hide. I swore if he hit Ma this time, I was gonna stab him. And I meant it. But me and Quincy's thinking just alike, and Quince grabbed the knife first. I couldn't believe it when he walks up behind where Pa's sitting on the floor."

My heart was racing.

Curly said, "Pa tells us, 'So I falls to sleep out by the big bend in the river, and all the sudden, I wakes up and it's got dark and the moon's high and I look and someone's bent over down by the river. I blinks a couple times 'cause I can't believe what I'm seeing. It ain't nothing but luck that I had my pistol with me. I ain't scared, but I grab it outta my coat. You can't never be too sure.

"'He ain't s'pose to be 'round here and he done thiefed from white folks his whole life, so I decides I'm 'bout to make one of them citizen arrests. I starts to creep closer to get this scalawag. I didn't make a peep, but what they says is true; he's got the hearing of a dog.

"'All the sudden he stands up and whips 'round at me. I done what I had to. I done what anyone woulda.

"'I yells, "Stop!!!" But he keeps coming! He growls like a madman and raises this club as big as a tree over his head and . . . and . . . I shot. He was gonna kill me and I got him 'fore he could! He dropped like a sack of rocks.'"

There were tears in Curly's eyes.

"Pa wraps his arms 'round Ma, stops crying, and begins laughing again. He stands up, sees Quincy standing there with his hand behind his back. I'm thinking, *Do it! Do it, Quincy!*

"Pa raises his arms above his head and tells us, 'Boys, don't ever let no one tell you no different. Your pa's a hero! There ain't no more bears nor wolves in these woods, and after tonight, there ain't no more lions neither. I done shot that wild South Woods darky! His thieving days is over.'"

I was stunned.

Curly said, "Pa didn't even notice that the knife fell outta Quincy's hand. He screams, 'They needs to build me a statue in the middle of Chatham!' Then he runs out into the night."

I don't know how long I stood there before I found my voice. "Curly, you said he shot him. Did he say he killed him?"

Curly said, "I don't know. He said he shot him, I guess. The coward probably fired and run off."

"Did you tell the constable?"

Curly said, "The *constable*? You know I don't have nothing to do with him. Besides, Pa's probably lying."

259

I said, "But, Curly, you're crying. You're crying. You must know he's telling the truth. You know he shot that poor man."

Curly looked at me like I was crazy.

"Poor man? You think I'm crying about that crazy Lion Man fool? You think I care one raccoon turd about him?"

He stood in my face like he was going to hit me.

"I'll tell you why I'm crying, Red."

He wiped his nose on his shirtsleeve. "Have you ever wondered what it's like to know you're seconds away from killing someone, Red? We've all got so mad we said 'I'm gonna kill so and so,' but that's just talk. Have you ever wondered how it feels to *know* you're going to do it? That if it don't happen tonight, it will tomorrow or, by God, for sure on the day after? That you're not just talking?"

"Well . . ."

"Well, I know. I cried 'cause Quince is gonna kill Pa. I cried 'cause I know, Red. I thought about it and I ain't gonna let Quince throw his life away. He's always been the good one. He's always done good in school and ain't been the burden to Ma that I been."

Curly was openly sobbing. "Ever since I can remember, we all knowed which of us was like Pa and which waren't. I thought hard on it and I ain't gonna have Quince toss out all the work he's done. *I'm* gonna do it, Red. I'm crying 'cause I know the only difference twixt me being a kid and being a murderer is time.

"There's a rope waiting for me at the gallows, Red, that's why I'm crying."

He raised his shirt to wipe at his tears. Tucked into the waistband of his pants was the butt of a huge pistol.

Curly was hurting horribly, and that probably should have mattered to me. But it didn't. The only thing I could think about was how the Lion Man had looked at me and apologized. That wasn't something one could easily forget.

Maybe Curly's father was telling the truth. Maybe the Lion Man was lying dead out at the river. Or maybe he'd missed him completely. Or maybe he hadn't been killed and was lying in the woods slowly bleeding to death.

"I have to go."

He yelled after me, "I trust you, Red. Don't tell no one you seen me cry."

If it weren't for the fact that I sounded so pathetic and silly when I practiced doing it at home in the mirror, I would have roundly and vilely cursed out Curly Bennett and his entire family.

→ Chapter 30 ←

The Emotion of Memory

BENJI

Miss Cary says for a news story to be something people will want to read, it's got to be like a well-written novel by a great author; it's got to touch on human emotions. She even gave me a list of what the most important human emotions are. I see this as proof of something I've suspected since we first met, that she doesn't think I'm real bright.

She told me, after I'd written something, I had to compare it to her list to make sure I was striking one of the emotions there. She says I have to do this until it happens without thought. The most important human emotions, in Miss Cary's eyes, are:

1. Anger
2. Fear
3. Happiness
4. Sadness
5. Surprise

I'm well on my way to being a good reporter, because another one of Miss Cary's lessons is that the best reporters always question what we've been told. Good reporters want to look deeper into whatever we're investigating; we don't just accept any old answer someone gives us. I've taken that lesson to heart and didn't accept Miss Cary's list of the most important human emotions as the undisputed truth either.

I'm not saying the list isn't a good start, but I think there are two more important human emotions that need to be included. I've never heard of them described as emotions, but they should be. From what I've seen, they have a stronger effect on you than feeling sad or happy do.

I'm talking about sounds and smells. There is nothing that can bring up memories quicker than a certain sound, or clearer than a familiar smell.

Someone singing a song can make you remember exactly where you were and what you were doing the first time you'd heard it. Hearing a belt get pulled out of its loops real fast can make your head jerk up whilst you remember a licking from a year ago like it just happened.

But the emotion of smell is even stronger.

A good whiff of something can quick-as-that pick you up and drop you in another place and time, just as surely as that contraption in the story *The Time Machine*.

I can walk into our home and if Mother has baked cookies, a memory so strong sometimes gets into my head that I can remember conversations from years ago, or even the way the light was falling through a window.

I was walking home from school when I was around six or seven. I know it was then because that was the year the mayor gave me a Hudson Bay capote for my birthday, and I was so proud of it, I didn't want to take it off, even when spring was edging close to summer.

I remember becoming very excited when I opened the front door to home and breathed in air that was drenched with the smell of cookies. I dropped my Hudson Bay coat on the floor and ran to where the warm brown smell was coming from.

Any time I smell chocolate chip cookies, I remember Mother's exact words when I came into the kitchen. She said, "I know you didn't just drop the mayor's coat on the floor. Do you have any idea how much that cost?"

I said, "Are the cookies done?"

She whirled around from the stove and snapped, "And I know those aren't your boots tracking wetness into my kitchen! You have to the count of three to get your clothes taken care of, Mr. Benjamin Alston, and the 'one' and the 'two' are silent."

I remember I had a moment of stupidness, wondering if it might be worthwhile to make a dash at the cookies that were cooling next to the stove. I wasn't particularly bright at six or seven years old.

But when Mother said, "Three," I was brought to my senses and went to do as I was told.

Or I can go tomorrow into the icehouse in Buxton and pick a coat off a nail and pull it around me, and in no time, the brisk smell of dampness and cold that are clinging to the coat will carry me into the middle of a snowball war that happened years ago.

Me and Spencer were pinned down in our snow fort while the twins and Pilot pelted us with snowballs. They'd cheated and soaked the snowballs in water to turn them into ice balls, and we were defenseless. Trying to protect my head, I pushed my face into my jacket and first smelled that smell that the icehouse coat brings up.

If I had closed my eyes, I would have been back in the ice fort, listening to Spencer's laughs, feeling his legs kicking at me as we lay huddled behind the crumbling walls of our soon-to-be overrun fort.

Spencer had said, "'Tis an honour and a pleasure to die in battle with such a wonderful chum, Benji."

I'd replied, "No, Spencer, the pleasure's all mine," just before one of the ice balls sent Spence crying home with a busted lip.

So even though Miss Cary was the first black woman in North America to have her own newspaper and had done a bunch of other things that people celebrated, she didn't know everything.

She had refused to publish another article, but that's not the reason today's headline was going to be:

SCIENTISTS DISCOVER NEW EMOTION. FAMOUS NEWSPAPER EDITOR EMBARRASSED FOR GETTING IT SO WRONG.

→ CHAPTER 31 ←

The Quandary

RED

I am not a coward. Fear isn't what slowed me while running through the woods toward the big bend in the Chatham River to see if Curly's father was telling the truth. It was careful thinking, not fear, that gave me pause.

Since Father was in London for two days, my first instinct was to run and tell the constable, but I knew I had to go check. If the Lion Man really was wounded in the woods, bleeding all alone, every second counted. But as I got deeper in the forest, I began to have doubts.

A debate raged in my head so fiercely that I sat on a fallen log and tried to work this quandary out.

Curly's father was a liar, that much everybody knew. But even a stopped clock tells the right time twice a day and even the most dedicated liar can accidentally be truthful.

He *was* indeed low enough to bushwhack another person. That was something else everyone knew. And even though Father said there wasn't enough evidence to try

267

him, the stories still fly about how it was Curly's father who'd murdered that railroad agent years ago.

I remembered what my grade six economics teacher, Mr. Camden, had said about how, decades ago, he used to hunt bears in these woods and how the worst thing to do was wound one, to not kill it cleanly. He said bears are vengeful creatures and, no matter what their injuries, will drag themselves around and ambush any hunter who wounded them. Maybe the Lion Man was out in the woods doing something similar; maybe he was waiting to take revenge on anyone who was white.

Maybe he *was* dead. Maybe his body would be flyblown by now. I'm not afraid of a dead body; I've seen plenty at funerals. But it reasons that someone who'd been shot and died in the woods would be a whole different level of dead than a neatly washed body in a casket. A level I wasn't particularly looking forward to seeing.

The doubts began weighing heavily on me and I knew there were two choices: Either run back to Chatham and tell someone, or go deeper into the woods on a wild goose chase.

Providence can guide one when the way seems lost, and it had to have been Providence that told me there was a third choice: Benji!

CHAPTER 32

Surprising the Spy

BENJI

The fish had given up on us, so me and the boys began swimming and swinging off the rope, seeing whose splash was most impressive.

The watched feeling wrapped its fingers around me again. I can't say why, but it was different this time. I realized in the weeks since I'd talked to the Madman, the feeling had changed from one of being watched to a feeling of being watched *over*.

And what I was feeling now was being watched. Whoever it was, was watching loud, not so loud that anyone else noticed but loud enough that within a few moments after they found a spot from which to spy, I knew right where they were hiding.

Even though the watcher kept ducking, they'd occasionally raise their head, and their brown hat stood out amongst the forest green.

I did nothing to alert my chums. When my turn to swing on the rope came, I sailed over the pond and, instead of trying to raise as much water and splash as I could, I took a quick breath and dove deep. I swam along the bottom of the pond toward the north side, where the reeds rose out of the water in a thicket a good twelve or fifteen feet tall.

Staying half submerged, I snaked my way to the pond's north bank and slinked into the trees. Once I was deep enough in the woods to be hidden, I looked back toward the pond.

The watcher hadn't noticed me slip away. His head kept popping out of the bushes, spying on my friends. I grew sore disappointed that none of my friends noticed I'd slipped away either; what if I'd been tangled in the lily pads and was drowning? They wouldn't have come looking for me until long after I'd met Saint Peter, gotten my golden slippers, and was stomping all over God's heaven.

I circled into the woods so I could come up on the watcher from behind. Just to be safe, I picked up two baseball-sized stones and held them tight. If he was carrying a weapon, the fact that I could sneak up on him might give me the upper hand.

I silently stole toward where he was.

He was flattened to the ground, raising his head every once in a while. From his size, I could see the spy was a boy, a brown hat covering his head. And he was unarmed. I grew emboldened.

I set the stones down and crept nearer.

I was close enough to hear his breath as he drew it in.

I waited for his head to go down one more time. I was only one leap away.

⤳ Chapter 33 ⤦

Attacked!

RED

Perhaps it's because of what I went through with the Lion Man before. Perhaps it's because there's a limit as to how frightened one can be, and once you get to that point, nothing else is as much of a bother. Whatever the reason, this time, when the wounded Lion Man pounced and began the process of ripping my throat out of my neck to gain vengeance on the first white person he came across after being so foully ambushed, I neither screamed nor moaned. I accepted the hand I'd been dealt and waited to be dispatched to heaven.

As I felt his icy fingers wrap around my mouth to stifle any of my dying wails, I had second thoughts. If I screamed loudly enough, maybe Benji and the other boys from Buxton would hear me and come to my rescue. Maybe my dying screams could serve as a warning and they could save themselves.

The Lion Man's hand was over my lips, so I opened my mouth wide, then clamped down.

I was shocked when the Lion Man cried out, "Oww! Red?"

I released his fingers just as he released my face.

The uncontrollable trembling that shook my body showed that my courage had been false.

Benji Alston furiously waved his right hand in the air and hopped from one foot to the other.

"That hurt!"

"I thought you were the Lion Man come to kill me!"

"What are you talking about? You're making me believe what they say about everyone from Chatham, that you're all addled in the head."

"No, Benji, this is kismet! I was looking for you."

"What? Why?"

"It's the Lion Man. I'm afraid a drunkard from Chatham has shot him."

"Shot who?"

"The Lion Man."

"Wait, what is it this man is lying about?"

"No, not that. Lion, l-i-o-n, the South Woods Lion Man."

Benji stared at me, and I can find no fault in the exasperated expression that worried his face.

He said, "Addled. Every single one of you."

"No, Benji, you must know of him, the escaped slave who lives in the woods with the lion's mane of hair!"

"*What!*"

"Surely you must have heard of him. We always believed he was from Buxton."

Benji's expression changed from bewilderment to horror.

"You mean the Madman of Piney Woods?"

He stopped hopping and shaking his bitten finger.

"It must be he. We call him the Lion Man because of his mane."

"You said he was shot?"

"Yes, I believe so."

"How badly was he hurt?"

"I don't know. I don't even know where he is."

"Did you tell the constable in Chatham?"

"No."

His tone changed, beginning to edge toward anger. "Who *have* you told?"

I was embarrassed by my answer. "No one. I discovered it myself less than an hour or so ago. I wanted to find you so we could go together to see if it was true. I figured if he was wounded, you'd be able to track him."

"Where did it happen?"

"I was told by the big bend in the river."

"Wait here, I need to get my clothes."

"Good, we'll need as much help as we can get. Bring your friends."

"No. This is something you and I will do alone."

I can't understand why he didn't want help. I hoped he knew what he was doing.

Benji Alston ran back to the other Buxton boys.

→ CHAPTER 34 ←

Starting the Hunt

BENJI

I only half remember running back for my clothes.

Spencer said, "Holy Michalamacalack, Benji, you near scared me to death! I didn't know you'd left. Where did you go?"

I pulled my trousers, shirt, and shoes on without saying a word. The other lads became suspicious as well.

"I've got to go back. I don't think I fed the horse today, and Mother will have my scalp for it."

Spencer got up and walked to the pile of our clothes.

"No, Spence. I'll do it alone. Stay. I'll see you later."

I hoped Red wouldn't easily tire. If we ran hard, we could be at the bend in the river in a little less than an hour.

→ CHAPTER 35 ←

The Scene of the Crime

RED

I'm glad Benji didn't want to talk as we ran toward the river. I struggled to breathe so much that I wouldn't've been able to say a word with the pace he was keeping.

He was leading me off the beaten track and we reached the big bend much sooner than if we'd taken the road.

When the sounds of the river splashing over rocks reached us, Benji slowed and began approaching with care. I followed.

He said, "Do you know on which side it was supposed to have happened?"

"No, he said he'd been sleeping and was disturbed by sounds at the river so . . ."

Benji pointed to his left. A bottle of Wild Kentucky bourbon was thrown on the ground at the edge of the woods.

He walked over and picked the bottle up. His brow wrinkled when he said, "Look, someone *did* lie here recently."

The dead leaves were disturbed as if they'd been scooped together for a pillow.

Benji sighed and stood at the edge of the forest, looking at the river.

After scanning the water and the other side of the river, he walked to the shore. "You go upstream," he said. "I'll go down."

"What am I looking for?"

"Anything that's unusual. If it happened yesterday, there may not be much left, but just look for something that doesn't seem right."

"How far up the river should I go?"

"No more than a half mile. If you find anything, whistle loud. If you go that far and don't see anything, head back here. Keep your senses sharp for my whistle as well."

Benji went downstream and I headed up.

→ CHAPTER 36 ←

Tracking

BENJI

My heart sank when I saw the empty bottle of whiskey. The label was fresh; the sun nor the rains nor the woods themselves had done anything to fade the colours of the huge turkey on the label. I smelled it, and the strong tang of alcohol burned my nose. It hadn't been out here for long.

This was the worst sign there could have been. It probably meant that at least some of the story the drunken man had told was true.

I hope Red didn't notice how scared I was when I told him to go upstream. He'd just slow me down and if I did come across something terrible, if I did find the Madman dead along the river, I think it would only be right that someone from Buxton be there first for him. Even though Red was nothing more than a newborn babe in the woods, at least he'd be out of the way. Who knows, maybe there would be a real obvious sign that he would notice, maybe not. I told him to go half a mile and whistle; that way I could come get him and double-check on the way there.

As I followed the river downstream, there was nothing out of place. A doe and her fawns had crossed here, one of the fawns losing its footing; a red-tailed hawk had pecked a fish into a skeleton there; a dog had stopped to drink in another spot. I'd covered a mile and not heard anything from Red, so I decided to go back.

Not a hundred yards upriver from where we'd first come out of the woods, my eyes were drawn to a muddy spot along the shore. There was a slew of raccoon tracks bunched together in the damp mud, like they'd been tussling over something. What was odd was that there were no fish scales or bones of any kind, so the raccoons hadn't been feeding. Atop the tracks were crow footprints, as if they'd bobbed in the area for quite a while.

I looked toward the land; there was nothing unusual there. I looked toward the river. My heart stopped.

Just in the river, in the shallowest part, a stone sat at the end of a smooth, foot-long furrow, as if it had been pushed there. I stepped into the water and stood over the stone, looking carefully where I stepped so as to disturb as little as possible. Someone's foot had pushed the stone to where it rested, someone who was in some sort of distress.

All of the pieces of the jigsaw were coming together.

My heart beat as if my blood had suddenly thickened.

Under the shallow water, almost exactly an arm's length away from the spot where the slid stone had come to a rest, were four small dents in the mud. Silt and debris were working to fill them but they were spread just far enough from each other that I knew what they were. They would perfectly match a person's fingers, the fingers of someone trying to pull himself out of the river.

And the spot where the raccoons and crows had danced was where those scavengers were doing their job and cleaning the forest, bringing it back to the way it was supposed to be.

Removing from the woods the memory of the poor Madman's blood.

And judging by the number of prints and the size of land they'd covered, there'd been a lot of blood.

I looked toward the forest and saw the spot where he most likely would have stumbled into the woods. I started to follow, but stopped.

I didn't want to do this alone. The idea of running to the mayor hit me with such force that I realized that was what I should do.

I ran through the woods but hadn't gone fifty yards before I stopped.

Red. I couldn't leave him out here not knowing what I'd found.

But he'd missed the signs. It would be just deserts if I left him.

But he *had* come to get help for the Madman. He didn't have to do that. And he was my responsibility since I'd sent him upriver.

And he was my friend.

I went back.

The moment I saw the prints, my courage left me again. I wished my eyes could see what Red had probably seen, just a group of animal prints. I wished the signs of what had happened weren't screaming at me, unwinding like a stage play.

I wished I didn't see a monster raising a gun and firing.

I wished I couldn't see the Madman falling into the river.

I wished I didn't know that he had struggled, trying to pull himself out of the water.

I could have easily batted my hand at my ears like I was being buzzed by a fly or a skeeter. I wished that much that the woods would quit talking to me.

I was comforted that the signs and prints couldn't tell me how long he'd lain in the river before he did try to get out.

But they also couldn't tell me how badly he'd been wounded.

I looked to the spot where he'd gone into the woods. Maybe he was close to death and the time it would take me to get Red would send him over. I should follow the trail.

I tried. It would be the easiest thing in the world to trail the Madman. I tried, I really did.

But I knew I couldn't do it alone.

I was glad my newest friend was here to go with me.

→ Chapter 37 ←

Joining Benji

RED

I'd seen nothing going upstream and had been walking back for only a few minutes when Benji's whistle reached me. There was a shrill urgency to it, so I quickened my pace.

He was standing not far from where we'd first come out of the woods.

It took me a moment to catch my breath.

I was stunned as he explained what the foot and claw prints meant. I was embarrassed that I hadn't noticed.

He said, "Don't feel bad. It would be like speaking French, I guess; if you don't know it, you don't . . ."

He peered at the river.

"Benji, what is it?"

He said, "The light has changed since we first got out here. Look."

I followed his pointing finger. The only thing I could see was a stick at a forty-five-degree angle perhaps ten yards from the shore.

Benji waded into the water up to his knees.

He reached down and pulled out something long, muddy, and dripping.

An old musket!

Benji looked toward the woods and, pointing at a spot that looked to me the same as every other, said, "There, that's where he went into the woods."

Chapter 38

Memory

BENJI

The farther we went into the woods, the more my spirits rose. If the Madman had the strength to wander this far, he couldn't have been hurt too bad. We'd been on his trail for close to half an hour and there hadn't been any signs of blood for quite some time.

What worried me was the direction he seemed to be running. It made sense to me that since he had been born in Buxton, he would head southwest to reach help. But he was running more in a wandering, northeast way, heading toward neither Chatham nor Buxton. This might mean he was hurt so bad that he was running in panic. If that were the case, we might reach him only after he'd run himself to death.

Red was about thirty yards behind me. I'd told him to follow me at a distance and double-check if there was anything I'd missed. Every once in a while, I'd see him through the trees, his hair a bright red flare. And even if I couldn't see him, he was making enough noise that I knew where he was. I wanted to keep him close so he wouldn't wander off and get lost. But also in case . . . well, in case of anything.

A good woodsman knows when he's near to whatever he's trailing, and the woods were telling me we were very close. The Madman of Piney Woods was close, but whether he was alive or not, I couldn't tell.

I froze. There was a sound that didn't belong.

I closed my eyes to try to feel where the sound was coming from.

The second I heard the dry wheeze, a memory began fighting its way from deep inside me. I should know why this sound was so familiar, but try as I might, I didn't. This was that same bad feeling I get when there's a word stuck on the tip of my tongue and nothing will make it fall off.

I waited, but the memory refused to cut itself loose. I opened my eyes and took a few more careful steps.

As the wind shifted, I flared my nostrils and closed my eyes. What I smelled caused the memory to explode from within me.

Clinging close to the ground like a low fog was a strong scent. A scent of rot and fear.

I gasped.

I remembered the lung-shot deer Father tells that story about!

Father *had* misremembered that afternoon in the North Woods those many years ago. It must have been May or June, because we had been hunting morels, not coming back from fishing. I remember how much fun it was seeing which of us could spot more of the mushrooms. I'd gathered twice as many as he had, though I had the feeling he was letting me win.

I'd heard the same dry wheezing sound I was hearing now, and I did tell Father to stop.

He heard it too and I pointed at a tangle of underbrush and vines to our left.

I had followed him, and what he said after he moved the underbrush aside and fell to his knees was spoken so low and so soft, it caught my attention like the loudest scream would.

He'd moaned, "Aww, naw, naw, naw . . . you poor girl."

There was a note in his voice that I'd never heard from my father. It was almost a cry, and it had scared me like I'd never been scared before.

I'd rushed to him and buried my face against his back, wrapping my arms around his neck, afraid to see what had forced those horrible sounds from the strongest, bravest man in Canada.

I was scared, but I looked over Father's shoulder anyway. I saw the doe lying on her right side, tangled in the underbrush. She drew another wheezing, bubbly, crackling breath. Her rib cage rose and fell like air going into and seeping out of a punctured brown-and-white balloon.

I remembered a moment of relief. I'd feared, when I looked over Father's shoulder, there would be some horribly hurt little girl lying there.

Father's hand was on the animal's neck. He stroked the doe and almost whispered, "It's all right, girl, it's all right."

That was when Father said, almost to himself, "Some ignorant . . ." and for the first and only time in my life, I heard my father swear.

He didn't say "fool" at all like he says in the story. Father swore.

And they weren't just mild swear words either; they were the type of words you hear from men who've drunk alcohol for hours. But the way Father spit them out was different. They weren't sloppy like the drunkards slur them. Father's words were crackling and alive with anger. The words jumped off his lips, and it wouldn't have surprised me if they'd started a fire as they sparked and danced through the dry brush and undergrowth of the North Woods.

I finally understood why adults are always telling us not to swear.

Father knew how swearing was supposed to be done, and when it was done right, it wasn't something a child would be able to handle. Even with me being as young as I was, the deep respect and fear I already had for the power of words grew even more.

He'd forgotten I was there. I squeezed his neck harder and he quickly changed his words to "Some ignorant *fool*'s lung-shot her."

He kept stroking the doe's neck and asked me, "Did you bring your knife, son?"

That was the first time the doe knew we were there. Its front legs kicked once and it wheezed again, drawing my eyes to where a ragged, black, blood-crusted hole interrupted the beautiful white of its underbelly. Maggots crawled there, so impatient that they couldn't wait for death.

I patted my right-hand pocket, then pulled my knife out as Father moaned again, "Aww, look at her teats; she's nursing a fawn somewhere."

The doe tried to get up but could only raise her head and neck a bit before she crashed back to the forest floor.

She looked at Father.

Her eyes swung over Father's shoulder and she looked right at me. There was so much fear and sadness and gentleness in her eyes that for the first and only time in my life, my heart skipped a beat. The injured doe wheezed again and began twitching. Her movements sent a foul, frightening smell into the air.

I can't believe I'd forgotten all of this, but I do remember thinking it was all too much.

I'm sure I could have easily handled any *one* of the things that had happened back in the North Woods all those years ago if they'd've happened by themselves. Maybe even two of them happening at the same time would not have bothered me so.

But when you added up Father's swearing with the ragged wheezing sound of death, with the way the doe looked at me, with the humiliation and shame of being eaten alive by the maggots, with the thought of a fawn slowly starving in the forest or becoming so weak it wouldn't be able to outrun whatever wanted to pull it down and kill it, the sum was way too much.

Father had been right about me leaving him right after we found that poor doe, but it wasn't like he'd said. It was much worse. Like a bad reporter, he'd left out all the details that gave the story its heart, its touch to human emotions.

I remember I'd set my knife on the ground, put my hands over my ears, and wanted to get away from all that I had just seen and heard.

Father *had* changed the story, and I knew why. It wasn't to teach me a lesson or because he misremembered or because he wanted to poke fun at me. No, Father had changed what happened because he knew the truth would embarrass me.

I hadn't just walked off into the woods, I panicked. I ran and ran and maybe screamed, because as I tore through the forest, I remember a sound trailing behind me.

I'd forgotten all of that until this moment.

Until the emotions of sound and smell triggered a memory of the forest.

I fought to find the courage to separate the twisted vines and discover what was making this familiar wheezing sound. If Father had done it, I could too, even though I knew *this* time when I looked I'd find what I'd dreaded seeing that late spring way back when. I knew this ghastly sound was going to lead me to a person, a human being, someone my Mother knew and used to be friends with, and he would be very near death.

As I began pulling at the vines, I hoped I wouldn't run. I hoped I'd be able to do what Father had done and supply some type of comfort.

I paused when I saw what looked like a strange-shaped, gnarled black root.

My mind reeled when I realized it wasn't a root at all. It was a man's foot tangled in the vines, his toes tightly clenched, folded down upon the sole of his foot.

My head spun, but I kept on.

My eyes followed from the foot to the leg of a pair of buckskin trousers.

I felt tears start to burn my eyes, but I kept tearing at more of the vines.

And once again my eyes fell upon the poor man we used to call the Madman of Piney Woods.

And this time I felt no fear.

→ CHAPTER 39 ←

Benji on the Edge

RED

"Red! Red! Over here!"

The sound bounced off trees, first seeming to come from this way, then that, giving me no clue to the direction from which Benji was calling. But the tone in his voice left no doubt that he had discovered something loathsome.

Each time he called my name, a chill brushed down my neck.

"Benji! Where are you?"

"Oh, Red, over here! Come quickly!"

The thicket to my right seemed to be the source of Benji's voice.

His broken sobs pulled me closer.

"Benji! I hear you but can't see where you are!"

"Here, just in front of you, on the ground. Pull these aside." He shook the vines to show me which ones to move.

I began tugging at the grapevines that choked this part of the forest floor.

Soon I came upon Benji's hunched back.

"Benji? Did you find him? Is he . . ."

Looking over Benji's shoulder, I could see a man's legs on the ground, covered by buckskin. He had one shoe off and one shoe on. His bare left foot was clenched like a dark brown fist.

"Oh, Red! He's barely alive."

I clawed at more vines until I was at Benji's side.

The South Woods Lion Man's head, with its mass of tangled hair, was cradled in Benji's lap.

I must've been in shock, because the thought I couldn't get out of my mind was that this must be some sort of mistake; we needed to keep looking. This man was far too small to be the South Woods Lion Man.

But it was he.

"Red, you've got to run to Buxton and get the mayor! And the doctor. I'll stay here and look after him."

Benji wasn't thinking clearly.

A sense of fear and panic rose in my chest as I said, "That is madness! I would never be able to find this place again."

He rocked the Lion Man's head and looked up.

"I can't leave him! I'll start a fire; you can tell where we are from that. Just climb a tree and you'll be able to see it. Just make sure you keep heading southwest, you can't —"

"Benji! You need to go. What if I get lost? It just doesn't make sense. You can cut hours off the time it will take to get someone here."

Benji muttered, "You're right."

He leaned forward until the Lion Man's head was completely covered by his sobbing chest.

"Come," he said, "cradle him and try to make him comfortable. You must promise me you'll hold him; you must promise me you'll not let go of him even if . . ."

"I promise, Benji. Please hurry. It won't be long before night sets in; I'm absolutely terrified to be out here! Please hurry."

Benji kissed the Lion Man's cheek and told him, "Please, sir, just hold on. I'm going for help."

The man's eyes blinked rapidly, but it was not an acknowledgment that he'd heard.

Benji stood, a stain of blood on his lap and chest. I took the Lion Man's head into my lap. It was surprisingly light.

I stared down at his mass of hair and at the smooth, dark brown skin of his forehead.

My confused mind thought about playing chess with Father.

During our matches, without knowing how or why, I'd so often find myself in a dire situation neither foreseen nor easily reversed. The only thing I knew was that the game was over. I had that same feeling now.

But in this dire situation, I found myself holding the dying South Woods Lion Man's head in my lap in a jungle of grapevines somewhere in the forest as night crept forward. It did seem as though the end was near; however, there was no king to tip in resignation to make it all end.

I raised my head and said, "Please, Benji, hurry!"

He was already gone.

→ CHAPTER 40 ←

The Run for Help

BENJI

I ran so hard, trees of the forest whooshed by me like I was on the 3:15 to Chatham. A forest of worries and thoughts whizzed by me just as fast. And just like I tried to avoid running into the trees, I tried to avoid running into those thoughts. If they stood between me and what I needed to get done, I sidestepped them and let them fly by. Not avoiding either would mean being knocked down.

The thoughts I *couldn't* afford to have were about what I was running from. I had to think about anything but this poor wounded man and Red and what a bad situation this was.

I figured it would take me no more than forty-five to fifty minutes to get to Buxton. Then there'd be at most another half hour to find the mayor and the doctor. By then the mayor would probably be preparing to leave the fields or would be sitting on the porch of Miss Aden, having a cool drink.

There'd be another fifty minutes to an hour to return to Red and the Madman. Plus, if I added another fifteen to twenty minutes for unforeseen events, I would be gone from them for at most two and a half hours. I also figured that if all went well, that would be probably a half hour before the sun set.

An unwanted thought intruded: The deepest parts of the forest have a love for darkness; they invite the night in an hour before the sun sets and hang on to it for an hour after the sun rises.

I let the thought zoom by.

I hoped for two things, that the Madman would not die during that time and that Red's courage would not abandon him. The thought of Red losing hope and leaving the Madman lying alone in the woods spurred me to run harder.

I would never blame Red for becoming so frightened that he'd run. He'd been right. He wouldn't have been able to find his way out of these woods in full daylight; in the black of a moonless night, there'd be no hope at all.

I let this thought go and turned my thoughts to figuring out how we'd actually move the Madman once me and the mayor and the doctor returned to them.

How would we carry him back? He was so deep in the woods that a wagon wouldn't be able to reach him and would take far too long.

Charming Little Chalet in the Woods came to mind, and just as I was about to avoid the thought, I knew why it had! Stubby and Pay used a travois to carry the tools and lumber that went into building their tree house. Everything they built was done with care and quality, so there was no doubt their travois would still be around and would be able to carry much more than the Madman, who couldn't have weighed more than a hundred and forty pounds.

That meant I'd need another half hour to forty-five minutes to get all of that together. My spirits sank. It would be well past dark when the mayor and I would get to them. The poor boy!

Even as well as *I* know the forest, being alone, lost in the woods on a pitch-black night would be enough to make *me* lose my mind. Plus, Red might be sitting with someone who was no longer alive. It would have overwhelmed even a woodsman like me.

I forced myself to run even harder. I also feared the dark would slow my progress so much that it might take me forever to find them. I cursed myself for not starting a fire before I left.

I let those thoughts go and ran until my eyes and lungs burned.

It's impossible to say the relief I felt when I began to notice certain landmarks, when I knew exactly what lay ahead. I was on the far north fringe of the Russells' land, only a fifteen-minute hard run from the mayor's fields!

My lungs felt like they wanted to come out of my chest by squeezing out of my throat. Every time my feet struck the ground, it felt like a wooden stake was being pounded into my chest, but the sight of known land and the glorious smell of familiar fields kept me moving on.

I burst through the tree line and looked the three or four hundred yards toward the back of the Russells' barn. Two tiny familiar figures moved there.

Could that be . . . ?

No! I ran harder. I waved frantically but was too far off to be noticed.

I had to stop to make certain my eyes weren't playing a dirty trick on me.

Air fought into me through both my nose and mouth. Stopping was a mistake. The moment I did, I weighed tons and sank to my knees.

I looked toward the Russells' home and once my chest stopped heaving and my eyes cleared, it *was* what I thought!

And what a salve for sore eyes!

Patience and Stubby!

They were building a shed not far from the Russells' barn. I'd never in my life been so happy and relieved to see those two!

They were so far off that the sound of their hammering reached me seconds after their arms actually went down. Shouting would be useless.

I waited for my wind to come back to me, struggled to my feet, and started loping toward them.

Once the sound of the hammering and the hitting of the nails started to happen around the same time, I stopped and began shouting.

"Pay! Stubby!"

Nothing.

"Patience! Stubby!"

She looked up and held off her hammering in mid-swing. Putting one hand over her eyes, she yelled, "Benji?"

Stubby looked up too. My strength gave way, the world began whirling madly around me, and the ground rushed right up to my face. I saw a flash of light, then darkness.

The world stopped spinning.

We were on a porch, and Patience was cradling my head. Stubby had brought a ladle of water, and its coolness was divine. The only thought on my mind was to cling to it ferociously so he wouldn't take it away.

I couldn't understand why Pay's voice was so angry. Plus, she was asking a million questions.

"Benjamin Alston? Benji? What is wrong with you? Who's chasing you? Is this a prank? If it is, I'm telling . . ."

I remembered!

I swallowed another ladle of cool water and said, "No! I swear it's no prank. The Madman of Piney Woods has been shot in the back and is lying far off in the woods with Red. He's nearly dead!"

"*What?*"

"Quick, we'll need a couple of fast horses and your travois. I'll get the mayor and Doc."

Pay said, "You wait here, we'll get everything. The Russells aren't home, but they won't mind if we borrow their mare. We'll go home to tell Mother and get the travois, then we'll get Doc and the mayor. We'll tell Mother we're taking Jingle Girl."

I said, "Wait, just let me catch my breath."

She said to me, "You'd only slow us down, Benji. This shouldn't take more than twenty minutes. We'll need you to guide us to them. Stay here and get your wind back."

As she ran toward the barn, she called over her shoulder, "And I'm telling Mother you're still calling him a madman. She's warned you about that."

I waited on the porch.

I was very happy that Patience was in charge.

Time dragged horribly, but finally the hurried clomp of galloping horses approaching grew louder. The mayor was atop his mare; Patience sat behind Stubby on Jingle Girl. The fabric of the travois was folded and its long poles were tied alongside a third horse I didn't recognize. Patience held its reins.

The mayor jumped off his horse.

"Benji! How bad is he —"

His eyes fell on the blood on my shirt and he cringed.

I said, "Sir, he was alive, but barely. He was breathing terribly hard. But where is Doc?"

"He's on his way back from Toronto. You and Patience take the mare and lead us. How far off?"

"An hour and a half." I climbed onto his horse.

He looked to the sky. "We gotta get there afore dark."

Stubby climbed onto the other horse while the mayor took Pay's spot and she settled in behind me.

I kept going over everything, anything to take my mind off how time was flying and how the sun seemed like it was trying to set faster than it ever had before.

Just as we turned into the woods, Patience said, "Benji! What about Red's father and grandmother?"

"What about them?"

"You said Red ran into the woods as soon as he heard about the shooting. Does his family know where he is?"

I hadn't thought of that.

"I don't see how they could."

"Stop the horse. Now!"

She pounded me in the back. "Stop!"

I pulled the mare up.

"Patience, stop hitting me! What is it?"

"What do you think Mother and Father would do if one of us didn't come home one evening? What would be going through their heads?"

Again I was forced to admit, "I just hadn't thought of that."

"I guess you hadn't. Have you thought how if it takes us a couple of hours to find them, it will take maybe four more hours to get him back and for Red to get to Chatham. Red's family will go insane."

She slid off the horse.

She told the mayor, "Sir, Timothy and I are going to have to ride to Chatham and tell Red's father he's not in any kind of trouble. We won't be able to go with you. Timothy?"

"Aw, Patience, I want to —"

"Don't be ridiculous. Timmy, let's go."

Stubby said, "No, I'm going with them."

Pay shouted, "Now!"

Stubby climbed off the horse that was carrying the travois, and the mayor took his place. Pay pulled Stubby up behind her on Jingle Girl.

As they rode off, the mayor said, "Now, there's a child with a great head on her shoulders."

I had no choice but to agree.

→ CHAPTER 41 ←

An Irish Lullaby

RED

Father's best friend, and the only person who consistently gives him a struggle in chess, the Honourable Justice Steven Mariotti, explained to me once how very fortunate I am.

We had been sitting on the front porch one evening waiting for Father to return from the courthouse, when Justice Mariotti said, "Alvin, there will come a time when you'll benefit greatly from your father's advice, and he won't be there to give it to you. It may not happen until you're seventy-five years old, but I guarantee a time will come that you'll desperately want to hear from him for guidance . . . and he won't be around.

"You, however, are blessed to have spent a great deal of time with your father and blessed to be wise enough to have an idea of what he would do, given a particular set of circumstances. Not many young people are so fortunate to be doubly blessed in this manner. When that time comes and, whatever the reason may be, your father is unable to directly answer your questions, simply ask yourself how he'd behave. Then do the same. Trust him and follow suit. You'll not go wrong."

If ever there was a time that I needed to talk to Father and was unable to, this gloomy evening in the forest was it.

What would he do?

I knew he would not abandon the South Woods Lion Man. That was a certainty. I knew no matter how frightening a situation this was and no matter what the cost to himself, he'd do what was decent and honourable. I'd do the same.

I'd promised Benji I'd stay and I would.

I'm certain one of the first things Father would have done is to try to soothe my fears with humour. But I'm afraid I don't know how he'd find humour or levity in this predicament.

"Alvin," he'd often say, "humour and tragedy are such close friends that one is always hand in glove with the other."

So even though this situation was loaded with tragedy, there had to be something comical in it. Maybe the fact that here I, who was rather timid about the forest, was sitting with the head of the man who'd greatly frightened me lying in my lap while night fell would tickle someone's funny bone. Maybe two people trapped within a strangled web of grapevines would be funny to someone.

I'm sure the lads would see some reason to laugh at this.

But they'd also be impressed. Hickman would doubtless compose a speech that would be clever and memorable.

Petey might look at me with admiration and simply say, "Good job, boy."

And the Bayliss boys? After they got over their embarrassment at running from the man whose head I now cradled, I imagine they'd find me to be the bravest lad in Ontario!

Father would doubtless trace that courage to my Irish blood.

He'd probably suggest . . .

The South Woods Lion Man caused all thoughts of comfort and humour to flee when he dragged in another lungful of air.

It was so dark now that the mane of hair circling his head like a halo was all I could clearly make out. I could see nothing two feet away from my outstretched hand.

I prayed more fervently than ever to be delivered from this tomb!

But no matter how much I prayed, this wasn't going to go away.

I imagined Grandmother O'Toole would at that very moment be planning how to punish me for not being home for supper. I imagined Father would tell her something comforting, something along the lines of, "Well, I'll wager when the lad gets home we'll hear about some grand experiment Mr. Victor Greene had him involved in where they lost track of time."

Most frightening was that it was impossible to estimate the passage of time in that accursed darkness. I felt as though I'd been there for days, but was it really hours? Or maybe even minutes? I didn't know.

I thought again of how Father might try to comfort me. Maybe he'd recount one of his funnier cases from long ago.

He always would start by saying, "It was so hilarious that when I told your mother she . . ."

Mother.

I don't know why, but I said the word out loud. "Mother." That's when I cried.

I was good up until that one word.

I hadn't cried for Mother in years, but the tears came so freely, they cascaded onto the South Woods Lion Man's face, causing his face to twitch with each drop.

My sobs quieted the croaking, chirping, cawing night-life immediately around me.

Justice Mariotti had been right; I did wish Father were

here to advise me. But more than that, I wished for something that I hadn't wished for in years: I longed, no, I ached for Mother to be here to tell me not to worry.

The sorrow and pain and loneliness I hadn't felt in years found me in this little cage of grapevines and made me wish for just one more chance to hold her hands to my face and deeply breathe in her scent.

My misery began to slowly rend my heart in two.

Fortunately, before I sank into complete melancholy, my training as a scientist took over. I changed one element in Justice Mariotti's advice to get a different outcome.

Instead of thinking what Father would do, I imagined what Mother would say.

The answer was obvious.

She'd scold me for thinking only of myself in this situation and not about the poor man who'd been foully ambushed and was dying in my arms.

She'd have been greatly disappointed in me, but she'd have been careful in letting me know.

She simply would have tousled my hair and said, "Alvin? First things first. Who's in more need of comforting here, you or this poor soul you're holding?"

An embarrassingly obvious question.

She would say, "We'll get back to you in a minute, but now, let us try to help ease this man's burden."

And I knew what would come next. She'd do one of those magical things mothers do that, on the face of the evidence, don't seem very important or powerful or capable of causing much change, but which do all of that and more.

I used the back of my hand to wipe my tears from the Lion Man's face and began singing the lullaby Mother sang to me those nights I tearfully fought off sleep. I was surprised how, though I hadn't heard it in years, it came back to me with no thought whatsoever.

The South Woods Lion Man and I rocked back and forth, and, heard only by frogs, crickets, and what I pray was a large owl, I sang to him and myself. My falsetto was nowhere near as beautiful as Mother's soprano, but I sang anyway.

Rest tired eyes a while
Sweet is thy baby's smile
Angels are guarding
And they watch o'er thee

Sleep, sleep, grah mo chree
Here on your mamma's knee
Angels are guarding
And they watch o'er thee

The birdeens sing a fluting song
They sing to thee the whole day long
Wee fairies dance o'er hill and dale
For very love of thee

Dream, dream, grah mo chree
Here on your mamma's knee
Angels are guarding and they watch o'er thee
As you sleep may Angels watch over
And may they guard o'er thee

The primrose in the sheltered nook
The crystal stream, the babbling brook
All these things God's hands have made
For very love of thee

Twilight and shadows fall
Peace to His children all
Angels are guarding and they watch o'er thee
As you sleep may Angels watch over
And may they guard o'er thee.

Mother's Irish lullaby worked. Not only did the Lion Man's breaths begin to slow and come more regularly, I also grew calmer myself.

The lullaby squeezed some of the fear and pain out of the little grapevine shelter where the South Woods Lion Man and I fought to keep ourselves in this world.

With the dark now more of a blanket than a prison, I sang the song again.

And again.

And again.

→ Chapter 42 ←

The Betrayal of the Forest

BENJI

I wasn't sure if the mayor noticed, but despair was on me like a bad smell.

I couldn't believe what was happening. The woods were failing me just when I needed them most. They weren't talking at all.

I knew better than trying to reason out where the Madman and Red were. That would just cause disaster and confused wandering. I only had to feel where they were and, like it always had before, the forest would lead me. But we'd made two passes in the area where I was certain they should be and called heartily to no avail.

The dark was inky. I couldn't read any of the signposts I'd memorized.

The swell of noise from crickets and toady-frogs and the cries of prey seemed to pull a curtain further over where we were.

The mayor *could* tell. He said, "What you think, boy? Maybe we should camp and start again in the morning."

Neither of us wanted to do that, but what was the point in getting more and more lost?

"Yes, sir. I'm terribly sorry, I know they're . . ."

"Son, we run outta time. There's no need to apologize for the darkness, Benji."

"Yes, sir. We passed a clearing about five minutes ago; we can camp there. I won't sleep at all and at dawn we can —"

The mayor said, "Don't you worry. . . ."

The mayor is very old, but his ears are just as sharp as mine. We shushed each other and turned our heads toward a sound that seemed to fall around us like a gentle misting rain.

After a few moments, he said, "My goodness, I've finally found out what an angel sounds like!"

He was right. The voice was light and winged and haunting, the beautiful singing of a girl from a heavenly choir. It floated and danced around us. It was near impossible to say where it was coming from.

The mayor said, "It's not the same song, but it reminds me of 'Down in the Valley.' That's the song my ma used to sing to me."

That was the same song Mother sang to me as well, and this angel's song did bring that to mind.

The mayor thought it was coming from one direction and I another.

He hailed, "Hullo! Hullo! Who's there?"

The singing stopped.

A voice cried, "Benji? *Benji!* Is that you?"

I jumped off the horse and ran toward the thicket of vines to my left.

I tore at the vines to get to my friend and the Madman.

Just as their forms emerged from the darkness, the Madman drew a ragged, shuddering breath.

Red looked up at me and smiled.

I smiled back and yelled, "Sir! Over here! They're both here! Red never left him! He's still alive!"

My admiration for my redheaded friend from Chatham burned in me so brightly that I was surprised this part of the forest wasn't lit up like a July afternoon!

Even though he was crying like a newborn lamb, Red was true to his word. He hadn't let the Madman down the whole time.

We spread the travois, and me and the mayor gently lifted the Madman into it.

Red and I rode the mayor's horse, and the mayor followed behind on the other horse, pulling the travois slowly.

Red was exhausted and soon asleep. The mayor said, "Hold on a minute, Benji. Unless we strap that boy to you, he's gonna fall off and break his neck."

The mayor cinched me and Red together with a belt. Red never even woke up.

We rode on, a small parade out of place in the forest. We found a slow easy pace that didn't jar the travois too much and settled into the long ride home.

Although he was quiet and seemed lost in his thoughts, I had to ask the mayor, "Sir, who is he and how do so many people know him?"

The mayor said, "He's my dearest childhood friend, Benji. Just like with you and Spencer, no one said one of our names without saying the other, like it was one name. Just like BenjiandSpencer, it used to be ElijahandCooter."

I waited, but he said nothing more.

"How did he get to be the way he is?"

The mayor said, "Who can say, Benji? I don't have all the pieces, but no one should be treated like this."

CHAPTER 43

Sleep

RED

I was surprised to awake in the dark on the back of a horse.

Even more surprising was I seemed to be strapped to someone else on the horse.

Most surprising of all was I didn't care.

I hoped when I awoke properly, someone would explain all of this to me.

But until then . . .

→ CHAPTER 44 ←

Madness Is Only One Letter from Sadness

BENJI

There was another five minutes when the only sounds our parade made were the every-once-in-a-while clomp when one of the horse's shoes hit a stone and the shushing sound the travois made as it was pulled along.

I figured the mayor was through talking. I guess it was too painful for him.

Another ten minutes passed before he surprised me. "Your mother was only a babe back then, Benji, back during the Civil War in the States. Everybody who was old enough was going to America and enlisting in Mr. Lincoln's army.

"Cooter always did look younger than he was, so 'stead of enlisting him as a soldier, they took him on as a drummer boy. He joined up with the Sixth Regiment United States Colored.

"He never would talk about it, but he had some times in that war that no one should ever have to go through. No one. Especially no one as kind as Cooter.

319

"From what other folk told me, I pieced together that Cooter had done something very brave in a battle. It's one of those things that never make the history books, but he come out of it a hero. The government of the United States gave him a huge ceremony, said he was the bravest coloured man in the army. Gave him ribbons and medals and all sorts of gifts. They wanted him to travel 'round the country talking to other coloured folk to convince them to join the army. He said he'd do it, but he wanted to come home to Buxton for a bit first. Told them that with his head as fogged up as it was, he needed to go where he knew he could clear it some.

"We thought for sure something horrible had happened to him. He was supposed to catch the train from Washington to Detroit, then from Windsor on up to Buxton. I remember how folks had everything set up to welcome him, but when the train pulled in, no Cooter. No message and no Cooter. We waited outside every train for a week afore we give up on him.

"Thought for sure he got waylaid somewhere. Folks speculated he had to be dead, 'cause otherwise why didn't he come home? How come he didn't send word?

"It was just last month he told me how come he wasn't on that train. Said back in eighteen hundred and sixty-five, when he was going from Washington to Detroit to get to Buxton, he got the first chance to be alone and think. Told

320

me he had time to see through most of the fog and knew he couldn't come home. Said he knew he wasn't a hero; he was the opposite and was deeply ashamed. Just walked off the train in Pennsylvania.

"It was nine years later he finally found his way back home to Buxton. Folks were so pleased to see him, they wanted to throw him that same parade and picnic we'd planned near a decade afore. Still wanted to celebrate him fighting for us, let him know he was Buxton's biggest hero.

"I could tell he was 'bout split in two over all the attention. Buxton had changed in that decade and Cooter had changed even more. They waren't no match anymore. Cooter refused to let 'em celebrate anything about him, got peeved if you called him a hero. Wasn't comforted being around most folk . . . no, he wasn't comforted being 'round no one, so he lived in the woods.

"He never would tell me what happened. I found out later that he was in a fight called the Battle of Fort Pillow. Fought side by side with white Yankee soldiers and all of 'em got overrun by the rebs. The Confederates were horrible harsh on the white troops they captured, but they were beyond harsh on the coloured. They cut the scalp offen any of the black soldiers they found, dead or alive.

"I know when he first came back, Cooter told me he couldn't sleep inside 'cause he kept hearing screams. He couldn't get the sound out of his head. I figure it must be the sounds of those troops being murdered that plagued him.

"Best I can figure, that's what set him off to go into the woods the way he did."

I wondered if Mr. Swan had told anyone about the Madman getting scalped. Probably not. He was one of the people who always looked to protect him. I wouldn't say anything either.

We rode on in silence.

Before long, the mayor said, "It waren't but in the last year that something changed. He started coming out of the woods whilst I was in the fields and began talking to me. Giving me bits and pieces 'bout what happened in the war, going over old times in Buxton.

"Seemed he knowed his time was short. He didn't say the words di-rect, but every time we'd talk, I knew Cooter's words had a lot of good-bye in 'em. I caint tell if he was just looking for some companionship or looking to get some things offen his mind. Whatever, he was slow and gentle 'bout doing it, like he used to be 'bout everything."

We finally broke out of the woods and were on the road to Buxton. Since we could go faster without jostling the mayor's friend too much, we'd be home in half an hour.

CHAPTER 45

Going Home

RED

Somehow, in spite of the darkness, Benji had led us back to Buxton.

It was after two in the morning when our tired group knocked on the Buxton doctor's door and aided the South Woods Lion Man, whose real name I was told is Mr. Cooter Bixby, into the doctor's house.

Benji and I rode to the Alstons' home and within moments of getting there, after a hurricane of hugs and kisses and tears, Mrs. Alston said, "Your father must be losing his mind, Alvin. No time for rest now, Benji. You two get back on the road to Chatham."

We began the forty-five-minute trip with me sitting behind my friend.

I was nodding to sleep when Benji said, "Red, the song you were singing."

"Yes?"

"How do you know it?"

"I'm not certain; it's something I've always known. It's

called the 'Cradle Song.' It's the Irish lullaby my mother would sing to me at night."

"*Irish?*"

"Yes. You know I'm Irish."

"Both me and the mayor think it calls to mind a song our mothers sang to us."

"Really? How's that possible?"

"It beats me."

I was far too tired to give it much thought. I only worried how even though Patience had warned them, Father and Grandmother O'Toole must be in a horrible state by now.

Those were my last thoughts before the soft clomping of the horse's hooves and the gentle swaying of our easy pace eased me to sleep. As I clung to Benji's back, I heard Mother's voice.

"*Sleep, sleep, grah mo chree, here on your mamma's knee. Angels are guarding and they watch o'er thee.*"

The terror and hopelessness I'd felt hours before were no more. And once again I was embraced by the words Mother would say to me at night, may peace, like a river, come.

Benji awoke me by saying, "Red? Red! You're home."

It is difficult to describe my joy when I saw our bay window illuminated against the darkness of the street.

Father sat in his rocker asleep, with his legs crossed, his head thrown back, and a shawl that Grandmother O'Toole must have placed on him draped over his shoulders.

The moment I saw him, it was as though he sensed I was there and jerked awake. He looked toward the clock, then out of the window.

Benji and I jumped off the horse just as Father arose and rushed toward the door. We met on the porch.

"Alvin! Thank God you're safe!"

He hugged me, then pulled Benji into his embrace as well.

He kissed the top of Benji's head. "Thank you so much for bringing him home, young man."

The tiredness that struck me on the road to Chatham finally grabbed ahold of Benji. He walked over to one of the porch chairs and sagged into it.

Father held me at arm's length.

"Are you all right, son?"

"I am now, Father."

"Do you want to wait until the morning to talk?"

I didn't. We sat on the top porch step, and I told my Father about the night.

He squeezed me to him and said, "I'm very proud of you, Alvin. You showed great character and courage. Your mother would neither be surprised nor have expected any less."

As my father smiled at me, I knew it had not been any grand show of courage on my part that had gotten me through this night. Rather, it was because this man, whose eyes fell upon me with so much love, had let me borrow enough of his strength to know that if I kept my head, I'd get through. It was because my mother had done a million small miracles to bring home the lesson of thinking of others before I thought of myself.

As Father and I hugged on the porch step, and Benji dozed in the chair, I'd never felt safer or more secure.

Those feelings fled when I heard, "Chester? 'Tis he? Is the lad safe?"

I could hear Grandmother O'Toole's bedroom door close and the rapid ting-a-ling, ting-a-ling of her cane as she walked quickly toward the front door.

She saw me clinging to Father on the top step and came through the door, her open arms stretched toward me. She cried, "Saints be praised! Our prayers are answered. I told ye, Chester, I told you there'd be no —"

She looked to the chair where Benji sat.

And she froze.

The oddest thing was that her expression never changed, not one bit of her face moved or shifted, yet her look went from one of great relief to one of absolute horror, absolute hatred. And although her hands remained in the exact same pose, with no movement whatsoever, they no longer seemed to be spread in welcome but were now angry claws aimed at my friend from Buxton.

The only physical change that took place was that she began to swell, growing with each angry breath she drew. Becoming huge again.

She spat, "And who is this little —"

Father stiffened and stood. I'd rarely heard him raise his voice, but he nearly barked, *"Mother O'Toole!* This is the young man who rescued Alvin in the woods. His name is Benjamin Alston and we are deeply in his debt."

Benji had awakened and now said, "Hello, ma'am."

Grandmother O'Toole began the process of shrinking.

Father continued, his tone sharp. "He was our guest for supper while you were in Windsor and it will be our honour to provide him with shelter tonight. Benjamin, Alvin will sleep on the cot and you shall sleep in his bed."

Grandmother O'Toole's body shook so violently and the cane bell tinkled so steadily that every sin ever done by every Irishman in all of Irish history was forgiven. Her eyes became slits and, without another word, she staggered back into the house.

Benji stretched and said, "Thank you, sir, but I promised my parents I'd come back tonight."

Father said, "Well, in that case, I insist upon escorting

you home. We'll go borrow a horse. Alvin, try to sleep. I'll be back in a couple of hours at the most."

Benji said, "I'll see you in Chatham next week, Red."

"Not if I see you first, you won't."

"Ha-ha."

Benji climbed back on the horse. Father took the reins and led them toward the city stables.

I called, "Benji?"

He looked over his shoulder. "Yes?"

"Thank you."

"No, Red, thank *you*."

"I'm serious," Benji said. "What you did was real important. Thank you."

"And I'm serious too. Thank you."

Each of us was too tired to continue thanking the other. I collapsed into the chair Benji had used and waited for Father's return. My intentions were to greet him when he got back, but sleep once again overpowered me.

I awoke with a start.

"Father?"

But the road in front of the house was empty.

I went inside to see what time it was.

The moment I stepped into the hallway, a most unusual sound greeted me. A strong, steady HAR-HAR-

HAR filled the living room and the foyer, as if someone in the house were sawing lumber.

It was coming from the kitchen. I opened the kitchen door and my reaction was shock. All the relief that had filled me this night was washed away by what I saw.

She was hunched over the sink, the steel wool that is ordinarily saved for only the dirtiest, most heavily stained pots squeezed tightly in her joined fists. She was scouring mercilessly at a plate. A plate from which she no doubt thought Benji might have eaten.

In five years of living with Grandmother O'Toole, I'd never seen her hair in anything other than the bun that sat in the exact same place day after day atop her head. I'd never before seen her hair loose. It was longer than I could have imagined. It hung down to hide her face, much like a silver curtain swaying back and forth as she bore down on the plate to scrub it clean.

Next to her on the counter was a pile of plates and silverware and glasses she'd already cleaned. Another plate, this one broken, was beside the pile of dishes. Apparently, she'd leaned into it so heavily that, unable to withstand her weight or her anger, it had snapped in half. Although most times, this would have been a major catastrophe and cause for mourning and curses on her part, she didn't even seem to notice, so fixated on sanitizing the kitchen was she.

She also didn't notice, as she rasped at the plate with the steel wool, the water had lost all of its suds and now splashed haphazardly, leaving flecks and specks of bright pink on the sink and counter and cupboards as well as the floor. So fiercely did she want to rid the dishes of any trace of Benji, she was unaware she'd rubbed her knuckles bloody.

I reflected on how my feelings had changed toward Grandmother O'Toole. Up until recently, I'd been so afraid of her. Not only because of the beatings she'd dish out with her shoe, or because of the ambushes that only the northern Irish cane bell had brought to an end, but more so due to her words.

While her shoe could do no more than sting and leave bruises, and the cane most often caused only bumps, both of which faded unnoticed with time, the words she said had wormed their way deep inside of me.

Maybe Benji had been right during one of our conversations, that maybe the adage "Sticks and stones may break my bones, but words can never harm me" is more a wish than a fact. Maybe it *was* made up by a person who was very good with words and used the saying as a way to hide their true power. For yes, the sticks and shoes and the stones and canes can cause pain and damage, but it was indeed the words that were truly deadly.

When I was a young lad, Father used to read to me every night. One of the things that stuck with me was the author who wrote, "If you want to know a person's true character, take note of the adjectives they use to describe other people."

No amount of time could make me forget the venomous names Grandmother O'Toole constantly called me . . . and nearly everyone else. But now, as I watched the way her hatred caused her to bleed, I understood what Father's author had been telling me. The names and vicious words weren't a description of something in me, or in the Canadians or the Englishmen or the people from Buxton, they were merely a reflection of this tiny woman.

I knew as long as I could keep an eye on her, she would never again be able to harm me. I also knew I'd never see her grow in size again. I finally clearly saw her for the tiny, angry, pathetic, hate-filled wee person she truly is.

Not so long ago, there was a common practice called "bleeding," wherein it was believed that sickness was caused by bad humours in the blood. It was thought the best way to cure an ill person was to cut them and allow some of the bad blood to escape. Barbers were trained to do this, which is why the barber pole is always red and white.

Perhaps Grandmother O'Toole's bleeding knuckles would drain away some of the sickness of hatred that ran through her veins. But no, that was ridiculous. I knew as long as she lived, her hatred would as well.

I closed the kitchen door and went to bed.

I would lose not one more night's sleep nor spend one moment more of worry and embarrassment for who she is.

I had no control over that.

I smiled and let my head sink into my pillow, content to know I am truly my mother and father's child.

→ CHAPTER 46 ←

A Madman's Final Wishes

BENJI

Two days after the doctor had done all he could and worked to make him as comfortable as possible, Mother, Father, and the mayor decided it would be best if the Madman of Piney Woods was brought to our home.

They thought the best place he could stay was Pay's bedroom.

Before they brought him, Patience and Stubby were sent to Uncle June and Aunt Nina's in Toronto. Mother and Father didn't tell them, but the plan was that they'd wait there until the Madman got better.

Mother and me had been keeping a vigil ever since. We would read to each other and wait for Father and the mayor to finish work before they came to sit with us.

On the second day after the Madman of Piney Woods was brought to us, Mother and me were sitting in the parlour when she said to me, "Benji, I want to talk to you about something."

"Yes, Mother?"

"Do you know by not sending you to stay with Uncle June, your father and I are placing a lot of confidence and faith in you?"

"Really?"

"Yes. Life can be a pretty brutal experience, and we feel you are mature enough to cope with some of the rough parts of being alive."

This was becoming more and more mysterious. I looked at Mother but kept my mouth closed. I didn't want to commit myself to saying I understood what she was talking about. Plus, a good reporter learns to wait for people to finish their say.

"The doctor has said he doesn't think Uncle Cooter's going to live much longer. And as sad as that is, there are other things we have to take into consideration. . . ."

She looked at me as if she needed some reassurance that I understood.

I nodded in a halfway way.

"I know my babies are not a superstitious lot, but I don't want Patience and Stubby to know, if it does come down to that, and he passes away here . . ."

She put her book aside and said, "Benji, I wouldn't want Patience to know he died in her bedroom. Am I clear, son?"

That only made good sense.

"Yes, Mother, I'll take it to the grave with me."

"That won't be necessary. Just make sure you don't slip up. I know you'll keep your word."

And I would.

On the third evening the Madman was in our house, the doctor clomp-clomp-clomped down the stairs.

Mother, Father, the mayor, and me looked up expectantly.

The doctor came into the parlour.

"He's grown quite weak. An infection is trying to set up in his right lung. I think he's close."

The mayor covered his face and drew a ragged breath through his hands. Mother and Father hugged, and I looked on, not knowing what to do.

Doc said, "He's asked to see all of you."

The Madman had been coming in and out of consciousness for days and was making sense only half the time.

They all stood up.

I said, "I'll wait down here."

The doctor said, "He asked for you specifically."

Mother said, "He asked for *Benji*?"

Doc said, "Yes. Well, he didn't ask for him by name, but he said, 'TooToo's boy who knows the woods.'"

Mother said, "But, Doctor, is he . . ."

The doctor said, "He's quite lucid."

Why did he want to see *me*? I wished I had time to get a dictionary and look up *lucid* so I'd have some idea of what to expect when I went in that bedroom.

Mother reached her hand toward me. "Come, son."

I followed them up the stairs. Father tapped lightly, then opened Pay's bedroom door. Heavy curtains had been put over the windows. The usual smell of the room, flowers Pay would keep in a vase on her bedside table, had been replaced by a quiet, stale-air smell.

The Madman was a bunch of small shadowy lumps under the covers of Pay's bed. He was still taking uncommonly long spells between each wheezed breath.

Father and I stood at the foot of the bed. The mayor sat on one side and took the Madman's right hand while Mother sat on the other side of the bed and took his left hand. Father draped an arm around my shoulder. I hugged his waist.

The Madman looked at Mother and smiled.

He turned his head to the mayor. "I know it don't make much sense. And it's straight-up foolish and prideful. But I'm worried 'bout what you and TooToo here . . . is gonna have to say 'bout me at my graveside."

The mayor patted his hand. "No need to be talking

nonsense like that. Doc said, far as he can tell, all signs are pointing to you still being alive, and as long as you want to stay that way, it won't change. Besides, might be some laws against us putting you in the ground afore you quit gabbing and cooled off proper."

The Madman chuckled, then winced.

"That's all well and good. But there's some things I don't need no doctor to tell me. Things I can feel. There's a tiredness I ain't got no desire to get rid of. Seems like it seeped right on into my marrow. Make me want to sleep deep. Make it so I truly don't mind not waking back up. That's where I'm at."

He looked right at Mother.

"TooToo, that biggest boy of yourn. What's his name?"

"He's right here at the foot of the bed, Uncle Cooter. His name is Benjamin."

A warmth washed over me as Mother, Father, and the mayor looked at me with just as many questions in their eyes as I had in mine.

The Madman said, "At first, when I knowed what was happening, I wanted to break the necks of him and that little white boy for not letting me just pass quiet in the forest."

He laughed softly. "I gots to say, though, there ain't nothing that'll convince you you's dead more than coming to and seeing some bright-red little white boy weeping and wailing right on top of you. I think them was the most confused minutes I ever spent in my life.

"After I thought on it whilst laying here, I sees I was wrong, I owes them two. By tracking me down and bringing me here, they give me the chance to get some things straight afore I crosses over.

"Yessir, I 'preciate them boys and what they done. Whilst I was laying out in the woods afore they found me, the only regret I had was that there was some things I shoulda said. There was some folk what I owed thanks to, some friends what needed to be clear on how I feel 'bout 'em. An' n'em boys give me the chance to do it afore I dies."

The mayor protested, his voice weak, "Now, listen here, that's enough talk about —"

The Madman cut him off.

"Please. Please. All I'm asking for is to get some words in and for some last requests to get filled. Can't you give me that?"

The mayor paused, then said, "Fine, you stubborn hard-head old man. What is it you want?"

The Madman said, "Look, we gotta be honest. Ain't nothing peaceful 'bout dying . . . with a hole blowed in your back. I know a restful death in bed at a old age . . . ain't what's been writ for me. But I needs you to say that's how y'all's gonna act. Y'all's got to believe me when I say I'm peaceful."

He looked at Mother and Father, then me. They nodded, so I did too.

He turned to the mayor, who slowly shook his head.

The Madman said, "TooToo, *you* gonna have to convince him I'm at peace, I'm at long last at peace."

He smiled at the mayor.

"Look at him. Old as he is, he still fra-gile. That ain't never gonna change. He a good man, yessir . . . he gunn come 'round. And, TooToo, you's close to the roots; you's half-blood African. You comes from strength. Even if he don't wanna do it, I'm-a need you to hold his feet to the fire till he do. Don't let him mourn too long or hard."

Mother said, "I'm giving you my word I'll do that, Uncle Cooter. Just let me know how you want your service conducted."

"Ooh, child, I don't want nothing fancy as no service. I just wants a few special folk saying g'bye to ease me over."

Tears ran down the mayor's cheeks.

The Madman squeezed his hand. "Don't cry, my friend. All I wants is for the three of you to say something what will . . . give me a good introduction to the folk on the other side."

He lifted his head slightly from the pillow and looked right at me.

"Benjamin?"

I couldn't help it, I held Father tighter.

Father nudged me.

"Yes, sir?"

"Like I tolt you, I always seent myself in you. In the way you know and respect them woods. Elijah done tolt me how hard you's working at being a reporter and all and that's good. You needs to take care your business."

His head dropped back into the dented pillow.

"You gotta be careful, boy. Life ain't fair; it ain't got no conscience 'bout letting one bad choice you make as a child be the thing what colour every waking minute you has thereafter. You gotta remember to treat each moment and each person as precious, treat 'em all with the same respect I seent you treating them woods."

"Yes, sir."

He chuckled and winced again and said to Mother, "See how I was right when I said he just like me? I could see them words going in his right ear and whistling out the left! But the boy smarter than me. Who know, maybe it's gonna stick."

He looked back at me.

"I wants you to choose where I's to be put to rest. And to say something 'bout how I loved that forest. Don't no one else in these parts but you and me know that feeling. I wants you to give my thanks 'bout that. 'Bout the good years it give me. You ain't got to do it at my graveside. Just go out in the woods. In the sunshine. You gonna know what to do, listen to the forest."

"I will, sir."

He pressed his lips to Mother's hand. Mother wiped at the tears pooling in his eyes.

"TooToo, our future, our hope, you know how special you been to all of us. Ain't no little girl been loved more than we loved you. I'm so sorry 'bout how things come to pass. I'd-a done more if I coulda, but sometime —"

Mother said, "Hush now. You'll always be my dear uncle. You've never shown me anything but love and I feel the same way about you."

He said, "Yes, TooToo, I always have. Could you say a word or two 'bout how I didn't never hurt no one, that . . . I didn't even understand what —"

Mother said, "What's all this, Uncle Cooter? You don't need to say another word. I'll celebrate your kind spirit and gentle nature. You let me say what I have to say about you. My heart will lead me to the right words. I'll tell about how much we prayed you'd get comfortable enough to come back and live with us, about how much we loved you. I only wish you could hear what I and so many other people in Buxton will have to say about you."

He sighed. "Another coupla things I want. Bury me quick. In a canvas shroud. I don't want nothing slowing me returning to the woods.

"You got to promise me. TooToo, you won't let 'em put my corpse to lay staring up at the ceiling of some church, neither. I seent some n'em funerals they calls celebrations, where the body's propped up there. Maybe it's just me, but I always found it a little hard to celebrate when one of the folks in the room is dead. Always thought that ain't no celebration, that's bee-zarre."

Mother said, "I promise I'll take care of all that, Uncle Cooter, don't you worry. I'm praying there's no need for it, but I'm going to see you get your wishes. You just rest easy knowing that's as good as taken care of."

He turned his head to the mayor. He brought their clasped hands to his cheek. They stayed that way for the longest, before the Madman said, "And you. My oldest friend. I been feeling different for the last coupla years. Been thinking 'bout easing myself back into Buxton."

The mayor said, "I know, I know."

"But I played my cards too late; it wasn't meant to be. 'Bout the only thing I feel cheated out of by leaving now is that you and me ain't gonna have time to talk 'bout our growing up like brothers. We ain't gonna have no chance to sit and remember.

"I gotta tell you, them memories been the same as friends to me in times when I felt low. Or lonely. Or scairt."

He chuckled softly. "Which was pretty much all the

time. Thank you, my dear brother, thank you for them memories."

The mayor sobbed, "I coulda done more. I shoulda done more."

The Madman smiled and said, "Uh-uh, none of that. You's a old man now; you shoulda got all that fra-gileness out your system long ago."

"Now, Timothy, Benjamin, Hope . . ."

For some reason, it was startling to hear him say Mother's given name.

". . . if y'all'll excuse us, I know this ain't something he's looking forward to . . ." — he cupped the mayor's chin and lifted his face — "but I'm 'bout to go home . . . and you and I needs to talk alone, Elijah."

The mayor looked into his friend's eyes, took a deep breath, then nodded.

"Yes, Cooter, we do. We waited too long."

I followed my parents' lead. We each kissed the Madman's forehead, then the mayor's. We closed the door behind us and left the old friends to make their peace and say their good-byes.

Two hours passed before the mayor opened the bed-room door.

We knew.

He was crying.

He said in a soft voice, "He's gone."

Mother stood and wrapped her arms around him. Father joined them and so did I.

Through tears the mayor said, "The only other thing he wants when we bury him . . . was a baby to be there. Didn't matter who, just wanted the fresh life of a Buxton babe to be there."

Father said, "Where you suppose he wanted to be buried, Benji?"

Without thinking, I said, "I know."

There was a small clearing north of our home where three deer trails crossed. It was a spot ringed by towering oaks, a sixty-foot-round spot where the giant trees had decided not to grow, like they were guarding the circle, like they were waiting. The place had a calmness to it. It was somewhere I'd stretched out and rested before. I'd even fallen asleep there.

Maybe it was the woods telling me, but that was the place.

Father said, "Is it in thick forest?"

"No, sir, it's a clearing."

"OK, you go get the horses. I'll get a couple picks and shovels. How far off is it?"

"About three miles."

"All right," Father said. "Mr. Mayor, you get home to your family till we come. Me and Benji's gonna dig the grave. TooToo, you telegraph Chatham and see if Red can be here early tomorrow morn. The sooner we get this done, the better."

We hugged again and went our separate ways to do what we needed to help the Madman of Piney Woods, Uncle Cooter, go home the way he wanted.

CHAPTER 47

He Has Passed

RED

Grandmother O'Toole was gone when I woke up.

The house had been quiet and peaceful in the days since.

I'm certain neither Father nor I missed the tinkling of the northern Irish cane bell, but after the third day, Father began to worry.

He'd made some inquiries, and finally Great-Aunt Margaret sent a telegram from Windsor, saying that Grandmother O'Toole was there safe and would be staying for a while.

I don't know what prevented me from talking with Father about what happened until the morning of the fourth day. I suppose Father had been waiting for me to bring it up, and I for him.

I'd made our breakfast and sat at the table.

I didn't realize how angry I was at Grandmother O'Toole until I started speaking.

With no preamble whatsoever, just as a forkful of scrambled eggs was about to disappear in my mouth, I dove into it.

"Father. It doesn't make sense. She told me there were things you had to twirl the cat to learn, but she's twirled the cat over and over again in her life and has learned nothing.

"She's twirled the cat about poverty, yet she hates poor people. She's twirled the cat about being mistreated because of one's circumstances, yet she hates me because my hair is red and hates *anyone* whose skin is darker than ours. She's twirled the cat about being beaten, yet she would club me to death if it weren't for the cane bell."

I slammed my fork on the table.

"Doesn't it seem only logical that if a person has been through all of the grief she has, they'd have nothing but compassion for anyone else who's been through the same? Shouldn't that make her realize firsthand what a horrible predicament other people are in? Who but an uncaring beast would heap more anguish onto someone else who's also been downtrodden? Who but a monster would inflict the same unfair pain that they'd been exposed to upon another human being?"

Father said nothing, but nodded again and again.

He was allowing me to vent my spleen, and I really wanted to. The fact that he didn't stop me encouraged me to go on.

"She should be institutionalized *immediately*! There's no need for me to visit which asylum she'll go to. If you

347

force me to pick, I'll choose the one that is the absolute worst. None of them could possibly be harsh enough to punish her."

I knew exactly what Father's next four words would be. I'd worked myself up into such a lather, he had almost no choice but to say in a heavy Irish brogue, "Ah, Alvin, me lad —"

I interrupted, "I must warn you, Father, I shall not easily be talked out of my anger."

Father looked very serious. "I have no intention of talking you out of the way you feel, son. If that's what you're expecting me to do, we can end the conversation here and chat about the weather. If, however, you and I try to understand together what is behind your grandmother's deplorable actions and deplorable condition, that we may be able to accomplish."

Father knew what I needed. I felt like begging him, *Please, let's do that,* but I only nodded.

"Alvin, I believe it all boils down to fear. Your grandmother is the most frightened person I've ever known."

"But, Father, what does she have to be afraid of?"

"Ah, son, I'd have to be much brighter than I am to know that. I only know that fear is a great corrupter. And I'm afraid that given enough time, fear is the great killer of the human spirit.

"She's only opened the door a crack and allowed you to

see a mere fraction of the horrors she's lived through. And though we may try, there's simply no way we'll ever be able to understand or be able to say we would have responded in a manner any different than she did."

Father put his fork down.

"I never imagined I'd tell you this, Alvin, but right after your dear mother passed away, there was a long conversation about Grandmother O'Toole coming to stay here in Chatham and help raise you. I had serious, serious doubts, son. I know this fear she is infected with is something that fights to keep itself alive; it wants to be passed from mother and father to daughter and son and on and on and on. It lasts for countless generations."

Father's voice cracked. "I loved your mother so much and was horribly lost back then, Alvin, horribly."

My heart broke for Father and at the same time a huge wave of shame swept over me. I'd always known how powerful my longing for Mother was, yet I'd never considered that Father was going through the same thing, or, and it seemed impossible knowing the depth of my own feelings of loss, his pain was perhaps even more raw and jagged. He'd loved her longer and knew her much better than I could have in the five years she was with me.

Father recovered, saying, "I didn't know if I wanted Mother O'Toole to be anywhere near you. But I did need help. Even though I was destroyed, I reasoned that since your grandmother's fear hadn't poisoned your mother, there was an excellent chance it wouldn't poison you either.

"You, Alvin, are the proof I was right. You, my beloved son, are the evidence that the human spirit is strong and resilient, that given a chance, without interference from so many of the indignities life pours upon us, our spirits want to soar. Want to love.

"Yes, for whatever the reasons, sometimes, as in Mother O'Toole's case, the spirit has cringed in the face of the horrors that have gnawed at it. It has slowly folded in upon itself, waging an unending war, fighting demons real and imagined, turning into exactly what it is that has so horribly scarred it, condensing and strengthening and dishing out the same hatred that it has experienced. These things happen.

"But some of the time, son, the opposite happens and we end up with Alvin Stockard. We are surprised and gladdened to look up and after thirteen years we have you.

"Someone who is kind, and loving and gentle.

"Someone who is proof that, though strong, hatred cannot endure.

"Someone who is not only my strength, but who is the hope for the future. The hope and the evidence that the Grandmother O'Tooles of the world can be overcome."

"Oh, Father."

It was childish of me and probably quite embarrassing for Father, but I left my chair and sat in his lap.

Father wrapped his arms around me, touseled my hair, and kissed the top of my head.

The beat of his heart comforted me beyond measure.

"Alvin, I don't know if she's coming back. If she does, fine; if she doesn't, that's fine as well. But as I've told you, we must remember she gave birth to the best part of both of us. For that, we are in her debt.

"And perhaps you can see her in the way I've chosen to. I choose to believe she has grandly taken a bullet, Alvin, not so much for me but for you. I choose to believe that so much pain and fear and hatred have racked her tiny body that perhaps the universe has said, 'Enough! It ends here,' and has taken pity and has not exposed her children and her children's children to quite as much."

I love my father a great deal. I know he is a very wise, very intelligent man. However, I choose to believe he didn't get to be this way on his own. I choose to believe much of what he's passed on to me were lessons learned from my mother. I choose to believe I have two loving parents wrapped in one.

Later that night, there was a knock at the front door.

"Evening, Judge. Telegram."

Father took the telegram from Mr. Dones.

"Oh, dear, Alvin."

I read the news.

ALVIN STOP PLEASE COME TO OUR HOME TOMORROW
6 AM STOP HE HAS PASSED STOP REQUESTED YOUR
PRESENCE STOP MRS ALSTON STOP

"What should I do, Father?"

"I suppose you should go to the stables to borrow a horse, then get directly to bed so you can leave here by four thirty in the morning."

→ CHAPTER 48 ←

Church

BENJI

The forest became so thick that me and Father had to tie the horses and, carrying the picks and shovels, walk the final two hundred yards to the spot.

Father entered the round clearing first. "It *is* beautiful, son. I don't know how many times I've been near here and never noticed this."

"I know, unless you know what you're looking for, you'd walk right by it. I'm going to ask Red to try to find out why the trees won't grow in this circle."

"So this is where y'all come when you and Spencer run off into the woods."

"No, sir, I've never brought Spencer or anyone else here. You're the first person I've shown this to."

"Well, I'm flattered, Benji, and I bet your Uncle Cooter would approve."

"I think he would."

Father said, "Should we lay him in the centre or closer to the woods?"

"I think the centre. There won't be as many roots."

I used the shovel to scrape away some of the carpet of dead leaves in the middle of the clearing.

Father was still looking up, admiring the trees.

"It's like church in here."

"Father! Come!"

As I used the shovel edge to move away the dead leaves, I found a spot where the earth had already been disturbed.

Father came to me.

"Look."

He said, "Looks like some animal decided this was a good place to bury something too, Benji."

"Only raccoons and foxes will bury their food, Father. This area is much too big."

Father said, "Well, let's just move off over here."

He pointed a short distance away.

"Wait, I want to see."

I dug into the loose soil. After going down only a foot, the shovel struck something. At first I thought it was a root.

I dug again. This time a piece of the root broke off. I bent over. It was too dry and too white to be a root. I picked the piece up.

It was an antler.

I smiled.

I shoveled the dirt back over the spot.

"Father, this is exactly where he'd want to be buried."

We began to dig right next to the Old Grandfather of the woods.

CHAPTER 49

The Service

RED

The place Mr. Bixby had chosen to be buried was beautiful. Huge trees ringed a clearing where Benji and his father had dug a deep hole, a pile of dirt and a gray canvas cocoon waiting by the side.

There were probably twenty of us who had made the journey to pay our last respects. The ages seemed to range from a woman in her nineties, who had been carried from where we'd tied our horses, to a quiet, darling, fat-faced baby. I couldn't help noticing I was the only white person to come.

Ropes were used to lower the canvas shroud into the hole.

Mr. Freeman, the mayor of Buxton, was holding the baby. He said, "Cooter asked that this be short and simple, and it will be. He asked that a few of us say some things to help him over.

"This is a lesson for me that's too late for the learning, but for the young ones here, for Patience and Timothy, for Alvin and Benji, for my son, little Levon David Freeman, don't wait. If your heart is directing you to do a kindness, to reach a hand out, don't wait.

"He who hesitates is lost."

He scooped up a handful of dirt and held his palm open so the baby could take some as well. He tossed what was left in his hand onto the shroud; the baby did the same.

The mayor hung his head and said, "Hope."

Benji's mother said, "Uncle Cooter was always kind. Even when storms raged in him that we knew nothing about, his kindness never left him. He'll be missed."

She threw dirt on the shroud and said, "Mrs. Solomon."

The woman who had been carried here walked carefully to the grave. Hers were the only dry eyes in the circle.

For such a frail, elderly woman, her voice was strong.

"We loved this boy. And he knowed it. It's time to let him be."

Someone handed her some of the earth and she dropped it into the hole.

Once Benji and his father and the mayor and I filled the hole, all the mourners held hands in a circle around the fresh grave.

Benji's mother started the song, her voice a beautiful soprano:

> *Down in the valley, the valley so low*
> *Hang your head over, hear the wind blow*

Hear the wind blow, dear, hear the wind blow
Hang your head over, hear the wind blow.

Roses love sunshine, violets love dew
Angels in Heaven know I love you
Know I love you, dear, know I love you
Angels in Heaven know I love you . . .

I didn't know the words, but the tune was familiar. I recognized it as the song the mayor and Benji told me Mother's "Cradle Song" reminded them of.

The song echoed eerily through the circle until it sounded as though we were singing a round.

For seconds after the last chorus, we were bombarded by gently fading music.

We left Mr. Bixby to his eternal rest.

CHAPTER 50

Endings

BENJI

A month had passed since we'd buried Uncle Cooter.

Nothing changed.

Even though now that school had started and I'd only work there on weekends, Miss Cary kept me running out of her office with "Now, off you go," Wimpy was still teaching me the strange language of printing, Pay and Stubby were still geniuses with wood and still pains in my buttocks, and Mother and Father were still where they've always been, there.

But I found out two things about myself.

First, I learned that I needed the woods. After Uncle Cooter died, I'd stayed away. When I first went into them, I missed knowing he might be watching over me. Instead of being reminded of that sadness, I stayed away.

But the forest called me back. And if I took Spencer with me, I didn't feel the loneliness quite so much.

The second thing I learned about myself was that almost as much as I need the forest, I need to write.

I followed Miss Cary's suggestion to write every day, and it had become a real habit. But I didn't follow her suggestion not to throw away anything I'd written. Some of the time, what I wrote was so bad I didn't want anyone to see it, and some of the time, what I wrote made me feel too sad and I'd toss it.

I'd tried a million times to write an article about Uncle Cooter, but the words refused to cooperate. I even pretended I had a deadline to see if that might make them come easier, but all it did was make me feel terrible when the deadline went whooshing past.

Whenever one of the older people tells Mother that bad news always comes in threes, she has an answer for them. She says, "Maybe, but good news rides in on the same horse."

And, as usual, she was right.

The first bit of good news came when Pay and Stubby agreed to take me on as *their* apprentice. It was kind of humiliating to ask, and I'm not sure why I did, but it always seemed like they had so much fun together.

The second bit of good news was when, early one Saturday, Spencer knocked ferociously on our front door.

"Benji! You'll never guess what happened!"

Before I could open my mouth, he blurted out, "Hickman Holmely's father got a job in Memphis, Tennessee!"

360

"That's good, but why are you so excited?"

"They're moving to Memphis! The Upper Ontario Forensics Competition is only for folks who live in Ontario!"

I was thrilled for Spencer! There was no way he wouldn't be the next champion.

The third bit of good news was delivered by Mother and Father.

They burst into the house, screaming.

"Benji! Have you seen it? Have you heard?"

"Seen what?"

Mother was holding a newspaper. I could tell by the type it was the *Chatham Freedman*.

She was so excited, though, that she'd balled the paper up. "What is it?"

Father smoothed the paper on the kitchen table and said, "Look!"

The headline read THE PASSING OF A LEGEND AND AN ERA.

Direct under those words, it read, BY BENJAMIN ALSTON AND SARAH CARY.

I was stunned!

"But why would she give me credit for this? I didn't give her an article about Uncle Cooter."

Mother said, "You didn't, but I did!"

"Mother, how could you put my name on something you wrote?"

Father said, "No, you silly boy, she dug one n'em articles you threw away out the garbage and thought it was so good, she snuck behind your back and give it to Miss Cary. Miss Cary said she was very pleased but not the least bit surprised."

"She didn't tell you to leave her office and say, 'Now, off you go'?"

"She told me, 'Thank you very much.' She said I should be very proud!"

Mother and Father hugged and kissed me and said, "We are, Benji, we are so proud!"

Good news had brought an extra horse along because the fourth piece of good news was the looks they gave me, looks of stunned disbelief!

I read my article:

A LEGEND HAS PASSED. AND LIKE so many legends there was more to him and less to him than was suspected. Mr. Coronado Aloicious Bixby, known as Cooter by his loved ones, was laid to rest on a beautiful August morning.

The service, held in a cathedral of oaks, was attended by only a few of those whose lives he touched. Although he eschewed the name hero, we at the *Chatham*

Freedman must respectfully disagree, he was a hero. Not only for the well-known bravery he showed in battle but more so for the way he lived his life afterward. He is a hero because, in spite of all the horrors he'd witnessed, he never allowed anger nor vengeance to poison his spirit. He is a hero because though surrounded by the ignorance of his fellow man, he never became bitter.

Mr. Bixby has left behind many friends, and many others who, though they aren't aware of the fact, have suffered a tremendous loss.

He will be deeply missed.

Miss Cary is a wise woman and has accomplished a great many things in her life. But that doesn't mean she doesn't make mistakes.

Major ones.

Some big enough they'll last for the ages.

She got the headline all wrong. It should have read:

STAR, HUMBLE NEWSPAPER REPORTER OVERJOYED
TO DISCOVER THE SPIRIT OF A MADMAN LIVES
ON IN HIM.

Author's Note

Most of my books have been written in libraries, both public and school. Why? I really can't say. I used to think it was because when I'm sitting in the library, there's always a wealth of research material only a few steps away, but the Internet and laptop computers have made that a moot point. Now an author can write from anywhere and have all the knowledge of the web literally at his or her fingertips. The library, however, was my spot from day one and remains my go-to place.

When I was writing my first book, *The Watsons Go to Birmingham* — 1963, I learned that if I reached a point where the story started to slow down, instead of stopping writing altogether, I needed to get up, go over to the stacks of nearby magazines, and read one of the writing periodicals. That way I gave myself a break and still remained involved in the writing process. It was during one of these slow periods that I read an article where an author described how she felt emotionally devastated every time she finished writing one of her novels. She wrote that there was such a feeling of loss it was as though someone close to her had died. I remember my eyes rolled like a slot machine at a casino and I thought, "Oh, please, get a grip." What a load of hoity-toity, artsy-fartsy nonsense that is.

Then I finished writing *my* book. When I woke up the next morning, I thought the rumbly, jumpity feeling in my stomach, the dizzy sense of unease, and the strong desire I had to bawl were due to my celebratory dinner the night before. I'd eaten the La Azteca special, a baker's-dozen of cheese, lettuce, and tomato tacos drenched in hot sauce, all for the suspiciously low price of $3.99. When the queasiness hadn't left by early that evening and I actually started crying, I knew I owed two people apologies: the owner of La Azteca and the woman who said she mourned when she finished her books.

I felt so bad when I realized I wouldn't be going back to the library to "talk" to the characters in *The Watsons* again, I did feel as though they had died. There really was a period of mourning that I went through. And much as in real life, when you lose someone close to you, one of the components of grief is that you will be overwhelmed by questions. You'll find yourself asking, "I wonder what my departed dear one would say to this?" or "How would they react to that?" or even "What would they be doing now?"

Some novelists try to answer these questions with a sequel, bringing old characters back to life and letting readers, and themselves, know what *did* happen next. That is risky. If a character's story is done, I believe it's best to let them rest in peace. But that doesn't mean I'm not curious as to what happened.

When I finished *Elijah of Buxton*, I was overcome with an even stronger-than-normal sense of loss. I'd always wanted to write a book about slavery but knew it would be difficult for me. I didn't think I could honestly put myself into the mind of a slave, a person whose existence depended on denying their own humanity. When the character young Elijah Freeman came to "visit" me at the library (remember, this is all going on in my head), I knew I had a way into the story of slavery. Instead of having the novel's point of view be that of a slave, a traumatized person who had spent his or her entire life brutalized and dehumanized, I could tell the story from the perspective of a slave's freeborn child; someone who was far enough away from the horrors of slavery to have not been absolutely poisoned by it, but close enough to hear the echoes of the screams in his parent's nightmarish memories.

I began the process of getting to know who Elijah was, listening to his off-kilter reasoning, laughing with him, worrying about him, and eventually falling in love with him. Then I finished writing the novel and he was gone. I'd lost him. I always wondered what happened next in his story, and what he'd say about this or think about that.

I knew I couldn't answer those questions in a sequel, but I couldn't let go of them, either, which is how I came to write *The Madman of Piney Woods*. With this book, I hoped to kill two birds with one stone: I was able to revisit Buxton and meet more of its extra-ordinary citizens, and I was also able to sneak a peek at what has happened in my dear friend Elijah's life forty years later.

And what a delight it is to come back to Buxton! I've always thought there was something magical in the place, a land where so many dreams came to life, where the very soil is infused with the hopes and unimaginable exultation of people shedding the cloak of slavery and being free for the first time in their lives. I imagined the newly freed parents' joy at knowing their children would not have to go through the life-scarring trauma that they had.

As I dove back into researching Buxton and learned more about its relationship with the nearby city of Chatham, I somehow stumbled across the story of Irish immigration in Canada. And much as my research taught me facts about Buxton that surprised me, I was surprised to learn about the horrors so many Irish people went through in their quest for freedom in North America. While reading descriptions of the coffin ships of the early

1800s, I was struck by how much like slave ships those boats were. I imagined the life-scarring trauma a young girl would go through after surviving being imprisoned on one of these ships. The more I read, the more I began to see other parallels. It was at that point I understood what my next book would be about. I also saw I could incorporate lessons my parents had taught me into the story.

My mother used to tell me and my siblings not to rush to judgment when first encountering people. "Life can be rough, and everyone you meet has been through hardships you're far too young to be able to imagine," she'd say. "Give folks a chance." My father would tell us about how extreme adversity could cut both ways, how it could either build or destroy character. He also said the way we react to the adverse situations in our lives will define who we are. Some of the time, the victims of horrific acts become angry, resentful, and hateful, even turning into ramped-up, blinded, carbon copies of the thing that hurt them so much. Some of the time, the victim's eyes are opened, and they realize the poisonous folly of behaving in the same way as whoever it was that caused them pain, and they are lifted through forgiveness. Think Nelson Mandela. At other times, the victims of unimaginable adversity are stunned into a state of nothingness, a state of complete withdrawal.

Taking my mother's lesson into account, I saw there's no point in judging one reaction as more honorable or better than the other. Who's to say why the burden that one person carries so easily absolutely crushes someone else? It's all a part of what makes us human, and it's another of the parallels that shows, no matter what our superficial differences, there is, as a redheaded lad from Chatham and an African-Canadian boy from Buxton discover, much more that binds us together.

Acknowledgments

My sincere thanks to the many people who aided in bringing this book to life.

I'm fortunate enough to have early readers who give priceless feedback, among them Jay Kramer; Caleb, Joshua, and Lisa Edmond; Ami Rosebud and Heidi Thomas; Howa Furrow; Annaliese Furrow-Casement; Camden Furrow-Casement; and especially, once again, Rose Casement.

This wouldn't have been possible without the help of my many friends at Scholastic who worked so hard to make this book the best it could be: Joy Simpkins, Rachael Hicks, Megan Bender, Caitlin Mahon, Jody Revenson, Susan Hom, and Elizabeth Parisi. And the biggest thanks of all to Anamika B. and Andrea D. P.; their skill as readers and editors amazes me. Thank you for the many hours of work you devoted to our madman.

Huge thanks are sent to my daughters, Ayaan and Ebyaan, and my son, Libaan. You guys make every day so special and interesting.

Finally, thank you to my dear wife, Habon. Your steadiness and patience have guided me through the storms. I love you so much!

About the Author

Christopher Paul Curtis grew up in Flint, Michigan. After high school, he spent thirteen years on the assembly line at Fisher Body Flint Plant No. 1, where his job hanging car doors left him with a lifelong aversion to getting in and out of automobiles. He graduated from the University of Michigan–Flint, where he began writing fiction. His first novel, *The Watsons Go to Birmingham — 1963*, was awarded both a Newbery Honor and a Coretta Scott King Honor. His second novel, *Bud, Not Buddy*, won the Newbery Medal and the Coretta Scott King Award in 2000. *Elijah of Buxton*, his sixth novel, was also a Newbery Honor Book, a Coretta Scott King Award winner, and a Canadian Library Association Book of the Year. Visit Christopher online at nobodybutcurtis.com.